CROWN JEWELS

THE AKASHA RECORDS

BOOK ONE

MARIA VANDENBURG

Cover Design by CRJ Design https://crjdesign.co.uk/

Published in the United States by
Vandenburg Lion Publishing.
www.justmariakv.com

VANDENBURG
LION
PUBLISHING

SEATTLE, WASHINGTON

"People will do anything, no matter how absurd, in order to avoid facing their own Soul. One does not become enlightened by imagining figures of light, but by making the darkness conscious."

- Carl Jung

Contents

Acknowledgements

Crown Jewels: The Akasha Records (Book One) is dedicated to my mother, who has been encouraging me to write for as long as I can remember. She has always served as my first editor, a tradition started with shared laughter over my spelling and grammatical mistakes from newspapers I created for her as a child. This book also would not have shifted into what it's become without the gentle guidance and suggestions of Steve Lockley. I will always appreciate that he "threw his hat in" to become its final editor.

I am also thankful to each and everyone of you. Whether the *Akasha Records* resonates or not, whether you love it or it doesn't strike a chord, you still invested some of your time into tuning into its words and its energy, and for that, I will always be grateful.

Finally, I would like to acknowledge and thank my own Shadow, who I am working on knowing and embracing each and every single day.

Foreword

There are these precious moments in life when I get to reflect and appreciate the creation that has flowed through. Writing this foreword is one of those moments for me.

Sitting, smiling wide, breathing deep into a heart full of gratitude. Coming to terms that what I want to express, seems impossible with words... as it seems to go with most life-transforming experiences.

Humaning with Maria has invited a natural flow of creative collaborations that continue to ripple into widening circles.

All in divine timing, Maria's journey of inner alchemy led her to Intention Inspired—a self-discovery project that blossomed from my own becoming as a person.

As Maria moved across the world multiple times, finished her MBA program, wrote this book, and explored life with an authentic embrace, I've had the pleasure of witnessing snippets of her journey while nurturing community with inspiring intentions.

To this moment, our connection continues to flow into a wondrous entanglement of a spiritual dance. So it fills me with delight knowing others will get to experience their own enriching insights through Maria's imaginative and luminary tales.

- Matthew Prindle
CEO of Intention Inspired

30 Days of Authenticity (a 30 Day Series designed to run with Crown Jewels to allow you to explore getting to know your own Shadow) will launch with Intention Inspired in August 2020. Maria Vandenburg will be hosting it live. It will be available on an on-going basis to anyone who is seeking it from then on. You can find out more details here: iam.intentioninspired.com

About the Author

I once had a job interview where the CEO of the company pulled me aside afterward to provide an unofficial mentorship opportunity. She told me to stop selling myself short, never say "I just" do this or "I just" do that. Well, my work is a celebration of the exact opposite. It's about coming to terms with who I am and stepping confidently into my own skin and living in my authenticity. Knowing that I am enough, just as I am, and hopefully a similar recognition for any and all who happen to come across these pages, my work and my voice.

You can find out more about me here: www.justmariakv.com

You can find out more about 30 days of Authenticity and go on a journey to get to know, embrace and love your own Shadow here: iam.intentioninspired.com

If you enjoy this book, I would encourage you to please leave a review on Amazon. It helps me to get the word out there so that others can connect to the magic, mystery, and love of their own Shadows.

Cast of Characters
(in order of appearance)

Avraham: Founder of the secret council within the Order of the Pragmatists and Alejandro's ancestor.

Athena: Goddess and protector of the Crown Jewels and the Two of the Royal Heart"

Raoul: Shadow is Ilan, a white stallion - Raoul is Akasha's first love and a master of plant Medicine.

Alejandro: Shadow is Mariam, a black jaguar - Member of the Order of the Pragmatists whose quest for knowledge has overpowered every aspect of his life.

Akasha: Shadow is Esmeralda, a dragon - Akasha is one half of the Two of the Royal Heart.

Thomas: Shadow is Peter, a mountain dog - Thomas is the guardian of the Temple of the Holy One.

Sophia: Shadow is Mystique, a black panther - Akasha's little sister who has a story in her own right.

Tariq: Shadow is Leo, a lion - Tariq makes up the other half of the Two of the Royal Heart.

Paul: Shadow is Rocky, a wolf - Paul is Tariq's first mate and best friend.

Abdul: Shadow is Juliet, a falcon - Abdul is the Leader of the Order of Pragmatists.

Isis: Shadow is Manu, a sphinx – Isis was Akasha and Sophia's mother, and the former high priestess of the Temple of the Holy One.

Khalid: Shadow is Amadeus, a white stag – Khalid is second in command at the Order of the Pragmatists.

Rashid: Shadow is Simon a lynx - He is the newest recruit with the Order of the Pragmatists.

Prologue: 573 AD

vraham rounded the corner to the Well of Remembrance that stood atop the hill above the town; the ancient Well that had protected the town of Gibraltar for thousands of years. Having had a dream the night before that he would receive direct guidance on the Crown Jewels, he perched silently by the edge and waited. He knew not for what.

If I can replicate them, then the Order of the Pragmatists can move into more powerful practices. Imagine us being able to move through time and space! Avraham had formed a secret society upon hearing of the powers of the Crown Jewels; long lost ancient relics linked to the history of their town, their lives, and their destiny. He dreamed of a time when he could travel at will to document and collect specimens to conduct his experiments without the current boundaries of linear time and space. *I could travel to LionsGate to study the Lions People and*

learn more about Sirius, our sun's own spiritual sun! All of these things had been told down his family line, but to witness them? To set foot in Ancient Egypt and meet the sacred people who had brought the Crown Jewels to this physical realm to begin with? Chills ran up and down his spine. He heard movement and suddenly came back to his senses.

A wagon came bursting up the cobblestone road, with two people seated up front. The man on the left was commanding the black stallion. His dark hair matted to his forehead with sweat as he looked around nervously, raising the crop to encourage the horse to move faster. Avraham immediately saw a sparkling gold Ring with a ruby red stone upon his hand. The woman beside him was dressed in white. She gazed stiffly ahead wearing a golden Crown. She jumped when the horse did as they moved along.

Avraham's heart leaped. Could that really be them? He rubbed his hands together in anticipation as he stepped forward. There was a slight crevice just beyond where he was standing, he could approach them without being noticed. *Human sacrifice for the cause of the Order is sacrifice for the greater good*, he thought as he pulled the alchemical knife from his side. The knife had recently been finished by the Order. The wooden handle and the golden blade had been designed with sacred geometry to cut into electromagnetic fields destabilizing the object it touched. This allowed the holder to capture the electromagnetic codes within the object and could be used for both living and non-living beings. Avraham had one intention when he suggested the secret society create it: he wanted to understand how to replicate the Crown Jewels and was prepared to do everything necessary to do so.

The wagon picked up speed as stones scattered in all directions. Avraham braced himself, leaning forward to calculate the appropriate distance to make his leap. He heard the horse below and knew it was time. Taking a deep breath with the knife in his hand he jumped.

Avraham felt no fear as he sailed through the air and landed with a thud right on top of the man. Startled, the black stallion neighed, jumped and bolted, throwing the women off the carriage. She shrieked as she fell, but the horse carried on. The man struggled to regain composure, throwing his hands in the air and shifting his weight, but his efforts were useless.

"You have something I need, you can either give it to me freely, or we can use harsher measures," Avraham placed his knees against the man's chest, forcing his weight upon him as he placed the knife against his neck. The man's eyes grew wide with shock. He looked to his right and saw that his companion was no longer with him.

"Where is she?" were the final words he managed to say as the wagon burst over a large rock which unintentionally plunged the knife directly into his neck. Avraham was in shock. While he had been prepared to kill this man, he hadn't anticipated it happening. The horse started galloping out of control. Avraham jumped again, leaning past the man pulsating in blood. He dived to his left, grabbing the reins and pulling to try and reel the stallion in. The horse did not stop. Avraham saw the cliff approaching and knew he had no choice. He quickly pulled the dead man's fingers up, removed the Ring and jumped.

He landed with a twist as a sharp pain shot through his side. The wagon and horse continued over the cliff to the sound of the creature's cry of panic. He had been aware that this could happen, but witnessing it was an entirely different matter. His heart ached as the horse flew to its death. Avraham had no words. He rolled over and put his hands on his knees.

"Avraham, I have been expecting you," he heard someone say. He looked up unsure if he was dreaming, to see a woman with long flowing golden-red hair, piercing blue green eyes and a green robe that seemed to float with the breeze. Although she appeared to be human, her presence felt more powerful.

"Who are you?" He paused and looked around, to find that no one else was present.

"You have been careless and I am here to provide you with a warning," the being said, she stepped forward and pulled out a wand with a black stem and an emerald green star. Golden energy seemed to emit from it.

Avraham stepped back. He didn't believe in magic and wands but there was something supernatural about this whole encounter.

"Your society has been created out of greed. The Crown Jewels have been gifted to aid the Two of the Royal Heart when it becomes time for their mission to begin. They had been given for safekeeping, but your search for knowledge has broken that trust." The being stepped forward and tapped her wand as the Crown appeared before them.

"With this death, I have no choice but to remove them."

"I hadn't meant to take anyone's life," Avraham said slowly. He had only wanted to understand how to recreate them.

"We know of your intentions, but now you must know of ours. The Crown Jewels will remain in hiding until the Two of the Royal Heart return and claim them."

"The what?" Avraham had never heard of the Royal Heart before.

"This will not make sense to you now, but in time you will have a descendant and his Shadow Mariam will have a vital role to play. For now, I have come to tell you to stop. You will not be able to recreate the Crown Jewels; they no longer exist in this realm"

"What other realm could they possibly be in?" Avraham felt a continued mix of emotions overwhelm him.

"Open your mind Avraham; more exists than meets the eye. I am here today to make you aware of that. There will come a time when I will work with One of the Royal Heart and your descendent, but for now, we ask you to stop. To end the holy war and make peace with those of the light." With that, the being vanished leaving Avraham alone in his thoughts and confusion at the Well.

Introduction

The Winter Solstice

homas had been struggling with his words for weeks.

Will I say the right things? Will people understand? His stomach was in knots as he rubbed his hands together and along his white robe in search of comfort. Although he was the guardian of the *Temple of the Holy One*, he still doubted his words and his power. Peter, his Shadow, sent him some unconditional love and strength through their telepathic connection as Thomas took a deep centering breath and walked into the main sanctuary.

He tried to make his steps look confident as he gazed at the large central opalescent oval crystal beaming from the altar stone, sending bursts of rainbow light from the setting sun around the large circular room. He felt peace as his energy connected with the crystal. He sensed a particularly strong gaze and looked over at the front row of the circular wooden pews. He made eye contact with Abdul, the current leader of the *Order of the Pragmatists* and felt an additional surge of support as he stepped into place and began. "What if this world is more than it appears?"

"What if there were things going on all around you that you aren't aware of, and at the same time, play a significant role in not only how you perceive your life, but also how you live it? I am here today, to help you see that both of these things are true. I ask you for just a moment to suspend your judgment." He took a deep breath, calling on Peter and on the universe for guidance with his words, so that his message would be clear. He knew what he was speaking about tonight was far greater than just himself.

"Tonight, I want to talk about two things; the importance of knowing and embracing all of who you are, and the importance of operating from a space of authenticity and pure intention, a space where you are able to tap into your essence.

"I want to talk about these things because, when you are able to embrace your entire being and are connecting and operating from it in a state of authenticity, magic can happen." He paused, looking around the room and made eye contact with the others, hoping his words would resonate as he took a deep breath and continued on...

Chapter 1

The Passing of Raoul

 leven days and eleven minutes earlier, Raoul moved stealthily through the forest, searching for a specific plant. *Where is it? Where is the herb?* He knew that if he could find it, it would complete the vision he had received with Ilan, his Shadow who appeared in the form of a white stallion. The plant medicine he was hoping to create would help change someone's mood; it would transmute the negative emotion and behavior into something positive.

"*Just think Ilan, we wouldn't have to go through struggle and strife! We could take this and Akasha and I*

could be permanently happy." Raoul was full of joy as he brushed his long dark hair out of his face and crouched down to dig through the bushes, the billowing olive trees shading him from the hot midday sun. He was anticipating bringing forth a new medicine that would help him and his love Akasha along their spiritual journey.

"*Raoul, what if we needed to become conscious of the darkness to recognize the light. If there was no contrast would life still be as meaningful? What if the darkness was also an aspect of the divine authentic nature of your being? Think back to our first interaction. You did not automatically accept me as part of you. You needed to become aware of areas in your life and deal with thoughts that weren't allowing you to see the full picture,*" Ilan guided him gently.

"*But you wouldn't have given me this vision for no reason Ilan.*" Raoul caught sight of a leaf that looked familiar and immediately crouched down on his hands and knees, reaching into the brush. He was so engrossed in his search that he did not hear the sound of footsteps as someone approached him from behind.

"Found what you are looking for?" a deep male voice asked.

Startled, Raoul turned and looked up. The man was unfamiliar, but he recognized him as a member of the

Order of the Pragmatists by his black robe and hood. He was tall, of a firm stature with a shaved head, and looked younger than his deep voice had suggested. He appeared to be of around his own age of twenty. Frustrated at having to stop his search, Raoul grunted in annoyance as he slowly stood up, brushing the dirt from his hands onto his robe. "Can I help you?" His tone wasn't nearly as inviting as his words.

"Yes, I do believe you can. My name is Alejandro. I am interested in how you acquired all of your knowledge of plants." A smile played across his lips, but there was a threat in his voice.

"I don't trust him or the secretive order he belongs to, nor do I know him, but what should I do?" Raoul focused on sending this thought to Ilan for guidance, knowing that Alejandro would not be able to see or sense him.

"I don't know that there is much you can do Raoul, unfortunately, which is why I tried to show you this, to prepare you." Ilan felt grieved at not being able to say or offer more. He knew that Raoul had misinterpreted the vision.

"I've heard a lot about you and your powers with plant medicine. I am interested in how you do it. I want to know where you learned your gifts," Alejandro said.

"I cannot possibly reveal all of my knowledge to you in a matter of minutes," Raoul snapped back. While Raoul heard the threat in the man's tone, he was not intimidated. There was too much at stake. His knowledge of the plants was sacred and something he treasured and guarded. He couldn't just pass this information along to anyone who asked, especially not to someone who was a member of the Order.

"Have you heard of the concept of your third eye?" Alejandro stepped closer to Raoul and reached up to touch his forehead.

Raoul jumped back although there wasn't really anywhere for him to hide. His fight or flight response was kicking in as he sensed how dangerous this man might be.

"Step away from me. I have not given you permission to touch me!"

"I don't recall having to ask permission. You see, the interesting part about our third eye is that it reveals to us information that is greater than our knowledge of this world. So, if you will not find it within yourself to help me in my quest for knowledge, then I may have to resort to… well, let's just say, alternative means of getting there."

Alejandro pulled a knife from his robe, it had a long black wooden base with the symbol of the Order carved into it, and a golden blade that seemed to radiate power.

He took a step closer, ignoring every word that Raoul had said.

Adrenaline coursed through Raoul's body. He couldn't just reveal this information to this man, even if he had wanted to. He didn't know how much he could even put into words. It was an ancient knowledge he sensed and remembered; alchemical compositions that just came to him. He could never write them down for others to use but knew enough to re-create when he needed to.

With each step that Alejandro took, Raoul's thoughts of finding the elusive herb were put aside. All he could focus on now was his own safety. *Perhaps I can stall him?*

Raoul moved backwards, and felt his feet firmly planted against the root of the great olive tree he had just been crawling beside.

"Have you heard of the valerian root?" Raoul found himself saying the first thing that came to mind.

"The root that is said to help with sleep? I am looking for deeper knowledge than that; one that spans your whole lifetime." Alejandro twirled the knife in his hand and looked intently at Raoul's third eye.

Raoul's instincts kicked in, he was not going to let this pass without a fight. He would not allow Alejandro access to his thoughts. He didn't know what the knife in his hand, but could sense that it was an ancient piece of technology. He knew he was in danger and was determined to protect himself and his knowledge. Without thinking, he rushed forward but felt his foot caught in the roots of the tree. He was snapped back. As his head bashed against the tree, his world went slowly dark.

"How can this be happening? I'm not finished yet! Have I protected the knowledge? Can he really tamper with my third eye? What about Akasha?" His heart started to feel incredibly heavy as a thousand thoughts rushed through his mind; the last being the powerful and deep connection he felt to the love of his life.

"Well, well, well, this might be a lot easier than I thought," Alejandro was grinning as he brought the knife up to Raoul's forehead to taper with the magnetic fields, codes and power. The minute the knife brushed the field, he felt an electrical reaction. "Ouch!" Alejandro screamed as he dropped the knife, his hand stinging from the shock.

A sharp shooting pain ran from the base of Raoul's spine, all the way up to the top of his head making it hard for him to gather his thoughts.

"Oh Raoul, I saw your passing from this realm, but I didn't anticipate this." Ilan was grave as he sensed the connection between them being severed from the impact of the mysterious knife.

Raoul grew weaker by the minute, and the pain was increasing as he was still within the confines of the physical realm.

"Raoul, you need to go. Go to the Spirit Realm. Move forward. The pain is too much for you to bear if you stay."

"Did he get access to the code? Is it safe?" Raoul was talking about the electromagnetic field that surrounded him, and the light codes established from his conscious awareness of the ancient alchemical knowledge of plants. He felt like he might explode into a million pieces and he knew he could not stand much more of this pain.

"I love you Ilan." Then he strained to send one last final message: *"Akasha, I will always love you."* With that, he left his physical body separate from his Shadow.

Chapter 2

Akasha and the Obelisk

is voice reverberated through her mind's eye. *How can that possibly be the last thing I will ever hear him say? Did I imagine it?* Akasha was beyond angry. Even now, twelve hours after Thomas had discovered Raoul's body in the grove outside the Temple, she still wasn't sure if she had heard it. The mark of the Pragmatists had been burned into his third eye. *Now, he's gone!* Tears welled up inside her. She wasn't sure which emotion she felt more; her profound anger at the *Order of the Pragmatists* for taking Raoul's life, or the depth of her sorrow in losing him.

"Sophia, I can't take this. I have to get outside!" Akasha yelled at her younger sister. When her mother Isis had passed five years ago, she hadn't been sure if she would be able to pull herself out of her grief to take care of herself and her little sister. Now, she felt like she would never be the same. Her heart felt permanently hardened.

Akasha threw on her warmest robe and her burgundy shawl then left their cottage without waiting on Sophia's response. She had to get outside. She had to get to Cleopatra's Obelisk. For some reason, she always felt solace there – a connection to something more. She hoped that would be the case tonight as she walked along the dusty road of Gibraltar to the central pillar that rose against the backdrop of the water.

What is the point of being on this planet if all we ever feel is pain and grief? She thought angrily as she kicked a few rocks along the way. The full moon shone bright above the Obelisk, making a perfect circle as if designed to shed light and compassion on her, if only in this moment. She felt the moonbeams touch her skin and tried to absorb some of its gentle light in an attempt to find some peace.

She reached the Obelisk and sat down at its base letting her fingers run over the hieroglyphs as she allowed her emotions to surface. Her robe bunched uncomfortably against her knees. She tried to catch her breath but couldn't; the pain was just too much. She gave into it and her body wracked with sobs. *I can't believe he's gone! My life will never be the same. How can I get up and run the stall tomorrow? How can I do anything without him?* It felt like she would forever be surrounded by sorrow. Raoul had been her rock. The connection between them had deepened with the passing of her mother. Akasha had learned that it had been okay to let someone else into her heart, to open up and truly allow someone to see her. She had leaned on him for support and knew that without fail, he would be there. Now that was all gone, it had been ripped away. She slammed her hand down on the base of the needle, trying to release some of her rage. *I can't believe what they have done. I don't understand! Why would they kill him?*

In the distance, she heard the roar of a lion as her hands collapsed into her lap. She knew that she should get up and go home, but her heart was too heavy, she wondered if she could even move. She had to listen to her body for the first time and recognize and honor her own needs.

For her entire life she had been holding in her emotions. She had told herself that it wasn't okay to truly express them, that it was a sign of weakness. With the passing of Raoul, Akasha realized just how wrong she had been. She had no choice but to get the poison and the pain of his loss out of her body. If she wanted to be able to get back up and move on, she needed to deal with the pain she felt. So, she cried and allowed her anger and sadness to surface. She sat against the Obelisk and let what seemed like never-ending tears flow.

Chapter 3

Leo the Lion

 er body tingled all over as the rain poured down. She looked up in confusion no longer sure where she was; water and darkness seemed to engulf her. She found herself on a mountain top with a swirling sky of twinkling stars above her and the majestic full moon. The stars seemed to move with her breath, creating a beautiful pulsating rhythm that took her to a state of awe as the rain dissipated. Although it was a dark night, the mountain top air felt warm and oddly comforting.

Disoriented, Akasha looked around trying to see beyond the mountain path she found herself on. Her eyes gained focus and she suddenly gasped, as she sensed a powerful presence. A massive creature emerged near her appearing in the form of a lion. He had a different type of energy to him, it was as if he came from the stars, like he was made of the stars. Akasha had never experienced anything like it. She trembled, unsure whether she was shaking in fear or wonder.

He moved in her direction and instinctively she took a step back. He was almost ten times her size with a golden mane that seemed to have the entire universe within it. She felt completely overwhelmed. Unable to see clearly, she was overpowered by his presence. Golden light surrounded and swirled inside and through him.

Suddenly, he arched back and roared. Akasha was surprised with the feeling this roar evoked within her. It was a roar that felt like it shifted the entire energy of the planet; a roar that shook every single atom, molecule, and cell in her being. Before she could control her reaction, her body arched in return and suddenly, she screamed. She both heard and felt the sound emanate from her and enter into physical reality. She screamed with all the passion in her soul that was heavy with the loss of Raoul. She yelled from her tears of sadness that had come earlier that night. She yelled with everything there was, is and ever will be.

She felt a huge sense of release, transformation, and transmutation but didn't understand it. The name Leo surfaced in her thoughts. She was puzzled with how she had made this connection; how did she know him? How did she know his name?

He looked at her with kindness and compassion in his golden eyes. *"Leo? What is going on?"* She couldn't speak, but seemed to be able to communicate with this creature through her thoughts. How did he seem so familiar? *Am I no longer scared of him? How do I know him? Why did it feel so freeing to yell as he roared?* It was as if he was guiding her with his presence. *How does he know of my pain?* Akasha thought in confusion as she tried again to make sense of everything.

He raised his head to the stars and roared again with such power that Akasha awoke, her body pressed against Cleopatra's Obelisk, her burgundy robe completely soaked.

"It's time to go," she thought. Shaken, cold and tired, she got up, and as the sun began to rise to greet the new day, she made her way home, not knowing if she would ever understand what had just happened.

Chapter 4

The Temple
of the Holy One

kasha walked down the cobblestone road that made up the main thoroughfare of Gibraltar, pulling her wet shawl closer to try and block the cold morning winds. She shivered and felt a knot in her stomach, her body was speaking to her again. *Well, what is it?* She thought as she felt called to make a stop at the *Temple of the Holy One.* That had happened several times recently; she would feel compelled

to do something without any explanation for it. Something seemed to nudge her along and move her forward, as long as she was open to listening to it.

I am so exhausted. Can't I just go home and rest? She wasn't expecting a physical response, but she hoped for some sort of direction. All she felt was a longing in her gut to go to the Temple, to step through its dark, ancient doors, and kneel before the crystal altar stone. It used to be such a place of solace as her mother had been the high priestess for many years. With her passing, it had become difficult to go inside. Akasha imagined her mother being with her, offering her unconditional love and support and that need for comfort, outweighed anything else.

She sighed and veered over to the left, slowly making her way toward the ancient tower of the Temple. A huge pillar standing amongst the beautiful greenery. The circular Temple was made of ancient stone with stained glass windows and a steeple at the top. There were many signs and symbols carved into the stone that she could not understand, but she knew held deep meaning.

Her ancestors had worshipped here in the Ancient of Days. *How I wish I knew their stories and had their insight.* She wanted something that could help her through this incredibly difficult time where she was grieving her lost love during the day and screaming with a mysterious, powerful lion at night.

She took a deep breath to calm herself down as she continued in the Temple's direction, slowly ascending the steep crest of the rock of Gibraltar, the Temple lay just beyond the base. Knowing that she would be here, along with the rest of the town, in a few weeks' time for the Winter Solstice service, she wrestled with her emotions. For years the town had been gathering on the Winter and Summer Solstices to usher in the new seasons. *I suppose it wouldn't hurt to walk through the doors now, ahead of that,* Akasha thought as the ancient arch of the sacredly designed wooden doors came into view. The intricate carvings made it look like the doors held the text of an ancient book that she had yet to learn how to read.

Akasha believed in the Spirit Realm. She knew she was more than just this physical shell of a body. There was still so much unexplained, so many answers she longed for. She had expected to have more time with her mother to have some of these mysteries explained. *It seems like everyone I love is being taken from me.*

She slowly approached the large ornate doors and hesitantly touched them to see if they would open. As if by command, the doors gave way to let her in. She walked inside and took a deep breath, her eyes adjusting to the darkness, the burning myrrh incense providing an additional moment of comfort as she connected to the scent. At the sound of movement she looked to her right.

"Why hello, Akasha. I wasn't expecting anyone at this time," Thomas pulled his robe tighter around his frail body. There was a chill breeze blowing in off the sea, and her opening the door had allowed it to enter. Akasha bowed to the elderly man that had acted as the guardian of the Temple for as long as she could remember.

"Thomas, I wasn't planning on coming but wanted just a moment of silence, if you don't mind?" Akasha bowed in greeting, placing her hands across her heart.

"By all means."

She approached the altar stone. It was a beautiful piece of crystal that seemed to exude its own magical energy. It had a huge stone base, with an oval stone that gave the illusion of rising all the way to the ceiling. The stained-glass windows reflected perfect geometric colored patterns onto the stone itself.

She knelt at one of the front circular pews and closed her eyes. Taking a few deep breaths, she focused on her heart. Her mother had once told her that the heart was the center for understanding those things that seemingly could not be understood. She felt so angry and worn out that she wasn't sure if she was going to be able to connect, but she had to try. When she felt her heart center, she knew she was tapping into the power that existed deep within her. She focused on her breathing. With each inhale, she gathered more strength, and each exhale, she released a little of her pain.

This isn't going to be easy, she thought as she continued to breathe into her center.

Suddenly, she felt a presence. She still felt her pain and her grief, but there was also support.

She inhaled deeply. *Why did this have to happen? Why do I always lose the people I love?* Her thoughts seemed to be her way of communicating directly with the divine as she exhaled them with an audible sigh.

"That is the wrong question to ask."

She didn't hear the words, but they entered her like a new train of thought.

"The questions to ask are, how do you become whole from this? What do you do next? How can you use the pain that you currently feel?"

She felt a rush of energy course through her body. She had never heard anything other than her own thoughts before. She almost opened her eyes but had an innate knowing to continue the process. She took another deep breath and sighed again, trying to release her focus on her own voice and open up to what wanted to communicate with her. An image of a Crown came into her mind. A beautiful gold Crown covered in lavender and emerald jewels. While she had experienced peace, love, angelic support, and stillness in communion with the divine before, this was the first time she'd experienced any sort of direct vision. She placed her hands on her heart to focus, and felt her spirit rising with a sense of wonder.

I don't understand. Next, she saw a brilliant ruby red stone at the center of a gold Ring. *But what does this mean?* She slowed her breathing to try and connect deeper. Intuitively she knew that the answers were tied to her ancestors, her heritage, but so much was still unclear. She often found that when she slowed her breathing, her connection with both the Spirit Realm and her body grew. It continued to amaze her how much her awareness could shift with just the practice of a few deep breaths.

The Crown, she sensed, was connected with leading, with being royalty. The ruby red Ring was also tied into her future, but how, she did not know. Akasha had always had a keen sense of intuition which only deepened the more she tuned into it.

I am so confused. Could that voice in my head please return and help me? She wanted more guidance and knew she had been communicating with something much greater than herself. She was determined to follow her heart and be open to the idea of communication. Suddenly, she felt another presence, a familiar loving presence, one that she deeply missed and longed for. She almost came out of her meditative state when she heard him speak. *"Akasha, I am here."*

She shuddered at the sound, *I'm not sure I can handle this.* She knew he could not physically be with her, but she didn't want to let go of her connection with him. *"What? How can this be?"* She almost said out loud, the tears flowed once more. She felt joy and grief at the same time, it was such a paradox.

"I may have left the physical realm, but I am still with you. I am still watching over you. There is much to be done," Raoul's voice spoke, he seemed to be communicating directly with her heart. It was almost as if he was sitting behind her, giving her strength, sending his energy to her. *This is so strange. It's almost as if I can feel him with me even though I know he isn't there.* Akasha continued to breathe deeply, connecting to her heart center, sensing that was enabling their connection.

"But how?"

"In time, Akasha, in time. Just know that you are not alone. I love you and I am here."

"*But where is here? I am tired of not under-standing!*" While Akasha was grateful to hear his voice again, she felt overwhelmed.

"*Akasha, just breathe. If you get upset or disconnect from your heart center, you will break our connection.*"

This was too much. Less than 24 hours ago he had physically left her life. "*How can I not be upset, Raoul! You are no longer with me! I'm alone. I don't understand what's going on or what's being asked of me. I miss you.*"

She felt a huge welling up of what she could only explain as love surrounding her, and relief as she sensed she was being guided through her grief and acceptance of the loss of Raoul. She couldn't stop the tears as she disconnected from her heart and returned to her physical reality.

Her eyes felt dry. She was so exhausted she wasn't sure if she had the strength to make it back home to Sophia, but she understood how badly she needed to rest. *Tomorrow will be another day.* She took one last deep breath, sent up thanks and energy to the universe, and opened her eyes.

It took her a few minutes to regain her equilibrium, but slowly she rose and made her way out of the Temple. She noticed Thomas as she was leaving. He nodded and she managed a small smile, then stepped back out into the newly starting day.

Chapter 5

Thomas and the
Book of Records

 e looked around in awe.

That was the first the Crown had been seen in over five hundred years. And the Ring? Simply amazing! Thomas approached the altar stone grateful for his extrasensory perception, spiritual gifts of extrasensory and telepathic communication of others in the same physical vicinity.

With Akasha's vision of the Crown Jewels, so much might now be possible. Thomas and others had long known that Akasha would play a key role in their return, but he hadn't anticipated her waking up to it so soon. *I agree with Raoul, though. There is still much to be done. How will she react to the fact that she is One of the Royal Heart? Is she ready to learn that it is her destiny to become the next high priestess of the Temple? Had Isis previously communicated anything?* He left the Sanctum to return to his private chambers, lost in thought.

"Breathe Thomas. You are getting yourself all worked up! One thought at a time, one breath at a time." Thomas heard Peter, his Shadow who appeared in the form of a mountain dog, echoing back to him.

Thomas had made the decision to become the guardian of the Temple after a fateful night under a full moon. He came from a line of holy workers and had many secrets to keep. The family knowledge was held in the *Book of Records* that dated back more than ten thousand years. He struggled with the responsibility of it all. *Can I carry all of this knowledge forward? The Winter Solstice is just a few weeks away, will I be able to communicate what I need to? Akasha is starting to wake up, and she needs to understand what has just happened!* Not listening to the advice of his Shadow, he entered his chambers and made his way to his desk.

When Isis was around, he felt supported. She had been the high priestess leading the way and he supported her, and the sacred knowledge. Her passing had changed that, and he often felt overwhelmed. He knew he was being divinely guided, but he worried he would fail to say or do the right thing. The sacred knowledge was powerful, although it required the eyes to see and the willingness to hear.

The emergence of the Crown Jewels through Akasha's mind's eye was extraordinary. All beings have the ability to tap into their own extrasensory perception through an energy center called the third eye. However, few actually use it, as they do not believe it is possible.

"It must have been Akasha's heartbreak over the loss of Raoul that opened her up to that expansion," Thomas thought. *"She tapped into her heart center and the authentic nature of her being, surrendering her will in an effort to seek comfort from that which cannot be explained. Her heart was broken open on a much deeper level than had been available to her previously."*

Thomas, at a very young age, had been able to open his third eye and connect to the Spirit Realm and Peter. As his relationship had grown, so had his senses, though he still sometimes questioned himself as his own doubts and fears surfaced.

"The Crown Jewels," he spoke aloud to Peter, "just think about the possibilities!" Thomas knew he needed to write this into the *Book of Records*. He would call it the Akasha Records; they were an important record to keep.

This vision of the Crown Jewels was no small matter. These Jewels, if manifested by the Two of the Royal Heart, had the ability to bridge worlds together. They could link the worlds of the past, of the future, and even of other dimensions. The Crown Jewels could completely change the course of the planet. They could bring in a whole new era of peace and prosperity as long as they remained in the right hands.

"I must write this all down immediately!" Thomas was starting to grow anxious as he stood up and made his way to where he kept the *Book of Records* hidden safely within the drawers of his desk.

Chapter 6

Sophia's Concern

kasha! Where have you been?" Sophia looked genuinely worried as the wooden door creaked open. She quickly grabbed her candle and rushed over as Akasha made her way inside. She often worried about her sister, casting her own needs aside to make sure that Akasha was alright. She knew that she should take better care of her self, but now was not the time. Her sister had been missing. She had woken early to find Akasha had still not returned, and spent the last few hours pacing the floor.

"I am sorry, Soph. I fell asleep against the Obelisk and then felt called to the Temple on the way home." Sophia took one look at her sister's bloodshot dark oval brown eyes and put her arms around her, placing the candle on the nearby table.

"I know we will need to go in a few weeks' time for Solstice, but I just felt pulled to go inside tonight." Akasha rested her head against Sophia's shoulder.

"Oh sister, I wish there was a way for me to take your pain," Sophia whispered as she kissed her cheek. She saw the pain in her sister's face and felt nothing but compassion. She helped her take off her shawl and ushered her into their kitchen. They often had the ability to pick up on each other's emotions without the need for words.

"I can't make sense of anything yet," Akasha replied. "I know you are concerned for me, and I am sorry that I worried you, but I really need to rest now." Akasha leaned back against the wall, her body slumping in exhaustion.

"Okay," Sophia was disappointed. *I feel like she is closing herself off to me,* she thought as she gently guided her safely upstairs to her sleeping chambers.

"I promise, Soph, that I will tell you everything once I am able to make sense of it. But now, I must sleep."

Akasha made no effort to even change out of her dress, something she was normally fastidious about.

Sophia kissed her on the cheek and covered her with a blanket. She looked outside the window as the sun was rising and there was a full day ahead. She sighed, a little anxious about what she had to do next, not really wanting to go forward alone.

Chapter 7

Tariq and the
Ring of Infinite Wisdom

 ariq stood on the deck of the Black Onyx, the single masted sailing ship that had been given to him by his grandfather. He was close to finding what they were looking for; he could feel it in his bones.

"Just be patient," he heard Leo, his Shadow, tell him quietly. Tariq looked over at Paul, his first mate, the only other one on the ship, and closest friend, half expecting him to hear Leo as well. In all the years Tariq

had worked with Paul, it was still hard for him to accept that Paul had not yet awakened to his own Shadow. Tariq knew Paul would have to be receptive and ready for it. It was an individual journey, and incredibly difficult at the start. He thought back grimly to the time in his life where he had first been introduced to his own. *"You know Leo, I am so grateful I opened myself up to the idea of you all those years ago. I don't know if I would have survived without you."*

He pulled out his magical compass, a gift Leo had given him years before. The compass circled in a ring, it was used on the physical realm to allow Leo to direct him to the right location. The dial stopped moving, letting him know that the treasure they were seeking was below.

"Paul! Just here! Let's drop anchor and dive in!" Tariq yelled in excitement as he prepared for the cool waters.

Paul did as instructed and joined his friend at the rail. "How will we know where to swim?" He stood hesitantly at the edge of their ship.

Tariq laughed at Paul's ever-present skepticism. "Paul, at some point you just need to surrender and trust! The treasure is below. The Ring is almost with us!"

Without waiting for his friend to respond, Tariq dived off the Black Onyx and into the Strait of Gibraltar.

He resisted the urge to gasp at the sudden cold of the water as he made his way deeper. He pulled the compass from his pocket, clasping onto it for direction from Leo. *"I'm hoping Leo, that you can guide me to where the treasure is."*

He kept swimming, feeling the darkness seep in as he moved lower and lower. His body started to demand oxygen, his lungs straining with the effort. He knew he wouldn't be able to stay down here much longer but he was determined to find the Ring.

Suddenly he saw the ruins of a large boat immediately beneath him. *Is this it?* He felt the presence of Leo urging him on. He wasn't sure if Paul had even made it into the water yet, but he didn't care. He could feel the presence of the Ring of Infinite Wisdom in front of him. He wasn't sure of the powers it held, but he knew it was within his grasp.

His lungs started to swell. *I have to push myself. I am so close!* He swam forward and reached the boat, and then he saw the treasure chest, and knew that what he sought was inside. *But can I lift it? Can I get it to the surface?* He was struggling to remain conscious and knew he wouldn't have much longer before he would be forced to return.

He placed his hands on the ancient chest, wrestling it with it, but it was stuck.

"Oh Leo, please help me. I can't have come this far to not be able to lift it." He fumbled with the chest, exerting all of his effort and energy. His heart pounded rapidly as he felt the power of the object inside. Tariq had the ability to sense the energy of the things in his environment and the Ring's presence was palpable.

"What have you relied on in the past?" He heard Leo's voice say.

"Well, you?" Tariq didn't want to give up, but he didn't know how much longer he could stay down there.

"Tariq, you do not have much time before you will have to return to the surface. Let me ask again, who have you relied on in the past?"

Tariq's head started to feel heavy, he couldn't think straight anymore. At that point, he saw what he thought Leo was referring to – Paul and he was carrying a rope. He had made it into the waters and was swimming frantically towards him. He saw what Tariq had, even without the connection to his Shadow.

Tariq felt a wave of relief. They worked to lift the treasure chest from its place, but it wouldn't budge. Tariq felt like kicking the chest in frustration, but he didn't have much energy left.

"*Leo, what do we do?*"

"*You trust.*"

"*I trust? That's supposed to help me when I feel like my lungs are going to implode and my world is going dark!*" He felt some of Paul's natural skepticism seep in. "*Trust what exactly? That this treasure chest doesn't want to leave its place? That the Ring isn't meant for me? Absolutely not!*" That thought went against everything he knew to be true, everything his heart seemed to be directing him towards.

"*I trust that this Ring and the treasure in this chest is meant to go and be with its rightful owner who will know how to use it in the correct ways and for the highest good.*" He felt this train of thought enter his consciousness as the chest began to shift and give way under the pressure of their hands and bodies. Tariq was tapping into the authentic nature of his whole being and that was enough. The chest loosened by the power of his thoughts, intentions and words. Together, Paul and Tariq secured the rope.

"*See what happens when you surrender to the power of your own consciousness and divine guidance,*" Tariq heard Leo say as they swam towards the sunlight.

They reached the surface gasping for breath. Tariq felt like his lungs were going to explode but that did not take away from the exhilaration he felt. They climbed back on board the boat and together they hauled up the chest.

Years ago, they had heard the story of a lost treasure and a magical Ring. Today? Well, today he had worked with Leo, tapped into the authentic nature of his being and they found it! Words weren't available to express the happiness and exuberance he felt.

Chapter 8

Thomas and the History of the Crown Jewels

 homas sat in his office and slowly opened his desk. He pulled out the ancient *Book of Records,* the golden cover coated with dust. He had made his last update five years ago at the time of the passing of Isis. It was used to record significant events and he knew he needed to capture the start of the Akasha Records, the title he felt appropriate to begin documenting Akasha's journey. He was almost scared to touch it for all of the sacred knowledge that it held. *If this was ever*

*destroyed or lost...*he shivered at the thought as he felt Peter's presence beside him.

He flipped through to an entry and read:

The Holy War between the Order of the Pragmatists when the Order of Melchizedek ended in the year 564. It had started over a disagreement about how the Crown Jewels should be used. The two opposing sides refused to compromise. The Light Workers, those of the Order of Melchizedek, believed in their use to connect to the Spirit Realm, the Pragmatists to bring further order and rational understanding of the physical world. They were powerful pieces of ancient technology.

The Order of Melchizedek was charged with the protection of the Crown Jewels. They are associated with those of the Light, who we consider to be ones that believe they are greater than just their human form, thoughts and mind and seek to embody that light. Left in their care, the Crown and the Ring of Infinite Wisdom were used at sacred ceremonies during the Summer and Winter Solstices.

The Order of Pragmatists operated from a base of rationality, pragmatism and the need for scientific proof. The Pragmatists had a member named Avraham, who upon hearing of how the Crown Jewels can be used to travel through time and space to gain knowledge of ancient wisdom, created a secret society to try and recreate the elusive elements of the Crown and the Ring of Infinite Wisdom. They developed the alchemical knife, which penetrated the electromagnetic field of anything it touched. The knife could then copy into code form the field for further study.

The Crown Jewels mysteriously disappeared with the death of the King in the Holy War, which also resulted in the end of the war. To return, both artifacts must be used by the Two of the Royal Heart while standing in the authentic natures of their being. There have been conflicting explanations of what it means to be authentic. It does not mean that one does not have their own inner turmoil or darkness, but that one is aware of it, working with it, integrating it, and transmuting it to understand that it is a natural part of life on this planet. The dark is a part of life, designed to be embraced to bring us all into balance. The light cannot exist without the dark. Neither is good or bad; both are necessary and should exist in perfect integration and balance.

The key difference between those of the Light, and the Pragmatists is that the Light Workers have made peace with the fact that there are some things that cannot be explained or known. Some things are beyond human comprehension. The Light Workers have faith in their connection to all there was, is, and ever will be. The

Pragmatists, with a few exceptions do not accept anything in faith. Although they have the same access and connection to all there was, is, and ever will be (as do all beings on this planet), some have lost sight of it.

Over time those of the Light and the Pragmatists were able to make peace. Some of our strongest discoveries were made with them working in tandem, but recently that has all changed.

Both those of the Light and the Pragmatists continue to exist today, though the root of their conflict remains and has resurfaced with the recreation of the secret society within the Order by a descendent of Avraham. The divide still exists between the Worlds of Light and Dark.

The Crown Jewels will reappear and provide the opportunity to balance the issues between the worlds when the Two of the Royal Heart come to claim and manifest them. Both will know what is needed and will be guided into action. The Guardians of the Temple ask that any and all who read these pages keep an open heart, open mind, and open will, as the universe is always there to guide you to what is to come, as long as you are open to listening.

Thomas absorbed the last few words of the *Book of Records*. He quieted and paused asking for direction as to how he should start writing this particular record. He pondered the divide that exists between the two worlds and felt swept up in thought.

"You have to go through the dark to appreciate the light," Thomas said aloud.

Thomas knew that the Crown and the Ring of Infinite Wisdom would be physically manifested by the Two of the Royal Heart. He had long since known that Akasha was one of the pairings; that had been told at her birth. What he did not know, however, was who the other was. *I had always assumed that it would be Raoul, but there must be more to this story*. He started to write down his thoughts:

The divide between those of the Light and the Order of the Pragmatists has only increased with the passing of Raoul.

He paused.

"How do we get the Light Workers and the Pragmatists to see that they should be in harmony with one another, that the strength and power of both parties would shift if they work with each other?" he asked aloud to Peter, and to the Spirit Realm.

"How much do I reveal to Akasha? Do I trust that wisdom will be passed down to her as long as she continues to seek and be open to receive it?"

He recorded his memories of Akasha's calls for help and dated it with today's official date:

12th December 1073 AD.

Chapter 9

Athena

kasha rolled over in her bed pulling her feather blanket closer to her. Unable to sleep soundly, she felt incredibly agitated.

She grunted in annoyance and opened her eyes, suddenly finding herself sitting with an older woman with golden red hair. It was braided along the sides with wisps of curls framing her face. Her skin was wrinkled with age, and she had a rather harsh look about her, yet her grey eyes were soft and caring. She wore a dark green robe with a gray sash and was carrying a beautiful emerald green star wand.

"Hello?" Akasha was on edge. She wasn't entirely sure what to expect as the last time she fell asleep she found herself having a roaring conversation with Leo.

"Yes, that was quite the conversation wasn't it?" the woman replied, seemingly reading Akasha's thoughts.

"Do I get any semblance of privacy anymore?" Akasha said, although she knew it didn't matter if her words were spoken aloud for them to be heard. She felt disoriented and didn't enjoy feeling like her inner world was being invaded

The old woman chuckled. *"In time, in time. You first need to learn how to harness your power and energy."* She looked deeply into Akasha's eyes.

"Right," Akasha stood up, her energy coming back to her, she refused to make eye contact. *"So, first I have to lose my love, then I am no longer allowed to sleep peacefully, then a Crown appears, and I am suddenly interacting with a lion. And now? Now I can't even have any private thoughts! I am not sure I like this rearrangement of my entire life!"* While she had felt some release with her yelling the night before, she still had a lot of anger and resentment within her.

"Stop," said the woman. *"Although, I care for you deeply, I am not going to let you see yourself as a victim. You are born to do great things Akasha. I know this is hard*

for you at the moment, but there is a reason why all of this is happening. In time, it will be clearer."

"That isn't very comforting," Akasha scoffed, upset with the woman's cool remarks, she wanted to get up and leave but there wasn't anywhere for her to go.

"You need to work on changing that," the woman replied.

"Changing what exactly?" Akasha could feel her inner fire growing by the second. *Why can't I just be left in peace to grieve?* She looked at the woman for the first time, taken aback by the power in her presence.

"You need to work on acknowledging and being with exactly how you are feeling, which in turn, allows you to let go of what is no longer serving you. When you hold onto anger, resentment, and pain, ultimately it is only you that ends up being hurt. These emotions can harm you and affect your mental well-being, especially if you don't take the time to recognize, acknowledge and then work to release them. You will meet someone in the next few days who will help with precisely that - acknowledging some of your inner thoughts that you might not even be consciously aware of at the moment," the woman explained, *"I hope that some of my words land within you Akasha and you can begin to realize how powerful your thoughts are, that you are, in fact, the creator of your own reality."*

"*How is it possible that you and Leo seem to know everything I am thinking? Actually, how is it possible that you are aware of things that I don't even realize I am thinking?*" Akasha was genuinely confused and started to feel overwhelmed and frustrated. *Who else am I supposed to meet? I've made enough new acquaintances for the time being!*

"*Things are more than they seem.*" The woman moved a little closer.

Akasha sighed and turned her back to her. This woman seemed to enjoy speaking in codes and she really wasn't in the mood to try and decipher them.

"*It's not codes, Akasha. I am here to remind you of who you are, to let you know that you are not alone. I am here to show you that we are all with you,*" she echoed back her thoughts once more.

"*BUT WHO ARE YOU?*" Akasha yelled facing her once again, starting to reach her boiling point. "*I don't understand any of this! What if I don't want to do great things? What if I just want to have my life back? And who the hell is this 'we' you keep talking about?*"

The woman sighed. "*Breathe, Akasha. Take a few deep breaths and get back to your center.*"

"*Thanks, Mother,*" Akasha responded sarcastically, she paused as she realized she could have upset the woman, but the woman laughed in response to her flippancy. Her laugh was contagious. Akasha looked over and could not help but smile.

"*My name's Athena. I have agreed to serve as your protector in this transition, in your awakening. What you are entering into is your awakening period, meaning you are starting to wake up to a clearer understanding of who you are and what you're meant to do.*"

Akasha could sense the power emanating from her. She wasn't just an ordinary protector, and with that acknowledgment, her mood shifted immediately. She wasn't sure what she had signed up for, but she felt an immense feeling of gratitude. *What is she protecting me from though?*

"*It's alright, Akasha. You will understand when you are ready. You are tired, so I will let you sleep. I just wanted to let you know that I am here. I am with you always. If you need me, all you have to do is think of me and I will come.*"

"*I'm still so confused, and what about meeting Leo last night? Who is he?*"

"*In time,*" Athena responded.

"*Oh yeah. Everyone's favorite response,*" Akasha stammered, recalling the conversation with Raoul at the Temple. Her heart jumped at the thought, and then

collapsed back into anger and sorrow as she remembered
he was gone.

*"I think that's my cue to leave. Hopefully, when we
meet next, you will be in better spirits."*

"I'm sorry," Akasha realized that she was taking out
her frustration and weariness on this being who was only
letting her know she was loved and protected. She wasn't
being fair.

"It's alright. Now, please rest."

With that, Athena vanished and Akasha laid back
down, finally falling into a deep sleep.

Chapter 10

Sophia and the Market

ophia left the cottage and walked along the road to the village passing the ancient Well of Remembrance, her stomach churning at the thought of running the stand alone. Gibraltar had a thriving marketplace filled with local produce, art, tapestries, spices, herbs, and the potions that they sold. *While Akasha sleeps, there is still work to be done. Our stall isn't going to make us any money without one of us being present to serve the community.* It had been five years since Isis's death, and they did not have the income they received from her role at the Temple. They needed to be

at the market daily to make ends meet, even if Sophia really didn't want to be there on her own. She slowly entered the marketplace, one of the first to arrive, hesitant and nervous for the day without the presence of her sister.

Normally, Akasha ran the stand. She knew so much more about the potions, but Sophia would have to make do. *I hope no one asks me any difficult questions,* she stepped inside their stall and started to prepare for the day, setting out the potions to display them.

Akasha and Sophia came from a long line of healers. While Raoul had been an expert in plant medicine, they had a gift with potions. Some called them magic. The secrets of the potions had remained in her family for years, passing through the female line. Isis wanted her daughters and the next generation to have access to the sacred knowledge. So, she had instilled ancient crystalline knowledge into each one of the potions, making them available to the public. The Earth has a powerful crystalline core that these potions contained the sacred essence of. Isis created a way for Akasha to replicate the techniques ensuring that the potions could be produced after her passing. Sophia longed to learn this ancient knowledge, but for now she was content with the knowing that there was a different potion for anything you could possibly imagine – love, lust, health, wealth – all of it. If you took the potions regularly and believed in them, you would attract what you desired, as long as it was for your highest good and didn't cause harm to others.

Sophia touched the rose quartz crystal she wore around her neck. It helped her feel connected to her heart. She felt it as a source of strength in feeling loved. *I know that to some it is just a gemstone, but to me, it is so much more. It's a reminder that there is more to this world than what appears. It is my way of feeling closer and connected to all there was, is, and ever will be.*

Lost in thought, she reached up to tie her brown curls back behind her head with a ribbon. She wiped her hand on her light blue dress and moved around their stall, setting out the potions on the table and preparing to serve the customers when they arrived.

Sophia saw Abdul, the leader of the *Order of the Pragmatists* approaching her stand in the typical black robe of the Order, a black turban upon his head. He was tall with dark features and a muscular build that intimidated and scared many, but there was something about him that had always seemed familiar to her. With the recent loss of Raoul to his Order, that feeling of familiarity had hardened. It seemed strange that a member of the Order was approaching a potion stand, but she didn't give it too much thought.

✠ ✠ ✠

"Good morning," Abdul said as he approached the counter. This would be their first encounter and he wasn't sure how she would respond. He was well aware of Raoul's recent passing and hadn't fully come to terms with the depth of his loss himself, nor the repercussions of it.

"Hello, Sir," Sophia replied, looking up and making eye contact.

"Please call me Abdul," he said as he placed his hands on the counter and slowly began to pick up one of the bottles.

"Abdul," Sophia responded stiffly.

"I wondered if you have anything to help with clarity?" He looked down at the potion in his hands. He understood her harshness and felt it within himself, the pain caused by Raoul's death. He had been hesitant to investigate within the Order and he hoped this potion would give him the strength he needed to own the Order's responsibility for the murder. *I need to figure out what I am so fearful of, or why I am resisting taking the investigative action I know I should be taking to restore justice.*

"The leader of the Pragmatists is asking about clarity?" Sophia's tone was far from friendly.

"Oh, Sophia, very well played," Abdul smiled and placed the bottle back down, her tense mood seemed to lighten a little. He appreciated the fierceness she was expressing. Abdul knew that it was important to express, acknowledge and release one's emotions, even if he was struggling to do that himself.

"I am sorry. You caught me off guard." She looked down at the table.

Sophia picked up the bottle he had just held. He noticed that her gestures in packing it up seemed anxious as she handed it back to him.

Abdul reached into his pockets to pay for the potion and complete this initial exchange. He sensed her nervous demeanor and didn't want to test the waters even further. He was grateful for the initial interaction and to have the bottle to begin with. He had closed himself off to the Spirit Realm and his own Shadow for years and knew he needed to open himself again; he was hoping for Isis' help.

Chapter 11

Abdul's Reflection

 bdul walked away with the clarity potion in hand smiling at how the universe worked. He wanted answers, he wanted to know how to unite the order, and what he ended up with was creation and guidance from Isis. He thought of Sophia's nervousness at their interaction and his own. Her sister, Akasha, normally set up their stall but she didn't appear to be there today.

I wonder if she is okay? He sighed. He knew that his *Order of the Pragmatists* were responsible for the loss of Raoul's life and was still reeling from it. *I don't understand*

how someone could have taken a human life. How could we have spun so far out of control, how could I not know who was responsible for it? The mark of the Pragmatists had been left upon him, upon his third eye. But how? The more Abdul thought about it, the tenser he became. He needed to call a meeting, but he was hesitating, scared of what might be revealed to him, scared to discover how out of alignment the Order had become. He thought of Juliet, his own Shadow who appeared in the form of a falcon. When Isis had passed, he had made the conscious decision to not interact with her, the pain of Isis' loss was too great for him to deal with anything else. At times like this, he missed Juliet's presence, although deep down, he knew she was always there.

After the end of the holy war 500 years before, the Pragmatists worked to create balance with those identified with the Light. What the Light Workers took in faith, the Pragmatists had hoped to replicate with science. They hoped to prove scientifically everything that the mystics of the Ancient of Days had practiced. They had hoped to bridge the divide between the world of faith and the world of matter so that the two could work together and balance one another.

Unfortunately, through greed and corruption, that aim had been lost over time. Rumors swirled within the order of a resurfaced secret society, and the Pragmatists had come to view those of the Light as the enemy. Their ideas were scorned and rejected, their hopes and fears were ridiculed. Abdul kicked the dust in frustration during his walk back to the Cave of the Pragmatist, lost in thought.

He hoped he would find a few minutes alone to gain some clarity to resolve this. *I am ready to do the inner work to get the Order to be open to the Light. To examine my old wounds and heal so I can open myself back up to divine guidance, no further lives can be lost.* He resolved as he re-entered the cave.

Chapter 12

Akasha's Meditation

kasha stirred. "Soph?" she called as she slowly began to wake up. There was no response. She looked at the position of the sun, noting its placement.

It must be around midday, Sophia must have gone to the market on her own. She felt a surge of pride for her. At sixteen years old, this would have been the first time Sophia had opened up the stall by herself. *I am so grateful for the bravery she must have displayed this morning.*

Akasha rolled over. She moved to get up but felt a knot in her stomach and realized that before she could do anything else, she needed to meditate. *I am exhausted; I don't feel grounded or fully present.* She needed to take a few minutes to get herself centered within her seven energy centers as her mother had taught her.

She lay back down, put her hands over her heart, and focused. She breathed deeply for a few minutes, paying attention and slowing down. She imagined she could follow her breath down to her stomach and then back up and out of her mouth. She felt her body relax as it began to feel very heavy, almost like the Earth was holding her and calling her back home to rest. Akasha imagined a long cord extending from the base of her spine traveling all the way down to the center of the Earth. Beneath the grass, beneath the soil, beneath the rocks, all the way down to the crystalline core. Breathing deeply, she sent love down that cord, an energy of comfort and compassion. She imagined breathing into the Earth as if she could connect with the crystalline center and remained still until she felt Earth's loving energy return.

She shifted her focus to her base chakra, located at the base of the spine. This was her center for safety, protection, and balance. She imagined a deep ruby red energy and focused her attention, imagining this red energy refueling her. She remained there for a few minutes before she felt herself connect into what felt like a cocoon of protection and then shifted her attention to her second energy center, the sacral, located just below her belly button – the center for her creativity and sexuality. She imagined an orange light focusing and harnessing the energy of this center, feeling something stir within her.

She moved up to her solar plexus, located between her stomach and her lungs – the energy center tied to her feeling of personal power, self-empowerment, and her gut instincts. She focused on sending yellow energy to her core and breathed deeply as she knew she needed deep healing here after the events of the last few days. Slowly, she felt herself gaining back some of her power and strength. *I am constantly amazed by the difference a little visualization, meditation and focus on the energy centers can do.*

After some time, she moved up to what her mother identified as her true authentic center of expression – her heart. When this space was energized, Akasha felt other-worldly, connected and able to conquer anything that came her way. Her heart had recently been broken, so she wasn't sure how far she would progress today, but she imagined a healing green light entering her. She drew in her breath and stayed there for quite a few minutes, soaking into the healing, loving energy of her heart.

"Akasha?" She gasped at the sound of Raoul's voice.

"Raoul?" she asked, unsure.

"*I'm here,*" he replied as she felt his loving energetic presence surrounding her own.

"*I don't understand. How can I hear you and feel you?*" She was grateful to hear his voice again, but her heart was still heavy from the loss of his physical presence.

Her eyes remained closed, and she breathed deeply. This conversation was happening deep within her. Even though she could still feel her body on her bed and the sun shining down on her face, her mind and soul seemed to be in a different place.

"*There is much more than you are aware of right now. I am in a different realm than you, but when you are able to tap into the energy of your heart, we can reconnect.*"

"*Really?*" She couldn't see him but she felt him in her presence.

"*It is easier when you let go of control and your ego to open yourself up to all there was, is, and ever will be. I am always here. I am always with you, even if it doesn't feel like it sometimes.*"

"*Raoul, why did you leave me? How could you leave me?*" Akasha was starting to get upset. It didn't seem fair. They had so much in front of them. He was understanding more each day about the medicinal use of plants, and she was perfecting the craft of potions, in addition to the profound love they felt for one another.

"Akasha, it was my time. I know this won't make any sense to you now, but it will."

Akasha didn't respond. She just yearned for more from Raoul, more than just these words and the feeling of his presence.

"Akasha. I love you. But you must not focus on what you think you lack."

"Raoul, you have just left me here, and you want me to try and pretend that everything is okay? You are telling me to not grieve?" She could feel his energy slowly start to dissipate. She needed to work on keeping her temper in check, but now did not feel like the right time.

"I'm not saying that you can't grieve. In fact, I was very proud of you the other night at Cleopatra's Obelisk. You needed to get those emotions out and you still do. You don't always have to be the strong one, Akasha. Once you have processed this, however, you will need to work on shifting where you put your time, your energy, and your focus."

"Raoul, I don't need a lecture right now. All I want is a hug and kiss, and that is impossible. Instead, I have you telling me that things will all make sense 'in time' which is not helping."

"Akasha, breathe. I'm losing connection with you because you are lowering your vibration."

"What the hell does that mean?" Akasha demanded, she was getting tired of people saying things she didn't understand.

She became more agitated and immediately snapped out of her meditative state.

"What is going on?" she said aloud as she sat up in her bed. Being able to communicate with a powerful lion and her recently passed first love was unnerving. She needed to try and center her throat, third eye, and crown energy centers, but after the conversation with Raoul, she wasn't sure how she was going to do more today.

I just don't want to do anything. I don't want to move. Frankly, I don't even want to think. All she could do was lie in bed surrounded by her sadness. *It's odd but there is some comfort in this; in just allowing myself to be sad and come to terms with not being at peace. I keep trying to pretend that I am alright, but if I'm being honest with myself, I'm not. I'm grieving. I don't know if Sophia will be alright on her own, but I can't find the motivation to care. Does that make me a horrible person?* Akasha pulled her blanket over her head and allowed herself to be with her darkness, knowing that her sister would come home in a few hours and she would deal with reality then.

Chapter 13

Tariq's Discovery

ariq sat on the deck of the Black Onyx, the treasure chest safely by his side. He reflected on how he had met Paul on the Isle of Cyprus. Having recently connected with Leo and learned of the Ring of Infinite Wisdom, he remembered their first encounter at the ale house:

"This Ring will change the course of your life." Leo had spoken to him telepathically before he had entered.

"But, how will I find it? How will I know what to do?"

"Tariq, you have me now. I know you have issues with asking for help or support from others, but you will know what to do because you will remember you are not alone." Leo spoke, allowing his hidden and unconscious thought patterns to surface.

Tariq was silent. The words Leo said rang true. With the passing of Cora, Tariq's first love, he struggled with the concept of his own needs and desires. Was it okay to want others? To feel the need to have them in his life? Would they just abandon and hurt him? He didn't like the feeling of having a vulnerable heart and did everything he could to protect himself. He told himself that needing someone else would ultimately just cause him pain.

"Tariq, that's not the truth of who you are, or truly honoring your own needs. You have embodied this internally, having recently made peace with me and accepting our relationship. A man will enter this ale house shortly who will become like a brother to you. It is important that you are open to this and not shut him out. Together, you will find the Ring with the help of this device." Leo had spoken as the compass appeared in Tariq's hand and Paul walked into the room.

Snapping out of his flashback, Tariq pulled out his telescope and looked ashore. His eyes caught sight of Abdul, the well known leader of the *Order of the*

Pragmatists, walking along to their cave, with what looked to be a potion. The Cave of the Pragmatists was as mysterious as the Order itself, no one knew what happened inside.

"How odd? Someone from the Order with a magic potion?" He remembered hearing about these potions being sold at the market, and decided to investigate, but he also wanted his best mate with him. He snapped the telescope away and went to fetch him.

"What do you want?" Paul asked agitatedly, as Tariq descended the stairs into the space below deck that had been divided into two sleeping compartments.

He opened his mouth to speak, but before he could even get the words out, Paul interrupted him. "Isn't finding the Ring enough of an adventure for one week, Tariq?"

"Oh, where is that sense of adventure I remember from when we met in Cyprus?" While Paul was incredibly brave, he was also resistant, and could often be quite cynical.

Paul shrugged. "My sense of adventure is tied to my sense of safety, and I have a feeling that you're about to suggest something that would jeopardize it," Paul said without moving.

"That's the spirit!" Tariq said, slapping his back with a smile.

"What do you want?" Paul repeated, not returning the friendly gesture.

Tariq put his hand on his compass for guidance, *"Leo, I seem to be drawn to investigating this potion, but I don't understand why?"*

"You will know when you find the stand at the marketplace tomorrow morning. More will be revealed then."

"I've always sensed there was more for me in this lifetime. I feel like I am meant to do more, carry more, pave the way, but I don't have clarity yet of what that might be."

"You have a great destiny Tariq, but it is only revealed one step at a time,"

Tariq sighed, knowing that he wasn't going to get any additional guidance from Leo, and turned to face Paul. "I want to go and find some magic!" He said with a grin as he explained his plan to visit the market.

Chapter 14

Thomas' Reminder

 homas sat at his desk to write.

"Just keep going and trust your intuition," he heard Peter say.

He knew he was here to guide others by documenting and recording significant events, so he continued what he liked to call the Akasha records. He struggled with what he felt was the weight of this responsibility. In addition to recording the events in the *Book of Records* he also needed to prepare his talk for the Solstice.

The *Book of Records* told of the Two of the Royal Heart and how they needed to operate from a space of authenticity. The Crown Jewels would reappear when they had both accepted their Shadows, were standing in their authentic sense of selves, and truly connected to their hearts.

The Light Workers and the Pragmatists had different definitions of what that meant. Those associated with the Light defined standing in their authentic sense of self in the form of high, holy, and lifted; operating from a space of love. The Pragmatists did not view the world in terms of spiritual concepts and required more rationality and scientific definition. They had defined something as being authentic which could not be scientifically proven wrong, something backed by facts, not from a space of love, but of evidence.

The uniting factor between the two—of which neither side seemed to be quite aware of—is that those living from their authentic sense of self must be in a place where they are connected and acting from the source of their highest good. They are connected to their highest truth in a way that serves humanity. For the Pragmatists, it might be related to scientific proof; and for the Light Workers, to their source energy and inner being.

In either instance, they are standing in their authenticity because the individuals processing it are working in alignment with their deepest individual beliefs and foundations, their highest levels of consciousness. The important fundamental fact is that both definitions of authenticity are, in fact, true, as they are deeply connected with their source of truth, and they operate from a space that allows them to recognize, appreciate, share, and reflect it to others.

Thomas knew all of this, but it wasn't clear to others. Learning how to truly show and be seen within the authentic nature of one's being and use it in a way that helps humanity was written in the Book of Records in relation to the reappearance of the Crown Jewels. He pulled out his quill and paper, feeling inspired to write. He would deliver his talk on the Winter Solstice in just a week.

"I hope I can speak with Akasha before then," he said aloud. It was becoming increasingly apparent that she needed to know about the Crown, and about being One of the Royal Heart. He needed to step in and guide her, to equip her with this knowledge so she could take the next steps into who she was meant to be, the leader she was born to become.

"You need to overcome your fear, your doubt, and step into your power, Thomas. You need to believe that you are capable of being so much more than just the guardian of the Temple. You are a light in this world, and you will not fail."

Thomas felt chills all over at that thought and smiled. *Thank you, Peter, I needed to be reminded of that.* He began to write with purpose. He felt the love and support coming in from Peter as he started to connect with his truth.

It was going to be a long week and he wanted to make sure he got this particular Akasha Record and his Winter Solstice message just right; the whole town would be there. That began with, as Peter had just reminded him, trusting in the power of his own voice.

Chapter 15

The Entrance of the Cave

 ariq knew Paul's temperament but he also knew his own. He couldn't help wanting to leave the Black Onyx to go and explore the cave he had seen Abdul enter. So much mystery shrouded it, he couldn't resist the intrigue.

"We have dark robes we can put on to disguise ourselves, we can't not explore it now, can we?" Tariq hoped that his enthusiasm would convince Paul. He also knew there were ample Pragmatists around. He grabbed the black robes and threw one at Paul as he quickly got into his own. Paul grumbled and remained seated, he had a level of cautiousness that Tariq did not.

Paul shrugged. "I have no desire to explore the cave in broad daylight. If you want to go, then fine." Paul said firmly without getting to his feet.

"That's the spirit!" Tariq said, slapping his back with a smile that faded as soon he realized Paul was not going with him.

"I don't have a death wish, Tariq. If you want to go, fine, but I'll stay on board." And so they allowed the ship to drift into the shallows on the tide, until the water was shallow enough for Tariq to slip down with barely a splash. Tariq dragged a rope attached to the prow of the boat and used a stake to secure it. Thus he found himself in the shadow of the cliff, beneath the ledge he would soon climb to. The tide would not be turning for another hour and he would be back long before then.

Paul might have had a point, how am I going to not raise any suspicion if anyone from the Order happens to pass?

"*Leo, can you make me invisible?*" He asked but only slightly in jest; he was hoping for some sort of miracle. He heard nothing, but sensed Leo's concern at his lack of caution.

"*Tariq, this is unsafe. You should return to the boat and wait with Paul; I will reveal more when the time is right.*"

"*Leo, when have you ever known me to wait? I go when I feel inspired; it's now or never!*" He quickly started to climb, placing one foot wherever he found a gap. Forging ahead until he reached the level of the cave. Sweat covered his body from the rising heat of the sun and the warmth from his the black robe. He grunted as he pushed himself to make the final lunge over the ledge, not bothering to look around.

"*That was incredibly stupid Tariq. There are hundreds of people in the Order, and only one of you. You are not invincible. You might feel inspired, but you aren't following your better instincts, which would have told you to stay on the boat and wait until we can work on this together.*"

Tariq didn't listen to Leo. He stood silently for a few minutes holding his breath. Not hearing anything, he moved forward. *As I just said, it's now or never and I'm going to go now!* He quickly pulled his hood over his face and dashed into the cave; he wasn't one for patience.

It took Tariq's eyes a few moments to adjust to the darkness, but then he heard voices. His heart raced as he quickly moved to the side, looking for a place to

hide. He scanned to the left and the right searching frantically, willing his eyes to adjust to the candlelit caves. The
voices got closer, he couldn't make them out, but heard
their footsteps approaching

I can't get caught; I've only just begun! He
suddenly saw a curve in the hall and dashed through it
hoping that he wouldn't be seen, that it wouldn't lead to
others. He had just made it around the corner as two men
appeared, deep in conversation. He ducked down praying
they wouldn't see him, although he knew where the exit
was if he needed it.

Chapter 16

The Cave of the Pragmatists

ut you know he picked up a potion!"

Abdul heard a voice scoff, he had made himself some food and was heading down the main entrance of the cave, eager to return to his chambers. He couldn't quite place the voice. *Could they be talking about me?* He realized he might need to wait a bit longer before having some time alone with his newly purchased potion. The polished granite cave walls were narrow, but the sound echoed through them. The stone reflected and amplified the light of the burning candles that hung along the way.

"And? Your point? The last time I checked that wasn't a crime," a different voice said wearily. Abdul recognized his trusted second in command; a man he had known more than half his life. He was the only other person within the Order to have embraced his own Shadow, and who he completely trusted.

"But, Khalid! It's of the Light!" The second voice answered in disdain.

"Rashid, I never known you to be so stupid," Khalid was quite frank. Abdul couldn't help but smile as he shuffled deeper into the shadows, keen to hear the rest of the conversation.

"The Light is not bad. We know that originally the Pragmatists worked in harmony with the Light. They inspired us to prove and justify. Hand in hand, we created many masterpieces of art, science, and the mind. Astronomy and astrology are cases in point."

"I have heard this all before. But a magical potion made of crystals used to set intentions? It sounds so ridiculous," Rashid said quietly.

How does he know I have this? I have only just returned from the market? Abdul was alarmed and intrigued by this young man, Rashid.

"I'm sure it does to your rational mind which has never been exposed to these things before."

"And yours has?"

Abdul could hear the shift in their tones and knew that he would need to step in soon, the tension between them rising. He didn't want to have any additional divides formed within his Order.

"Rashid, don't take this the wrong way. There is much more to this world than just the Pragmatist's point of view. If you don't open yourself up to it, you will be missing the full story. You could miss the next great discovery because your mind won't be able to see the possibility," Khalid said gently.

"Are you sure you joined the right community?" Rashid snarled.

Abdul was hesitating, but the young man's words strengthened his resolve, a huge faction had appeared within the Order recently with the younger generation vehemently opposed to those of Light and closed to the outside world, treating them with contempt.

As the leader of the Pragmatists, he was doing what he could to avoid conflict. Unfortunately, it was not completely in his control. *There are others who want to experiment, who want to further the divide.* He could feel himself getting worked up all over again. *And now, it's too late. A human life has been lost! Too many things within the Order are going awry.*

Khalid sighed, "Rashid, I would watch your tone with me. I know you are new to the Order, but there is much to be said about respect here."

"I have no respect for anything to do with the Light, and there are others here that would agree with me."

That was the trigger he needed. "Gentlemen! What are we discussing here?" He rounded the corner and stepped into view.

"Abdul!" Khalid jumped, but quickly regained his composure. "Welcome. Let me introduce you to our newest member, Rashid."

"Welcome, Rashid," Abdul said amicably. "I hope you come to find your home here as I have. We have a few things to work through, but Khalid has been instrumental in helping pave the way where we have lost sight of our original intentions." Abdul hoped Rashid would sense the purity in his voice and tone, he really did want him to feel at home here, although his words alarmed him.

"Thank you, Abdul," Khalid said. "We are all doing our best."

The both stood there awkwardly saying nothing. Abdul knew he could stay and further defuse the situation, but he felt confident that Khalid could handle it. He also felt the urge to finally seek out his Shadow.

"Well, I won't keep you then. Nice to meet you, Rashid. I hope to spend some more time with you over the next few weeks." Abdul bowed as he parted ways carefully clutching the potion in his robe.

❈ ❈ ❈

Rashid was dumbstruck. He wasn't sure how to respond. Here was this man, Abdul, the leader of the Pragmatists from which so many had secretly turned away from following with Alejandro's influence. Abdul's purchase of the potion made Rashid question him. Khalid's conversation about new ideas and being open frustrated him, but at the same time, he felt a connection to both of these men, even if their viewpoints were different from his own.

Rashid shrugged. He knew that he would need to report these things to Alejandro later on tonight.

"What are you thinking about?" Khalid asked, immediately bringing him back to the present moment.

"Oh, nothing sir," Rashid responded with the disrespect now completely removed from his tone.

"Please call me Khalid. There is no need for formalities with me."

"Yes, Khalid."

"Now, if you don't mind, we should probably carry on with your lesson," Khalid started moving back in the direction of the instruction area of the cave with Rashid gently following suit.

Chapter 17

Alejandro's Catch

lejandro scratched his head. *I thought I knew everyone in the Order, but here is a face that I do not recognize.* He peered down the hall at the strange man crouched in the corner.

Alejandro had joined the Order ten years ago and a lot had changed since then. In recent years, he'd felt compelled to create an inner circle to hold true to his family's legacy within his ancestor Avraham's vision. This secret council formed to resurrect the use of the alchemical knife that had moved down the patriarchal lineage of his family. He was starting to see those of the Light as specimens to experiment on rather than human beings. He wanted to sequester them, to study and understand how they are able to perform the acts they do and be inspired as they were, the plant medicine of Raoul was an example of this.

Unfortunately, my last experiment went awry. I wasn't able to extract all of the codes that I needed, I will make them work though. I will uncover Raoul's genius. The alchemical knife had failed him. The electromagnetic codes were typically recorded into the base of the knife for study and future use. However, the shooting pain that happened when Alejandro had touched Raoul's third eye had not allowed for the full capture. Alejandro watched as this foreign man stood back up, looked around cautiously, then quickly ran back to the cave's entrance.

Who is this man? And what did he want? He made a note to himself to keep an eye out for him over the next few weeks. He would find out who he was, because the one thing that Alejandro couldn't handle was anything he viewed as a threat to his Order and his way of being.

Chapter 18

ᗧariq and the ᗎlan

 ariq climbed back on board the ship lost in thought after releasing the mooring rope. *It was interesting that the younger man was so judgemental of the Light. I agree with the older voice's comments about the rational mind, that if we become too caught up in our mind, we limit the possibilities because we aren't necessarily open to them.*

"*That is exactly what happens, Tariq, when you are open and working with me. You move beyond the boundaries of your human thinking mind. Next time, you need*

to do a better job of staying in tune with me. That was reckless, and there is more involved here than just you."

Tariq felt partially guilty for not paying attention to Leo, but was too exhausted and happy to be safely back on board to give it much thought.

"Paul! I went inside!" Tariq yelled as his feet hit the floor, and he saw Paul standing in front of him.

"Yes," said Paul as he went to prepare their meal for later.

"You sound nervous."

"Well, I don't know if sneaking around the *Order of the Pragmatists'* was your greatest idea yet, Tariq, especially as we only found the Ring this morning. We don't want to attract attention and put ourselves in danger," he said bluntly. He salted some recently caught fish for preservation.

"Valid points," said Tariq. "On all counts. But at the same time, how could I not? Do you know how many mysteries the *Order of the Pragmatists* has? No one knows what they are actually studying or doing within those cave walls!"

"They are guarded for a reason," echoed Paul anxiously. "We have been hunting for this Ring for years. We found it and you immediately placed us in danger."

"It appears that there may be tension within the Order," Tariq continued, ignoring Paul's concern.

"And you got all of this from your brief excursion today?"

"Oh, ye of little faith!" Tariq laughed and sat down beside his friend to help. "I am now even more convinced that we should pay a visit to the market and find this Clarity potion that is causing so much turmoil within them."

"Why?"

"The young man I heard was disgusted by Abdul's purchase. Why would Abdul want one? Why does the fact that he wanted one disturb this particular member of the order so much? The only way we can find out Paul, is if we investigate and try some of these magical little potions ourselves." Not to the mention the fact that he was eager to learn about the more that Leo had spoken to him about.

Paul was silent and Tariq smiled inwardly knowing that he would have his way. *Yes, more will be revealed, but what?*

Chapter 19

Akasha and her Shadow

kasha heard Sophia come home and groaned. She should get out of bed, but she just didn't want to. *I wonder how much longer I can get away with just lying here.*

"Akasha, are you alright? I kept expecting you to come down to the market." She heard the concern in her little sister's voice as she sat down beside her and felt guilty. She had let her down.

"I don't know Sophia, I honestly don't. Yesterday something happened that I can't explain and now I'm not sure if I will ever make peace with it." She knew that she must sound dramatic, but was struggling to put into words her recent experiences. She hoped Sophia would understand. *How would I begin to try and explain that I have had a vision of a Crown, screamed and yelled over Raoul's death with a magical lion, spoke to Raoul himself and then met Athena?*

Sophia was silent.

"Sophia, I know you are worried about me," Akasha said, "but honestly I think the best thing you can do for me right now is to just leave me alone. I don't mean to be rude, but I need some time, space, and energy to heal." She saw that her words would hurt her, but she was unable to say anything more clearly.

She saw the tears in Sophia's eyes as she left her room. *I really must be a horrible person. I honestly don't know who I am anymore.*

❈   ❈   ❈

Akasha lay back down, devastated to have hurt her sister. Her heart felt heavy so she decided to give it some focus, intentionally breathing in and out, praying that it would center her. She imagined sending love and light with each inhale and releasing some of her emotional pain on each exhale. She viewed her heart as something similar to her brain, it was an area of her body that she could think, feel and be guided from. After a few minutes she felt her consciousness expand, as her energy felt greater than her physical body. She continued to breathe into the experience and for the second time in the last few days, she didn't know where she was.

The moon was bright above her and the sky was full of stars. She felt a breeze, but despite it being night, it was still warm. She was standing on a mountain top, wearing a long white dress with a pleated design looking over a vast beautiful gulf. Her long dark curls blew in the wind, but she was not cold. By moonlight, she could see the water below, and the luscious landscape around her. *How does this keep happening? Where am I? Why am I losing control of everything?* She felt uneasy as she sensed something else; something dark; something sinister. As with Leo and Athena, she could sense a great power in it.

She turned and saw a pair of deep green eyes; giant eyes with flecks of gold in them and immense dark wings. Fear ran through every membrane of her body. Towering above her stood a giant dragon of a shimmering shade of indigo blue and black its large wings expanded. Akasha felt terrified.

"*Who are you?* She struggled to find her words as she didn't want to breathe or even move. She feared taking any type of action might lead to immediate danger.

"*It's okay, Akasha,*" she heard. The voice was familiar, although the words were not spoken aloud.

"*What are you?*" Akasha racked her brain trying to remember where she had heard the voice before. She was surprised that she could form coherent sentences and thoughts despite her fear. This was a lot. She missed the days where she could sleep soundly, and felt like she understood who she was.

"*I am with you always, although you are not aware of it. My name is Esmeralda,*" the dragon said.

Esmeralda felt like a mystery to Akasha, something she could not understand. The energy she felt coming from her was different from anything she had previously experienced. It felt powerful, confusing and hostile. Esmeralda made her incredibly uneasy, not to mention the intimidation from her physical shape and stature.

As this dragon bowed her head and moved forward to be seen more clearly, Akasha's fears exploded into form and rage.

"STOP!" Akasha yelled. "I don't know you. I don't know what you are. I don't know why you're here, and most importantly; I don't know if I can trust you!" Akasha's feeling of immediate threat transformed her fears into anger as they all came out at once. *Well I suppose that's a good thing, I'm not bottling them up?* Akasha had been keeping her emotions trapped for years. The release at Cleopatra's Obelisk had been her first real acknowledgement of them.

"Akasha, I am a part of you, I am aware of every thought, feeling and emotion you have." Esmeralda said. "The sooner you accept that, the easier this will be."

"What? Are you crazy? You expect me to believe that!" It was the most ridiculous thing she had ever heard. Akasha was backing away from Esmeralda but soon realized she had nowhere to go. She felt her fear rise and course through her body. *How can whoever this Esmeralda is expect me to think she is a part of me?*

"Akasha this needs to stop. You are allowing yourself to be swallowed up by your fears and doubts. You are capable of so much more." Esmeralda had wanted to come across with compassion for Akasha but her attitude in the current moment was not allowing for it.

Akasha snapped, "And what exactly is that? I have just lost the love of my life and I can't even have a minute to grieve for him." *Why can't I just be left alone? I don't need a dragon's opinions on my life, I don't need her scaring me, I just need some peace!* She looked around for an escape route. She couldn't just leap off the mountain but she didn't see any other way out.

"You have had the entire day alone Akasha, you didn't move. Now, tell me how good did that feel? Did you feel good about yourself today?" Esmeralda snarled as she was starting to allow Akasha's emotions to control the situation. She was reflecting back to Akasha her current emotional state, that was how the relationship worked. The more consciously aware of it Akasha became, the easier it would be for the two of them to work together. She would start to see how Esmeralda was working for her, not against her.

Akasha's inner fire continued to flare, "So, now you judge me for taking care of myself?! I don't need any more judgment in my life, thank you very much!" Akasha took a few more steps backward.

"I am not judging you, Akasha. You are judging yourself. I reflect back to you your inner thoughts, so you become aware of them. I am what they call your Shadow. Did you feel like you were taking care of yourself by refusing to leave your bed and shirking all of your responsibilities?"

"You know what! I am sick of this! I don't want any of your supposed help or reflection, or whatever the hell you are talking about. I JUST WANT TO BE LEFT ALONE!"

Esmeralda tried to withhold her flames, but when she was upset, it was impossible. She stepped back, but before she knew it, it was too late. She turned away and her blue flames flew out of her into the night sky.

Akasha stood shocked, her mouth wide open, it felt for a second like her heart had stopped beating. Not only did she not understand Esmeralda and their connection, but she now felt in immediate danger of sudden death.

"Akasha, breathe. I didn't want you to see my flames like that, but like you, when I get upset, I cannot control them,"

Akasha was shaking. "I don't have any words. I don't understand."

"Akasha," Esmeralda said, but soon she faded away as Akasha returned to her conscious reality in Gibraltar in the here and now.

Chapter 20

Sophia's Tears

 ophia was upset. *I can't believe her. All I wanted to do was help and she's shutting me out.* She stormed into her room and retrieved her journal from her desk. She had previously found release in getting her thoughts on paper, even the ones she had judged as bad or negative. She found solace in acknowledging and allowing them to flow through her. It helped to get them out of her system. *I'm so incredibly angry! I know she has just lost Raoul, but I feel like I am losing her.* Frantically, she began to write.

It was in her nature to want to help; she had been doing it all her life. With the passing of their mother, her maternal instincts had kicked in. "I know I'm the younger sister, but at this point, there isn't another role for me to play. I want to make sure Akasha is alright, and right now she is not letting me. I don't know what to do." Tears streamed down her face as she wrote.

She felt stifled and the writing didn't seem to be helping. *Maybe I can go for a walk? I just feel so lost and hopeless.*

It was late, but she couldn't stay in the cottage. She was too upset and needed to do something to calm her nerves. She pulled on her beige robe, shawl, and sandals, and headed outside, hoping a walk would help. *It's not like Akasha will even notice I'm gone,* she sulked as she moved out into the darkness.

As she walked, she didn't feel any better. Her nerves were shot and her worry about her sister was overtaking her own well-being.

Something happened to Akasha at the Temple, she remembered from her conversation with her earlier that evening. *Maybe if I go there myself, something similar will happen to me.* Sophia was terrified that things wouldn't go back to the way they were before, that her sister wouldn't recover.

Changing direction just past the ancient Well of Remembrance, she hoped beyond hope that some comfort or guidance would also be shared with her.

Chapter 21

The Sacred
Garden Gathering

 thena met with Isis in the Sacred Garden in the Spiritual Realm. The garden had many magical elements, including a plethora of sparkling rainbow flowers, a beautiful canopy with be-jewelled tables and chairs, ancient oak trees that seemed to touch the sky, distant mountains surrounded by a shimmering lake and an infinite amount of sunlight. Every element of this garden held healing properties.

"I don't know if that's the best use of your flames," Isis said, her tone a little bit sharp as Esmeralda came into view.

"Oh, Isis! You know   I am sorry. I want her to embrace me just as much as you do. I didn't mean to release them at our first encounter, but I couldn't let her just wallow in her victim mentality." Esmeralda landed abruptly and started pacing the sacred garden, inadvertently causing mass destruction. Akasha was capable of so much more than how she was acting at that moment. Tough love appeared to be the only way to get through to her.

"Esmeralda, I know you know this, but you are playing with fire, quite literally! There is a lot that Akasha does not know and understand yet. You have been connected and aware of her all of her life, but she is beginning to open to you. We need to be patient. I know that you want to integrate with her, but that will only come with time."

"I wonder if there is anyone on the physical plane we could ask to help," Athena pondered as she soothed Esmeralda, stroking her deflated wings.

"What about Thomas?" Thomas had been with them in the Temple of the Holy One and during Akasha's vision of the Crown. "Maybe he can help her to make peace with everything unfolding and not be so hard on herself." Esmeralda suggested.

"Yes, and also be more open to the idea of you. Thomas is a great idea. We have always been able to communicate directly with him, even in his waking state," Athena mused.

"Well then, let's get to work," Isis replied.

Chapter 22

Thomas' Guidance

homas shifted gear to work on his talk for the Winter Solstice but was struggling to get the words he wanted. *With the timing of the portal at the Winter Solstice, it's more important that ever this message resonates.* Thomas paced his office, picking up books, dusting them off, and then carefully putting them back on his cluttered ancient bookcase. His office was often in shambles.

"Thomas, are you hoping that those books will magically give you the information you need?" Peter said.

"You need to trust in the power of us and your connection to the Spirit Realm! You are not alone."

"I know, but I can't help but feel that a lot is riding on my shoulders." He thought back to his inspiration a few days ago, the moment he had chills all over. *I know that it's time to discuss the concept of Shadows. But how do I open up the space to those not consciously aware that they even exist?*

"I was terrified when I first met you. Khalid and I had no idea what we were doing, and suddenly you appeared. Tall, powerful, and incredibly daunting. I honestly thought you might take my life."

"It's not easy to meet your Shadow for the first time," Peter said gently. *"But remember Thomas, as you spent more time with me, we worked on the things within yourself you needed to integrate. Eventually, you saw that I am here to help you get to a place of wholeness. Others will realize this as well. Remember that once you learned to truly embrace me, the Spirit Realm opened up for you."*

"I know this, Peter, but my struggle is in how to share this with others? I can't just make everyone's Shadows appear in front of them, forcing them to accept these concepts now, can I? I need to talk with Akasha, but I am worried about saying the wrong things and overwhelming her. Being One of the Royal Heart is a huge responsibility."

Thomas continued to pace when he suddenly felt surrounded in a loving familiar energetic presence.

"Hello, Thomas," Isis said, appearing in his office amidst the clutter of his space and thoughts.

He stepped back, astonished. He'd had visions before, but not an apparition like this. Isis was surrounded in soft golden light, and just her presence put him at ease. "Isis. I have no words!" Although his words were unnecessary with their heartfelt connection.

Thomas dearly missed Isis and was overjoyed to be in her presence.

"It is lovely to see you, and I miss you too." Isis smiled tenderly, her warmth filled the entire room in a shimmering golden light.

While Isis' presence calmed him, it did not take away from Thomas' current fears. "Isis, I could use your help. I need to guide Akasha and others, but I don't know how much to reveal."

"I understand and that is exactly why I am here. We are farther along than you think. Esmeralda made her first appearance to Akasha just moments ago."

"Really? That's fantastic news."

"Yes, but Akasha has been overwhelmed. She did not leave the cottage yesterday, and Sophia had to run the potion stand alone. She is not holding herself from a place of unconditional love, or owning her grief and anger, so they are taking over. She is shutting out her sister, and while she has become aware that Esmeralda exists, the conversation ended with her being terrified and confused. I know you are well aware of the complexities of truly getting to know your Shadow."

"If Akasha isn't processing what has happened, then how ready is she to hear about her destiny?" Thomas made his way to his desk. He had a feeling he might need to capture more of this Akasha Record in the *Book of Records*.

"She is not aware of the power in her bloodline yet. We need to take it one step at a time, starting with her coming to terms with Esmeralda and building a relationship with her."

"But how do we do that? How do I help?" Thomas pulled out the Book of Records to see if there was any guidance he might glean.

"It is key that she realizes she is not alone, that you have been in a similar situation, you know what it feels like, and are willing to guide her along the way."

"And what of Sophia?" Thomas raised his eyebrows. He put the book down, realizing that Isis was asking for him to share his story, not the ancient records.

Isis sighed, "She is so close to being able to connect to us, but still doesn't quite believe. I hope that Sophia will start to release some of her fears and doubts. They are currently stopping her from being able to commune with us. Like you, Thomas, she needs to believe in her power and ability to do so. Sophia has an incredible heart. I believe she will get there, but she too, may need some help."

Thomas nodded his head in agreement, it was all true, even he forgot the power in his voice and connection at times, but he had Peter to remind him.

"Oh Isis, it is a pleasure to spend time with you again. I am grateful for all of the gifts that the Spirit Realm has bestowed on me, and I am happy to help in any way that I can." Thomas bowed deeply, only to raise his head to an empty room.

Chapter 23

Sophia's Adventure
at the Temple

 ophia walked through the Temple doors and saw that the Sanctum was empty. *I know it's late, but I still thought someone else might be here. I have never felt so alone before.*

She felt the urge to sit down and just breathe, to focus on the beautiful crystal in front of her and see if she could find some hope or inner peace. Her mother had taught her that the power connected to her heart was her true center of being. She wished she could talk to her now.

Sitting down in one of the pews, she focused her attention on the altar stone, and closed her eyes. *Mother, I don't know if you can hear me, but I need you. I need help from the Spirit Realm. I feel hopeless and isolated, and I don't know how to change this.* She continued to breathe deeply in and out, imagining that she could breathe directly into her heart. Deep breath in; she visualized love and light entering into her heart center. Deep breath out; she pictured that she could release all the chaos and disconnection she currently felt. She kept this pattern up for a few minutes, but nothing changed.

I don't believe it. Why is nothing happening? What is wrong with me? Sophia collapsed in tears. She had hoped she would feel comfort, not more pain. *This isn't fair! I don't understand!*

She remembered that within the walls of the Temple was an ancient library she had once been shown by her mother. It was forbidden without access from Thomas, but at this point, she didn't care. She wanted answers. She marched past the altar, determined to follow her gut instincts.

"Atchoo!" she sneezed from all the dust she disturbed as she entered the library, a separate room slightly down the hall from the Sanctum. She grabbed a candle and stood silently, her heart pounding. *What if I get caught? I'm fearful, but I have to do something.*

A book with a sacred symbol and the word "Chakras" on its spine caught her eye. She had not yet learned of all of the energy centers, but she had heard of them. Her mother had passed away before she had been able to teach her. She was intrigued, so she quickly and silently pulled the ancient book down. She cracked the pages open, glancing around nervously to make sure she was still alone. She was. She tried to read but realized that the candlelight was not sufficient.

As she rose from her position, she saw Thomas down the hall in the Sanctum lighting candles. She couldn't be caught, but she needed to go through the Sanctum to leave the building. *Maybe I can be unnoticed?* She took a few steps forward and dashed out of the library but tripped over her robe as she stepped into the room. *The book! I can't let him see it!* She landed on her side with a loud thump and immediately shuffled the book underneath her robe, hoping he wouldn't notice.

He looked up from his work and smiled, "Sophia, how lovely to see you."

"Thank you, Thomas." Sophia steadied herself and stood back up, trying to be casual, willing her tone to sound calmer than she felt. She was surprised at his gentleness. *Does he realize that something is wrong?*

Thomas paused in his actions.

"Well, I'd better get going. I just wanted to stop in the Sanctum for a second." She started to make her way to the door, knowing her story didn't make much sense at such a late hour.

"Sophia, I know that you have been through quite a lot recently. I want to make sure you know that I am happy to help in any way I can," Thomas offered.

Sophia shuffled nervously. *I suppose it wouldn't hurt to tell him some of what is going on. He doesn't seem to realize what I have.* She carefully made sure the book remained hidden within her robe and then turned to face him. She felt uncomfortable, but now that she was there, she might as well solicit his help.

"I feel hopeless, Thomas. I feel I am doing something wrong, and I can't find any support. My sister is upsetting me too. A lot has happened to her in addition to the passing of Raoul, but she isn't willing to tell me anything yet." Sophia was surprised by how easy it was to say what she wanted to.

Thomas paused, lost in thought, "Sophia, you know how to meditate, yes?"

"Mother taught me how to focus on my heart center a long time ago," Sophia responded, unsure if that was what he meant.

"Have you ever tried to go beyond that? Have you heard of the concept of chakras, the energy centers that exist within our bodies?"

Sophia gasped. *Did he know?* "Not really," she responded full of unease.

"Well, I would suggest you start there. Start tonight in meditation at home. We all have energy centers that exist within us. They start at the base of our spine and work their way up to the crown of our heads. Each center has a different color, resonance, and feel. I know your sister meditates, so perhaps you could ask her for some guidance."

"Well, I would if we were talking! Part of the reason I am here is that she asked me to leave her alone." Sophia's tears came back. There was nothing she could do to stop them. She clutched at the book behind her back, knowing she would need to leave soon, and dearly wanting to dry her eyes.

"I know you are looking for answers from me, but I am suggesting this because everything you seek from me, you should be able to find within. We are our own best teachers but often lose sight of that. Learning about your energy centers, the different colors, tones, and sounds associated with each of them will help you to connect to what you already know but have forgotten," Thomas walked over and gently placed his hands on her shoulders.

"I just wish the Spirit Realm made more sense to me," Sophia said, temporarily forgetting her unease. "I feel there's some reason I don't have access, like I'm not good enough." She looked down at the floor as she spoke, embarrassed, but also strangely relieved to be able to express her emotions, ones she wasn't even fully conscious of having.

"Oh, Sophia, you are not cut off at all," Thomas said softly. "Every single person has access to the Spirit Realm. What limits them is their lack of belief in being able to know it."

"I don't understand," said Sophia.

"I am trying to say this as gently as I can," Thomas responded, "but you absolutely do have access to the Spirit Realm. The only thing that has been preventing you are your thoughts and your belief that you don't.

"That is why I suggest learning more about the energy centers. Once you start to meditate and work on cleansing them, you can realize that the Spirit Realm is already yours. I hope my words are making sense."

"Yes," Sophia said softly, "they are."

Thomas waited patiently. "If you ever have any questions as you start working your way through this process, please know that I am always here. My talk on the Winter Solstice will help both you and your sister deal with everything that is happening to you."

"Thanks, Thomas," Sophia slowly backed away again. The more she thought about the book, the more anxious and excited she became. "I had better get home now, but I appreciate your help."

"My pleasure, Sophia. Any time."

Chapter 24

The Secret Meeting

y fellow Pragmatists, thank you for gathering," Alejandro called the secret council to order. It had been a few months since they last met, but with Raoul's recent death, he knew he needed to bring them together again. *I need to make sure they are all still with me*, he thought as he moved to the center of the room.

Alejandro was only thirty years of age, but old in spirit, as though he had lived many lifetimes and carried the knowledge and lessons of each within him now.

His ancestors had also passed on the traditions he was currently trying to uphold within this secret council.

"Raoul's death was unfortunate," Alejandro spoke, "Unfortunate, but ultimately it was necessary."

The twenty or so council members were gathered in the chambers in the back of the cave. They sat close to one another, intent on hearing from their leader. Rashid was among them as they sat in silence.

"We formed this council to resurrect the use of the alchemical knife gifted to me by my family. While I regret the death of the young man, what we will be able to discover through the electromagnetic connections with his third eye will be truly astounding! I hold in my hands his electromagnetic codes." Alejandro pulled the knife from his pocket and displayed it to the group. "How was he able to develop cures for diseases and illnesses that we have been unable to create ourselves. What did Raoul have access to that we don't?" Alejandro spoke loudly and clearly, making eye contact with each of the members, hoping that his energy and enthusiasm would spread. "We will soon know!"

"I saw a vision when I entered the field of Raoul's third eye. It caused an electrical reaction that was captured in the knife. I saw a pyramid with geometric patterns along the base, but I don't know what this means. I have made copies of it so that we can all study further. Once we have decoded it, we will need to test again. For now, we have our work cut out for us in deciphering what has been revealed."

The room remained silent.

"But Alejandro, what of his death?" Rashid asked after a few moments.

His tone doesn't seem challenging, but I need them to understand. Alejandro scratched his head as he gathered his thoughts. "Rashid, thank you for speaking up as I am sure your question is reflected in the thinking of the others. Raoul's death was unfortunate, and we will do all we can to avoid further upsets. However, think about it this way. We now have information that previously existed only with him. We just need to figure out the codes and translate this knowledge for our use. We can all have a more scientifically based understanding of plants for medicinal treatment. His death could ultimately aid us!"

Rashid didn't look convinced. In fact, he looked very uneasy, but he remained silent.

I need to keep their attention. They need to be reminded of why we are here. Alejandro had another thought, "Also, thank you, Rashid, for your report on Abdul's purchase of the Clarity potion." Alejandro smirked hoping to turn the attention away from the tension he sensed. *The Clarity potion should get them*, he thought.

The council members whispered to one another.

"See, this is who is currently running our Order!" Alejandro raised his voice and stamped his feet to gain momentum in his speech. *I seem to have their attention now. This is good.*

"Is this the man we want running things? Someone who instead of being passionate about science is using magical crystals and potions!" he scoffed.

The council murmured in support.

"Someone who isn't capable of leading! Someone who hides in the face of danger!" Alejandro shouted, as the energy of the group increased.

"We are capable of great things! We are capable of discovering things that will benefit everyone! We need to continue with this work!"

Alejandro had convinced himself, but had he convinced the others?

Chapter 25

Sophia's Study

ophia ran home under the cover of darkness and quietly entered their cottage. She crept silently up to her room with the book, eager to read.

"There are seven main energy centers starting at the base and working their way up to the crown of the head," she began to read. "Each chakra has a corresponding color that helps to visualize them when focusing on energizing and cleansing."

Sophia paused. *This is new information!* She felt her spirits begin to lift as she read on eagerly about the root, sacral, solar plexus, and heart, pausing to take in every line.

"Then we move into our fifth energy center, the throat, corresponding with the color blue. This is about how the individual communicates with the world. It's connected to their sense of truth."

Sophia followed the diagram and moved her hands up to the center of her forehead.

"The third eye chakra. The corresponding color is indigo. This center is tied to awareness, while the heart center allows us to connect to all there was, is and ever will be. The third eye – when properly opened and cleansed – can allow the individual to become aware of the things beyond themselves."

"So, the Spirit Realm is connected to the third eye? Maybe if I can somehow cleanse my own, it can help me access it!" She realized she was speaking aloud again and clamped her mouth shut.

"Finally, we have the crown chakra, located just above the head, with the color of white or violet. The crown chakra connects the individual to the whole, to allow the individual to step into a place of oneness."

Sophia gave a sigh of relief. Even though she hadn't started working with these energy centers yet, it felt powerful to learn about them. Her fears and anxieties turned to excitement as she began to dive deeper. How powerful a little awareness can be.

She didn't fully understand yet, but she was grateful to have found the book. *I will ask Akasha how to meditate and cleanse these. Maybe by seeking her help I can pull her out of her current mood.* She blew out the candle and placed the book underneath her pillow. She would try to return it in the morning, before the market.

Chapter 26

Akasha's Call for Help

kasha woke up still feeling exhausted. She was confused about everything that had been happening, both in her dream and meditative states. She also felt guilty about yesterday. *Am I abandoning Sophia? The way I feel I have been abandoned myself?* She knew her sister just wanted to help, but she had no idea how she could. *I don't even know how to help myself. I'm not even sure I understand how to breathe anymore,* her thoughts seemed to pivot her back into the depth of her sadness.

Akasha was used to finding a feeling of peace through meditation, not the anxiety caused by the events of the past week. She was worried about her ability to cope.

It started with connecting with Leo. How did she know his name? How could she sense his emotions and compassion? It was as if she'd met him before, as if he was intimately connected with her. It made no sense. Next came Athena, her "protector throughout this transition and awakening." *Transition into what exactly? Losing my sanity?* She could feel that both Athena and Leo came from somewhere else. They had this power connected to them that felt otherworldly. *And the Crown, the Ring, and Raoul?* She started to tear up at the thought of him. He had felt so real to her in those moments they had connected. *But how can I be having conversations with him?*

Finally, came Esmeralda. Akasha had no idea what to think there. Esmeralda felt terrifying and incredibly hostile. She was utterly beyond knowing, something menacing.

Thus, it was that Akasha awoke, uncomfortable, and confused. She didn't want to burden Sophia with any of this. She knew she had upset her sister, but she wanted to make more sense of it before letting her in. She racked her brain to think of someone she could talk to, someone who could help her understand, and remind her this pain was all temporary. Suddenly, she had an idea.

"Okay, Athena! If you really are here and my protector right now during whatever the hell this is, then I'd like your help," Akasha said out loud.

She heard nothing. Then she remembered something her mother told her, that we need to be clear in asking for what we want. She had told her there is always help and support around us when we are brave enough to ask for it. To receive it, it was important to ask clearly, set the intention, and believe in it. Akasha tried again, trying to center herself and her thoughts a little more to speak with pure intention.

"Okay. I need someone I can talk to that is still alive, someone who can help me to understand what's going on."

She waited.

"Thomas." She heard the name silently, but she heard it distinctly.

"Oh! Thank you!" she exclaimed.

Her heart filled with gratitude, and she sent that loving healing energy to the universe. She felt it returned. She smiled for the first time in days and got out of bed to ready herself. She needed to stop by the *Temple of the Holy One* before trading at the market began.

"Soph! I need to head out a little early. I will meet you there, okay?" Akasha yelled to her sleeping sister, not bothering to wait for her reply. She threw on her shawl and dashed out the door

Chapter 27

The Temple of
the Holy One

kasha hesitated at the entrance, unsure of how she would feel. This space was sacred to her but still so strongly associated with her mother. The powerful visions and interactions had left her feeling weary, and she was not sure if her nervous system could handle any more. Taking a deep breath, she entered and was surprised as she instantly felt a sense of ease. She sighed gratefully.

She took in the calm, still environment and realized she hadn't had a chance to balance all seven of her energy centers during the past couple of days. She kept getting interrupted after connecting with her heart, and hadn't felt emotionally balanced enough to focus on cleansing her throat, third eye and crown. Akasha had a daily morning practice that was essential for her to rebalance and align, a practice she had lost sight of recently. She sighed, thinking back to her outburst with Sophia. *I hope she still isn't upset with me. I probably should have waited for her response.* For now though, she came back to the present moment and set these thoughts aside. *I need to find Thomas.* She walked past the pews, slowly making her way beyond the altar stone to his office.

As if he could sense her presence, Thomas walked through the doors to join her. She nodded in greeting. He seemed to have a deep inner knowing about him that emanated from every part of his being. Akasha had always appreciated that.

"Akasha," he bowed, "I've been meaning to visit you as I might be able to help."

"Thomas," Akasha greeted him in return, shuffling forward. "So many things have been happening, and I'm at a loss as to how to deal with them. The line between what's real and what isn't has become blurred." Akasha peered towards his office, hoping he would invite her in.

"I know it has been a lot, Akasha, for both you and your sister. Can I offer you anything to drink? A little water or some tea?" Thomas gestured towards his private working chambers and they slowly made their way inside. Akasha shook her head. Seeing all the dust and clutter, she wondered how one of the most calming presences in her life could live amongst this.

"Please make yourself comfortable. I have some-thing to show you that I think might be helpful for you to read."

Akasha continued to peer around his office as she moved towards one of his chairs. His chambers were rustic at best.

Thomas pulled a book out of his desk, and walked around to the other side, "Before I give this to you, I want to tell you a few things that might help to make sense of what is happening with you. You are starting to wake up, Akasha. You are starting to connect to your inner being. With that awakening, a lot of things will surface in the conscious mind that haven't been exposed to before, like meeting your Shadow."

Akasha took a second to take this all in. Thomas knew about Shadows? Wasn't that what Esmeralda had said she was? *That fire breathing being was an actual thing that could kill me?* She sat down on the opposite side of the desk in an effort for stability.

"So that terrible, horrible dragon is real?" She said eventually.

"Yes," he answered simply as he took a seat at his desk and placed the *Book of Records* in front of her.

She stammered, "But, how? Thomas, you wouldn't believe me if I told you about some of the things that have been happening to me."

"I would believe you, Akasha. I went through very similar experiences when I woke up. It began when I connected with Peter," Thomas spoke gently.

"Peter?" Akasha raised her eyebrows.

"My Shadow. Your own Shadow shows up in the form of Esmeralda."

Akasha gasped, entirely taken aback. "But how do you know that? How do you know about Esmeralda?" Akasha wasn't sure if she wanted to leave the room or stay and listen to what he had to say. She decided to explore the fear rising in her with curiosity.

"The same way I know about the Crown Jewels."

Akasha was dumbfounded. *He also knows about the vision?*

"Akasha, I have had access to the Spirit Realm for many years. We all have the capacity to tap into it and connect, but we have to reach the space where we are willing to do so. We also need to believe it's possible, truly surrender, let go, and trust."

"I still don't understand." Akasha, as with everything in her life in her current moment, was struggling to take this in. She shifted her hands uncomfortably along the seams of her dress and looked down. *Will I ever?* She thought sadly.

"I wouldn't expect you to right away. I just want you to know it's okay. You're okay, and everything will make sense in time."

"In time." Akasha cut him off sharply. "I've heard that from both Athena and Raoul." She couldn't help but get frustrated as she got up from the dusty chair and started to pace the room.

"I am glad that you have been able to connect with Athena. She will be a wonderful source of protection, but also of love and guidance." Thomas stood beside her.

Akasha sighed and rubbed her palms against her forehead. "I just wish I knew more. I wish I understood. I wish I wasn't so fearful. It's disrupting my life. I didn't get out of bed yesterday, Thomas, and I fear that Sophia is incredibly upset with me."

"It is scary to wake up and have everything you thought you knew to be true turned on its head. The thing to keep in mind though, Akasha, is that most people don't want to know and understand more. The fact you have come this far is truly astounding. You should be proud of how much you have been willing to embrace. It's important you come to truly love yourself, recognize your inner power and strength, and embrace every aspect of who you are. This will allow you to step into who you are meant to be and will be facilitated by embracing and getting to know Esmeralda."

"So, I need to embrace an imaginary dragon who wants to murder me?"

"Exactly!"

Akasha threw her hands up in the air in dismay, "but that makes no sense!"

"Your Shadow is a part of you. It might seem strange and unknowable because right now, it's brand new, and you consider her to be outside of who you are. Esmeralda represents all that you aren't consciously aware of, although you are slowly starting to wake up and get to know her.

"I went through a similar experience myself with Peter. At first, I was terrified, but eventually, I realized that he was there to guide me, to help me to embrace all of who I am. This, in turn, has allowed me to show up and serve others."

Akasha just sat in silence.

"Akasha, I know this is a hard time for you, but I am always here. I am always willing to help in any way that I can. I think this book will be of service. It cannot leave these walls as with the other books in the Temple's library, but you are welcome to return and read it at any time," Thomas handed her the *Book of Records*.

Akasha's hands trembled. She sensed there was a wealth of sacred knowledge within this handwritten book. She sat back down in his chair, flipped it open, and read the first passage she came across:

The Crown and the Ring of Infinite Wisdom make up the Crown Jewels and will reappear and provide the opportunity to balance the two Orders when the Two of the Royal Heart come into the authentic natures of their beings and act with pure intention to claim them. The Two of the Royal Heart will know what is needed and will be guided into action. We ask that any and all who read these pages keep an open heart, open mind, and open will as the Universe is always there to guide you to what's next as long as you are open to listening.

Akasha's heart began to pound. This book talked about her vision! It spoke of the Crown Jewels! She took a deep breath.

"Thomas, how is it possible? I thought the Crown was just something that appeared to me a few days ago."

"Akasha. I've given you a lot to think about for one day. I will be spending the next week preparing the Winter Solstice Talk. Can I count on you and Sophia being there?"

Suddenly, there was a loud crash outside of the chambers, they looked up to see Sophia holding a book and staring angrily at them.

Chapter 28

Sophia's Return of the Book

ood morning sister. I'm so glad to see you safe and sound. Thank you so much for making sure I was alright this morning, considering how you shut me out yesterday. It is comforting to know how much you care about my well-being," Sophia's eyes pierced her sisters with her sense of betrayal. She was breathing heavily, and her anger was clouding her vision.

Akasha was alarmed, she immediately stood up from the desk and walked to where her sister was standing, "Oh Sophia, I am so sorry! I did call to you this morning to tell you I was leaving, but you are right. It was incredibly inconsiderate of me. I should have made sure you were alright and that you knew where I was going." She stepped forward to try and comfort her sister.

"Enough! Akasha, enough! You can't just say you're sorry and expect things to be fine. I'm worried about you; I'm worried about me. I feel cut off, and it makes it even worse when it feels like you are abandoning me," Sophia was practically yelling. She hadn't realized that was how she felt until the words were pouring out of her mouth. *That's it, isn't it?* She thought silently, *I feel like my sister is abandoning me.*

"Sophia, try and calm yourself," Thomas said, also moving in.

"DON'T TELL ME TO CALM DOWN," Sophia raged. "You told me yesterday I had access to the Spirit Realm, the same access that Akasha does." She yelled at Thomas, pulling the book out and pointing it directly at him. Then she twirled around in a fury to face her sister, "I borrowed this book last night and wanted to ask you, my dear beloved sister, to help me develop my awareness of these energy centers this morning. Only, I wake up to find you not there! I head to the Temple to return it, which yes, Thomas," she turned to Thomas again frantically gesturing with the book, "I am aware I should not have taken in the first place, but I was desperate for help, and I find the two of you in a secret meeting WITHOUT ME. It makes me feel even more isolated!" Sophia screamed, so caught up in her anger. The sense of betrayal ran through her so deeply it all seemed to course through her all at once as she slammed the book down on the floor.

"Sophia, I don't know what to say," Akasha jumped, but again tried to move forward to soothe her sister.

Akasha's words brought Sophia right back as she looked deeply into her eyes. "Why don't you try not saying anything. You've been doing a pretty good job of that lately," She turned, and stormed out of the Temple. *Is that what it's like to feel your emotions? I hadn't realized I had been holding back and suppressing so much. Despite my anger at my sister, this feels, well, good? How strange?* She thought as she marched down the road and off to their stall leaving a stunned Thomas, Akasha, and book behind.

Chapter 29

The Path to Greatness

kasha, let her go. She is upset and needs time to clear her head," Thomas said, reaching for her arm as Akasha started to chase after her sister. As she stopped, he released her and reached down to pick up the book that Sophia had so forcefully thrown. *How interesting, she might be a little further along the path than we initially thought.* He noticed the title and placed the book against his chest.

"I have never seen her behave like that, Thomas. Usually, I'm the one to get all worked up. The last time I saw her this upset was when mother passed." Akasha rubbed her Temples and moved uncomfortably towards the bookcase wanting to get some of this nervous energy out of her body.

"Look at the book she was drawn to, Akasha," Thomas said. pointing at the sacred design on the cover. "She is already seeking hidden knowledge, which is an excellent sign. Perhaps you could guide her? She had mentioned she wanted you to. That might ease the current dynamics?"

"Perhaps."

She is still incredibly upset, and understandably so. Perhaps now might be a good time to introduce her to her role. It might give her the boost that she needs, Thomas thought, as he placed the book back on his desk, making a mental note to return it to the library.

"Akasha, I know that a lot has happened with you in the last couple of days, but your path is a great one, and with that will come many obstacles. The brighter the light, the darker the shadow, as they say." Thomas paused to make sure he had her full attention. *She is listening, Peter, please be with me to help me believe in the value of my words.*

Thomas, I am here, and you are connected, Peter spoke silently to Thomas through his mind's eye.

"You are destined to do great things, but that must start with belief in yourself and your acceptance of all of who you are. I know Esmeralda seems terrifying at the moment. I know you are grieving for Raoul and confused by your visions. But know that I am here, Esmeralda is here, and that others are here to help guide you, love you and help you realize what it means to be One of the Royal Heart."

"One of the what?" Akasha looked confused.

"We don't need to go into that today but know that your path is one of greatness. You might not see this, but I see it in you, and you can help Sophia see it in herself." Thomas saw Akasha's eyes light up at the suggestion of helping her sister.

"Thank you, Thomas, you have given me a lot to think about. I deeply desire to understand, but for now, I must make sure she is alright," Akasha bowed and quickly left the Temple.

Chapter 30

The Encounter
at the Market

he market was already alive with people when Akasha found her sister.

Sophia couldn't even look at her when she noticed her approach. "You know, with all of the time I have spent in the stall because you have been too lazy to get out of bed, it's practically become second nature for me to open up the stand now, alone." Sophia huffed, not allowing her sister the chance to speak as she slammed some of the potions down on the counter.

Akasha sighed as she smoothed her apron and stepped into the booth behind her, "Sophia, it was one day, and you know that I'm incredibly sorry for it." Akasha picked up the potions and gently placed them one by one in their correct rows on the table.

"Do I? How would I know that, dear sister? By you dashing off this morning and not even letting me know? And you know what else, Akasha? I know that you are better and special and have access to all of these things that I don't, but one of these days, it would feel great if you didn't lord that information above me; for example, all of our potions." Sophia had to put the bottles down quickly, otherwise, she knew she was capable of smashing them. She was usually quite calm, but this morning she had reached her breaking point. "I don't know how they work. I don't know how they were bottled and created. I don't know the magic behind them, but you do. And apparently, I'm not worthy of sharing that knowledge." She sat on the chair at the back of the stand. "And, I hate that I can't stop crying!"

"Oh Sophia, that's not it at all. The knowledge of the potions has been withheld only to protect you, not because you aren't worthy of it." Akasha dropped down to her knees to put her arms around her. Sophia allowed her comfort, too emotionally tired for anything else. She rested her head onto her sister's shoulders and let the tears flow.

"Sophia, you are worthy and have access to everything that I do; it just starts with having that belief in yourself," Akasha said gently. Opening up the stand and dealing with the first customers would have to wait.

Chapter 31

Tariq's Resistance

 ariq and Paul brought the Black Onyx into the harbour the next morning at sunrise and made their way into town.

The market was a lot bigger than either of them had anticipated. There was row upon row of stalls of fruits and vegetables, spices, meats, and cheeses, anything they could possibly imagine. The smell of cardamom and cinnamon waffled through the air as Tariq tried to locate the potion stand. He smiled at an elderly woman at a nearby stand as she raised a sample of her roasted almonds for him to taste. He kindly shook his head, determined to stay focused.

Everything seemed to be there, and so did the entire town. They all seemed to rush past, old, young, male, female, in what appeared to be a mission to pick up their goods before anyone else.

Paul glanced around the vast array of stalls, picking up an apple that he quickly set down as a young male in a turban glanced up at him warily.

Tariq paused and pulled out his compass, knowing he needed to ask Leo for help. Leo had said that more would be revealed today, and he was ready for it.

He took a few deep breaths to ground his energy and get centered. Though the market was in full swing around him, it was as if time stopped. Tariq's centering practices helped him to reach a space where he was operating authentically from his heart. So, he focused on his breath, waited for clarity and connection and then eventually came back to the present moment.

"Right," Tariq said as he walked forward, not entirely sure where he was going, but trusting that he was being guided.

They rounded a row of stands, and then they saw it, the magical potion stand, although it didn't appear to be anything out of the ordinary. Two young ladies were behind the counter, one of them trying to comfort the other.

"Is this it?" Paul asked as he moved toward the stand.

"I think so," Tariq said hesitantly, stopping in place. He couldn't explain it, but there was suddenly a strange feeling in the pit of his stomach. It was almost as if he felt nervous, which wasn't an emotion he was used to experiencing.

"Well, then, what are we waiting for, Tariq?" Paul asked, turning to his friend.

Tariq held back, knowing how out of character it was for Paul to be taking the lead. He knew he needed to find out more about the potion that Abdul had purchased, yet somehow, he was utterly reluctant to do so. *"Why am I scared to move forward?"* He held the compass in his hand, hoping that Leo would help him.

"Resistance is a natural human emotion Tariq, one that you have battled with before. Think back to the last time you felt this emotion." The voice of Leo was clearly with him.

"When I first met Cora?" He held onto the compass, trying to remember that moment. She was breath-taking, but she had intimidated him. *"I wasn't sure how to*

approach her, or what to say. I was scared she would reject me. But what does that have to do with this potion stand?"

Then he saw her. Her dark curls framed her beautiful face and gorgeous dark oval eyes. His heart jumped, and his nervousness grew at the same time.

"Who is she?"

"She is the other One of the Royal Heart Tariq. She is your destiny."

Tariq swallowed and put his hands in his pockets. He seemed frozen in space and time. *She's my what?* He looked up and saw that Paul had almost reached the stand and knew he needed to follow. He had to move past all of these fears and anxieties that were surfacing, but he didn't want to.

Nothing will change for you if you don't make a conscious effort to push through this. What are you afraid of? What's the worst that can happen? Leo communicated silently.

He sighed, breathed in deeply again, and followed his friend and the incessant thumping of his heart.

Chapter 32

Akasha and Tariq's First Glance

"Hello there," a man Sophia didn't recognize approached the stand.

Sophia quickly stood up, wiped her eyes and greeted their first customer of the day. "Hi, can I help?"

Luckily her tone is a bit softer than it has been, Akasha was relieved as she resumed setting up the potion bottles for the day. Her back was to them, but she looked up quickly. He looked kind, with short dark hair, piercing blue eyes and a gentle face.

"I'm Paul. My friend Tariq and I were curious about your potions and wondered if you could tell us a little more about them," he said, reaching out to grab one of the potions from the counter, making eye contact with Sophia. Akasha noticed that his eyes lingered a little too long.

She sensed Sophia's fear and knew she needed to jump in to support her. *I will have to sort out the rest of our supply later on,* she thought as she turned around to face the two new customers.

"Well, that depends on what you would like to know," Akasha said, she stepped forward and placed her hands on the table.

Tariq approached the counter and their eyes locked.

Akasha gasped, or at least she thought she did. Looking into the eyes of this stranger sent her into a completely different world. She couldn't look away from him. *It's like I know him; like I have always known him.* Her heart started beating rapidly and she felt her face get flushed. She brushed her hand up to her forehead to try to calm down, and then quickly placed them back on the table, grateful for the balance and support the firm surface provided.

"Well," Tariq said, not breaking his gaze. "We had heard of someone from the *Order of the Pragmatists* purchasing a potion and wanted to learn a little more about it."

Akasha came swiftly back to reality. *Oh, of course. I should have known.* Her defenses rose as she broke eye contact.

"So, you are one of them, are you? And why, may I ask, are the Pragmatists suddenly seeking out our potions? Is this some sort of fun game for you?" The inner flutters of her heart were shut down by her own sense of security and protection.

"No, no. Calm down. We aren't with the Order. We just heard the story and wanted to know what they were looking for." Tariq's voice was full of intrigue. He stepped a little closer, which caused her guard to be raised even further.

"And what story is this? The last time I checked, I don't believe that anyone from the *Order of the Pragmatists* would go around broadcasting the fact that they had purchased some potions from our stand, nor would they seek us out in the first place!" Akasha snarled. *I will not take any of this. I don't care who he is, or what the connection between us is, I will not be hurt and he doesn't feel safe.* She was determined to keep her heart guarded. It had been cracked open, bruised, and broken in the last few days, and she did not want to feel that way again.

"So, the Clarity potion then!" interjected Paul as he read the label off the bottle in his hand. "Let's not get too worked up over this now shall we, we aren't from the Order. We are just curious about your potions."

"Yes," Sophia, jumped in. "Akasha, it doesn't seem like these men mean us any harm," she said, raising an eyebrow at her sister. She smiled at Paul and he smiled in return.

"Abdul purchased the Clarity potion. It's actually one of our most popular sellers," Sophia continued coyly.

Akasha froze. Abdul had been here? He had purchased a potion? She hated him! She hated the Order! She didn't know if she had the mental capacity to process this new information. *If these two want to buy a potion, then fine, but this mysterious man – whose eyes seem to bore directly into my soul – and his ulterior motives need to make a decision and go.*

"We are just visiting for a few days. I apologize for any confusion," Tariq couldn't stop looking at Akasha.

Akasha could feel his eyes on her, but had had enough.

"That's great, I hope you enjoy your visit. Why don't you just buy one of our potions then and be on your way? We have a lot to do yet to prepare for the day," she pretended to be busy with other things hoping they would get the message, unwilling to deal with the emotional storm that was engulfing her.

Paul paused as he got some money out of his pocket and smiled again.

"I'm Sophia," she responded, "and this is my sister, Akasha." Sophia ran her fingers gently through her hair.

Akasha wanted to kick her sister under the table. *What is she thinking! I don't trust these two, and I'm certainly not ready to reveal any personal details about our lives. I realize that Sophia is upset with me, but really.* She slammed her mouth shut and just glared at them both, silently willing them to leave.

"It's a pleasure," Paul's eyes lingered on Sophia. He quickly caught himself and sheepishly looked over at Tariq.

"Yes, yes, it is. Are there any other potions you would recommend besides Clarity?" Tariq continued to stare intently at Akasha.

"I would suggest one for stupidity, but somehow we don't seem to sell it," Akasha said making eye contact with him. It hit again. Each time she looked into his eyes she felt a sensation she had never felt before. *What is going on? Does he have some kind of dark energy? Whatever it is, I don't like it.* She sighed and decided to stay with the moment, holding his gaze. She felt a rush of energy go to her heart center yet again, it continued to un-nerve her.

"What my sister meant to say was why don't you start with the Clarity potion?" Sophia said calmly. "It should help you with the answers you're seeking. Start there. That should point you in the right direction of whichever one you might need from us next. The potions are designed to help you seek the answers within yourself."

Akasha turned around to finish sorting out the bottles. *I really have had enough. I can't take much more of this.*

"Two bottles of Clarity it is then," Paul said. He handed Sophia some money in exchange for the bottles, their hands gently touching. Paul looked at her again curiously as they turned away.

"Now, would you care to explain to me what exactly that was?" Paul asked Tariq as they walked from the stand.

Tariq looked at his friend and shook his head.

"I don't think I could if I wanted to. It almost feels like I have known Akasha my whole life, even though I don't know her at all."

"Oh yeah. Makes perfect sense," Paul said, rolling his eyes.

Tariq laughed as they moved away, looking back at Akasha one last time.

Chapter 33

The Sisterly Debate

kay, Akasha. Can you explain to me what just happened?" Sophia's anger and emotions seemed to dissipate with concern. *I have never seen her act this way before, even when she first met Raoul,* Sophia thought back to Akasha's and Raoul's first interaction at the Well of Remembrance many years before.

"Oh Sophia, I don't know," Akasha said stiffly, her hands firmly clutching the table behind the stand. "Do you know who he is? And also, Abdul visited the stall?"

"Yes, I've been meaning to tell you. I think I channeled some of you with him looking for clarity of all things." Sophia felt such relief to feel the communication channels with her sister opening up back up again.

"And no, I've never seen either of them before, but this reaction from you? I know you have a lot going on, but at one point, I was worried for their safety!" She tried to soften the mood, her maternal instincts kicking in.

"Sophia, I was just so taken off guard by him. This Tariq person. His eyes. There was just something about him. The minute he mentioned the *Order of the Pragmatists* though, I was immediately on guard and learning that Abdul now has one of our potions took me completely over the edge." Akasha turned to face her sister, still visibly shaken by this encounter.

"Yes, I know. I was there for the whole thing. I get it. You were upset. But even before that happened, he affected you," Sophia said. *If she would just start opening up, it would help!* Sophia had been attracted to the other man, but not nearly at the level Akasha had been affected by Tariq.

"Sophia. I really don't think I can discuss any of this at the moment. I don't know why I reacted the way I did. I don't know why it felt like he could see deeply within me. What I do know is that it unnerved me, and I need time to get my head around it. I am sorry. I know this is all coming from a good place, but please, just let me be. I don't mean to come off as abrupt, but I honestly don't know what else I could say." Akasha looked earnestly at her sister.

What a surprise, Akasha is still shutting me down and her emotions off. I know this isn't healthy. They will end up surfacing one way or another.

"Fine, Akasha. Keep this all to yourself, keep everything bottled up," Sophia was tense and upset again. *I guess we are right back to square one,* she thought angrily, feeling her frustrations with her sister come up all over again. She stepped away.

"Sophia, please. This is a lot for both of us, I know. I am sorry I have hurt you recently, that has never been my intention. I am just struggling to deal with everything. I don't have the mental space right now to think about this, or to fight with you." Akasha looked at her sister as she herself started to tear up.

Akasha, cry? Sophia felt her anger turn to compassion yet again. *Ultimately all I really want is to help.* She reached out to put her hands on her sister's shoulders but remained silent. She wasn't sure what else she could do.

"I'm also sorry that you feel like I have been keeping things from you. Perhaps you'll allow me to show you how to cleanse our chakras. I have never been above you

Sophia; we can all access the same information. Could we try this evening?"

Sophia was still upset, but realized her sister was putting forth effort to make amends. "We can try," she said, grabbing her hands and squeezing them to try to energetically clear the space.

Chapter 34

Toning Lessons

hey sat quietly at the table after dinner having eaten most of the meal in silence.

Please let this help, Akasha thought as she wiped down their mats. They were dusty from their lack of use. She carefully placed them on the rug and gestured for both of them to lay down.

"Alright, Sophia. Let's begin. First off, I am sorry for all the pain I have caused you. It wasn't intentional. I hope that by opening up this cleansing practice for us, we can begin to heal together." Akasha put her head down on the mat and centered her spine. *And, I can begin to process my emotions.*

Sophia lay down and closed her eyes, remaining silent but showing she was willing to be guided by her sister.

Akasha began to facilitate the meditation. "Now, I will start by just asking us to focus on slowing down by focusing on our breathing. Let's spend a few moments here, observing our thoughts. Don't follow them through, observe them and then let them go. If you find yourself getting attached to any one of them, go back to focusing on your breathing." Akasha knew this was the start of any meditative practice, quieting the mind and getting to a place of really tuning into the core of her being. Not attaching to any thought, but observing them to reach a larger perspective that then allowed for greater awareness.

Sophia listened and followed.

"Now, we will start at our root chakras and imagine a cleansing healing red energy going in with each breath. We breathe in this healing energy purifying the energy center and releasing any toxins on the out breath. When we feel centered here we will sound the activating tone for this chakra which is LAM."

Akasha heard Sophia breathing deeply and continued, "Imagine an energetic cord coming from your root chakra and traveling down to the crystalline center of the Earth. Beneath the grass, beneath the soil, beneath the rocks. Take a few moments to imagine that cord connecting with the love and energy of Earth. Send love down and feel it return to you," she led.

Akasha felt a sense of grounding and comfort when she focused on this energy center, like the Earth was a motherly figure protecting and holding her. She hoped her sister felt the same. She waited a few moments, took a deep breath and started toning "LAM," as Sophia followed. They could hear their tones go from strained to clear with focus as they worked together to purify their root chakras. Using sound, tone, and color was an ancient practice designed to cleanse their energetic fields and corresponding centers.

"We will now move to our second center, our sacral chakras. Imagine a healing orange energy surrounding and purifying us, the activating tone for this chakra is VAM," Akasha said softly, as she felt her own sacral center begin to stir. It was powerful, spending just a few minutes visualizing the purification of these energy centers. She took another deep breath and toned "VAM."

Sophia continued to follow. The sisters had grown up singing with their mother, so Sophia was familiar with the use of sound, just not in as intentional focus as Akasha was teaching her.

When Akasha felt her sacral chakra cleared, she moved onto the next. "With our solar plexus, we focus on the color yellow and the activating tone of RAM. A shining, shimmering yellow light that we can breathe in to cleanse this space. We breathe out to release anything that doesn't serve us." Akasha was feeling her own energy levels rising, and it felt really good. She took another breath and toned "RAM."

They both spent a few minutes there before Akasha continued on. "Now, we move into our heart space, focusing on the color green and the activating tone of YAM. What you should feel here is a sense of love, a sense of connection, and a sense of wonder. Breathe in that purifying green energy and light to open this energetic center up," Akasha said, spending a few minutes here connecting to her heart and deeply feeling it. "YAM" she toned.

"Now moving up our throats and imagining a blue energy swirling around to cleanse and heal us with the activating tone of HAM." Both sisters continued breathing deeply in and out. "And now up to our third eye, focusing on an indigo healing energy and light and activating tone of SHAM."

Akasha heard herself saying the words to lead her sister through her first chakra cleansing but felt her environment and awareness change. It wasn't scary; it was just larger and more expansive. She took a few minutes to breathe deeply in and out, to keep herself centered, spending a few minutes in the indigo energy and light of her third eye.

Suddenly, she sensed a presence around her. This time, she knew who it was.

"Esmeralda?" Akasha felt a sense of fear and mild annoyance in being in Esmeralda's presence. She wasn't in the mood to interact with her but wanted to see this through. She remembered Thomas' words, but Esmeralda had made her angry the last time they interacted, and she resented it. *"You have no right to judge me. I don't care who you are, or how you say we are connected, or even how scared I am of you. What gives you any right to tell me how to live my life?"* she thought angrily, wondering if this would bring her immediately out of meditation. She saw she was on the same mountain top again, surrounded by darkness and stars

"I know this is a lot, Akasha," Esmeralda said, her voice calm and not reflecting back the anger in Akasha's emotions so they could actually come to work together. *"I know a lot has happened to you in the last week. I know I seem mysterious, but that is only because you are just*

starting to get to know and accept me. The more you allow yourself to do so, the more you open yourself up to the idea of me, the more familiar I will seem."

"Yes, I heard you before. You are my 'Shadow' and I should work with you." Akasha spoke the words but didn't believe them. "I wish you would just go away and leave me alone, Esmeralda!"

"Akasha, I don't know what to say,"

"So, don't say anything!" Akasha snapped. "Just in case I wasn't clear the first time, I don't want to have anything to do with you. In fact, I want to be left ALONE." She knew she was being harsh, but she also wasn't capable of expressing anything other than how she was authentically feeling. She looked around to see if there was anywhere to escape to. She peered down the path and saw a mysterious looking cave a little further along.

"Akasha, I will not rise to your anger, there is no point. I will go, but I will leave you with this. You have a great destiny to fulfill as One of the Royal Heart, and it is only through working with me that you can truly begin. I cannot force you; it is up to you to decide."

Akasha was silent for a moment and still fearful. She really didn't want anything to do with Esmeralda, in fact she wanted to go hide in the cave. She wondered why she hadn't noticed it the last time she found herself here.

"I don't want you to tell me to leave you alone again so I will go. But know that I will be here if and when you need me, and that every part of me is ultimately part of your transformation."

Akasha paused, her words reverberating in her head, every part of her? Could that mean what she thought it did? Every part of her would include the last thing she had witnessed Esmeralda do. *"Wait a second. I'm supposed to have something to do with your flames?"*

Esmeralda paused. *"Yes, the power and presence of them will heal you, but only once you are ready for it."*

Suddenly, she felt herself start to shift. She deepened her breath and went with it, finding herself back in the room with her sister by her side.

❇ ❇ ❇

"Spend a few minutes envisioning the color violet while focusing on the energy center located just above our heads, our crown. The activating tone here is OM. It is here that we are able to realize our connection to all there was, is, and ever will be. We spend a few minutes in this state where we realize that we are all interconnected. We are all one," Akasha said slowly, coming back into her conscious reality. "And when you are ready, come back into the room, and into the present moment."

Both sisters breathed deep and paused. Akasha gave her sister a few minutes to re-center and balance.

"How was it, Sophia?" she asked

Sophia just looked at her, her face downcast and full of sorrow. Not answering her question she quickly said, "I think I need some fresh air." She grabbed her robe and shawl and went to leave.

"Do you want any company?" Akasha yelled after her, hearing no response except the sound of the cottage door slamming shut.

Chapter 35

Sophia and the
Well of Remembrance

 ophia ran into the cold night, unsure of where to go but knowing she needed to move. *Nothing happened again! What is wrong with me?"* She started to cry, but even that didn't make her feel better. She picked up her pace. Seeing the Well of Remembrance, she decided to make her way there.

She ran up the hill, her legs struggling to carry her, heavy with the weight of her emotions and sadness. She stopped, panting and out of breath. When she reached the top, she gazed up at the stars and the moon, and placed her hands against the Well.

I don't understand what I'm doing wrong. Why can't I gain access and guidance to the Spirit Realm? I just feel more and more alienated. She collapsed with her back against the Well and let her emotions overcome her.

Suddenly she felt a presence. She didn't know what it was, but it felt safe and comforting. *"Focus on your heart."* She felt the thought enter into her stream of consciousness.

"But I have tried that before!" She was too upset to focus on anything other than her pain which resulted in the disconnection from that presence. There was no response.

This is so frustrating. Why can't I just feel better! Why am I alone? This isn't fair! She got upset again and stood up. She needed to get these emotions out, but she didn't know how. *I am tired of people telling me to focus on my heart, to just believe. I do believe! But nothing is showing up!*

Again, she had no response. She wanted to scream. She looked at the Well in front of her. *I don't know why I thought this would help. Why I thought coming here would make any difference. I am obviously not good enough.* Sophia was cold. The cool night air was stronger than her robe and shawl, but she was too exhausted to move. She collapsed again against the Well and let the storm of her current emotions wash over her, not sure if there was any peaceful way out.

Chapter 36

The Shadowy Confrontation

lejandro sat at his desk frantically working on the codes he had retrieved from the alchemical knife.

"Alejandro," Abdul entered the room without waiting for a greeting.

He jumped, so caught up in his work that Abdul's entrance startled him. He looked up, registered him and scoffed. *What does he want with me? This person who leads the Order in no more than name. He does nothing to move us forward.* Abdul infuriated him, and he did not feel the need to hide it.

"Well, I'm not entirely sure if that's the appropriate greeting for your leader," Abdul said.

"What can I do for you, Abdul?" He made no attempt at pleasantries.

"I have heard some disappointing things about you recently, Alejandro," Abdul stopped suddenly as he caught sight of the alchemical knife.

Alejandro stiffened, realizing he should have hid it upon his entrance, it hadn't been seen in the last 500 years, but it's sacred design had long been documented and would easily be recognizable by one who has studied it before. *Does he know of the secret council? Could he know of the tie-in to Raoul's death? Has someone within the council betrayed me?* He said nothing in return, waiting for Abdul to say more.

"I know you have been speaking ill of my purchase from the potion stand," Abdul continued, his eyes still fixed on the knife.

Alejandro breathed a huge sigh of relief but hoped it wasn't noticeable. *He knows nothing! All he cares about is his infuriating use of potions!*

"Oh. Yes. The last time I checked, *The Order of Pragmatists* didn't stoop so low as to buy magical little fairy potions," he said with disgust as he put the knife back into his desk drawer and out of Abdul's piercing gaze.

"I will not put up with this treatment, Alejandro!" Abdul said. "You seem to forget who brought you into this Order in the first place, who took you in when you had nowhere else to go, and who taught you the things that we do and the way that we do them!" His voice grew louder and angrier by the minute as he took a step closer to Alejandro.

"You will treat me with respect, or you will leave this Order! We are not 'above' anyone. Yes, Light Workers approach things from a different perspective, but that does not mean they should be treated with contempt or disgust. You might not understand the potions or their use, but that does not mean you should judge. Who gives you that right? This Order was founded upon truth and knowledge through science and rationality. Just because we don't know something does not mean we close our hearts and minds to it. How could we have ever completed anything if we hadn't been open to the fact that we don't know it in the first place? It's curiosity about the unknown that causes us to start all of our experiments. You are closing yourself off to so much, Alejandro, and your attitude is poisoning those around you," he pointed a finger directly at him.

"I treated you like a son," Abdul continued, "I believed in you. You have great promise and potential. In fact, I still believe that, but you need to get yourself together, Alejandro. You must learn that we can't know everything. Some things are beyond our understanding. You also need to show some humility and respect."

"As you are showing me right now?" Alejandro fired back. He would not allow Abdul to yell at him and say nothing in return, he stood up quickly from his chair to challenge him.

"You're right, Alejandro. I need to treat you with respect, and I need to honor you as a human being, but your behavior recently has been atrocious. If you are not able to come to terms with the fact you are not above any of us, but our equal, and stop your judgment, I will have no choice but to ask you to leave. I hope it does not come to that." Abdul looked deeply into Alejandro's eyes, pausing for a moment before turning around to leave the room.

Alejandro sat back down in his chair in silence. He was dumbstruck. Am I really being asked to leave the Order? He scratched his head. *That just means I need to move quickly; I need to decode everything from Raoul.* He became more determined to break the codes and move onto his next experiment. I need more insight though. Who can help me with that? He pondered as he pulled the alchemical knife back out of his desk and got back to work.

Chapter 37

Paul's Inner Journey

aul was lost in thought as they headed back to the Black Onyx.

There was something about Sophia that was unnerving him. He ran his fingers through his hair and and explored this further, following his thoughts back to how they had found her in the first place. *Tariq seems to have an innate sense of direction and guidance, that he can tap into whenever he needs to. Why don't I?* It had always seemed to guide them in the right direction, whether that was to their next treasure or, like this morning, the potion stand. *What is it? I want to understand.* Paul looked up and realized they were already at the harbour, fast approaching the ship.

"Tariq, I'm feeling tired," Paul said as they climbed aboard. "Do you mind if I go and rest for a while?" He wasn't tired, but he wanted to spend some time alone.

"Are you okay, Paul?" Tariq's voice was concerned.

"Yes, fine. I'm just a little tired," Paul lied again. He wasn't ready to tell him that he was hoping to use his bottle of Clarity to understand whatever his guidance system might be. Paul shrugged and hoped that was enough, as he made his way below deck.

He examined the bottle once he knew he was out of Tariq's sight. The label said it was infused with the essence of opals. *Whatever that means.* Paul's knowledge of anything outside of the physical realm was severely limited. He only paid attention to the things that surrounded him.

He opened the bottle which seemed to sparkle and held it beneath his nose as he sat on his bed. It smelled like something fresh, like something hopeful. Not being able to ask how much an appropriate dose might be, he decided to take a single sip and then lay down on his bed.

The potion tasted as it smelled: refreshing and rejuvenating. He read the label on the bottle again: *"This potion is designed to help you with clarity. After consumption, spend some time focusing on the item you are* seeking. *If you can, go to a quiet space where you will not be disturbed to allow the answers to unfold."*

Well, it's at least worth a try, Paul thought as he placed his head against his pillow and closed his eyes. He decided to ask his question aloud to make sure there wasn't any sort of confusion on the matter.

"I want to understand whatever it is Tariq has access to that I don't? I want to understand if I have the ability to have my own direct guidance," he rested his hands by his side and waited.

He had watched Tariq do that in the past, take a moment to pause, to focus on his breathing. Paul didn't understand what was going on, but he had noticed that clarity usually came after this.

Paul carried on, breathing in and out slowly, deeply. He began to feel drowsy. His body started to feel heavy, but his mind remained alert. A few minutes went by and nothing happened. *I want to understand!* He took a few more deep breaths, and just as he was about to give up and go back on deck, something shifted within him. *This is strange; it feels like the energy in the room has changed.* He knew he was still lying on his bed, but it felt like a completely different space had opened up to a limitless amount of possibilities.

"*Keep breathing slowly,*" he heard a voice, but it wasn't spoken out loud. Paul was surprised, his heart started to race but he listened and slowed down his breathing.

"*Who are you?*" he thought, continuing to breathe deep. In and out. In and out.

"*I am part of you,*" the voice said. "*It will make sense in time.*"

"*Okay?*" Paul was skeptical. He was hoping for clarity but seemed to be getting the exact opposite.

"*Breathe. Slow down. Stop worrying. It will all become clearer in time. For now, that potion will allow us to connect until you are more aware of me. When you worry, you lower your vibration. When that happens, it lowers your connection to the Spirit Realm.*"

"*The what?*" Paul was trying not to let his thoughts get too carried away. He was conscious of the need to remain calm and open. Even though he did not understand it, he still wanted to know more. He sensed he was accessing something powerful for the very first time.

"*The Spirit Realm exists beyond the realm in which you currently live. Everyone has access to it, but few are able to connect. It takes a belief in your ability to do so, as well as achieving a high enough vibrational state.*"

"*The Spirit Realm?*" Paul was confused, but wanted more of an explanation. "*So, is this what happens with*

Tariq? Can you tell me more about the Ring we found earlier this week?"

"Yes. This is the start of your connection with me, and your direct access to all there was, is, and ever will be. The Ring of Infinite Wisdom can only be used by Akasha and Tariq when they have stepped into the true authentic nature of their being. Its use is to help the Two of the Royal Heart recalibrate as they adjust through various shifts in their energies and environments. They will use it when they start their destiny to bridge the divide that exists between the Worlds of Light and Dark."

"I think I understand about fifty percent of that," Paul said sceptically, "Who are you?"

"This will make more sense in time. You will know who I am when you are open to the idea of me. I suggest you ask Tariq about his relationship with Leo. It will help you," the voice said.

"None of this makes any sense!" Paul's eyes were still closed but he felt himself coming out of his deeper state.

"Paul, if you become frustrated, we lose connection. If that happens, know that you can reach me through the Clarity potion or when you can reach a state of acceptance of all there was, is, and ever will be. I know that you're confused. When you can start to believe these experiences are real, you will see the truth in our connection."

Paul felt this presence and voice fading, but he was absolutely fine with it. This whole encounter seemed to only deepen his unease. He didn't know how to even begin processing what he had just been told. *So, the ruby red Ring is called the "Ring of Infinite Wisdom?" And, Tariq is One of the Royal Heart? What does that even mean? And, he has access to this so-called Spirit Realm because of his relationship to a man named Leo?*

"Leo?" he mused as he returned to the physical realm. "I thought I knew everyone in Tariq's life, and I can't remember there being a Leo anywhere in it."

His brain had too much to unravel. So, instead of focusing on the details, he concentrated on what felt so much better, sleep. He would rejoin the rest of the world in a while.

Chapter 38

Bringing Back the Order

halid went to visit Abdul, as his conversation with Rashid did not sit well. Something about the young recruit's tone when he spoke of Abdul's purchase of something "of the Light" struck a nerve. Especially as they still did not know who was behind Raoul's murder. *We need to pay close attention to dissent and judgement of any kind.*

It reminded Khalid of the time before he knew his Shadow, Amadeus, who took the form of a white stag. He had originally been repulsed by anything he didn't know or couldn't understand. Amadeus allowed Khalid to see the beauty in the mystery of not knowing everything. Some of Khalid's greatest discoveries had been made because he allowed himself to listen and connect to his guidance. *I know this, and Abdul knows this, but I worry about the others.*

"Abdul," Khalid said in greeting as he entered Abdul's chamber.

"Khalid! My old friend," Abdul smiled. His face looked weary with hidden burdens, as he stood to greet him. It felt like ages since he had spent time with his oldest friend in the Order. They had joined together and followed a similar progression.

"It is good to see you, although I come with concerns for the Order," Khalid said. "I'm worried about the younger generation here. We have a death on our hands, Abdul. We cannot take this lightly, Gibraltar is not taking this lightly, and yet you have done nothing." His tone was soft but firm. *I know I am being harsh with him, but we cannot continue with inaction.* Khalid knew that only he could have this conversation with Abdul and propel him into action.

"Yes," Abdul nodded. "I know. I saw something similar in Alejandro. His head seems to be in a different place. They are not open to others, not open to the world. They are closed off to anything they don't understand, and can't relate to. He also had something that looked like the alchemical knife."

It was Khalid's turn to be alarmed. It couldn't be? The last time they had heard of its existence was 500 years before with the death of the King.

"Abdul, this is a grave matter. We are talking about the loss of a life here, and you may have just found the weapon! One we did not even know was still around. He could have murdered Raoul!" Khalid paused, understanding the gravity of the accusation and discovery. "It would explain how the mark of the Order was found on his body and yet we knew nothing about it. The knife would have left it's mark when it penetrated his electromagnetic fields. We have not properly investigated this Abdul, and that lies with you. We are a fact-based group. We don't take anything in faith, and yet you have been unwilling to unravel this mystery." Khalid knew he was being stern, but he also knew he needed to be. *That has been my unofficial role for years now, to make sure that Abdul fulfils his duties as the leader of the Order.*

"You are right. I have been afraid of what I might uncover," Abdul stood up and sighed, distraught. "How could the Order have reached the place where there are experiments, activities and demonstrations going on of which we were unaware? Activities we would never condone! I have been scared to dive in because I didn't want to believe that an ancient murder weapon has resurfaced within these walls."

"You must take action! We cannot have things return to the way they were during the holy wars, to the time when members of the Order lost sight of the integrity of human life in their quest for knowledge."

"I know," Abdul said, reaching for the Clarity potion that was lying on his desk.

"It reminds me of how we operated before we knew our Shadows," Khalid continued.

"We were so closed off before, and I see that now in their eyes. What about the future of the order? What else is lurking out there in the dark." Khalid's concern was genuine, the Order was very far off track and Abdul seemed to be slipping further away with his inaction.

"I plan to seek help, and I am starting to take steps. That is one of the reasons why I have this," Abdul gestured to the potion. "I know Isis is no longer with us, but I'm hoping for guidance on how to approach the matter. I need to speak with Alejandro about the knife. I plan on doing that once I have connected with Juliet. I worry that if I am too harsh with him, things will only get worse. How do you get to a closed mind? How do you reach people so convinced they are right, that they are blind to anything else?"

"As you said, maybe Isis' potion can help. She was such a force for good while she was still with us and I remember your connection with her. I hope you get the guidance you seek, but you need to move quickly, Abdul. You need to call a meeting to communicate that we are investigating and will not tolerate dissent. Otherwise..." Khalid placed his hands on Abdul's shoulders, *I am growing tired of having to repeat myself, he must listen!*

"I appreciate you raising your concerns Khalid. I realize that I have let this slip for too long now. I will try the potion tonight. Can I ask that you call the Order together tomorrow?"

He is asking for help, and for that I am glad. At least he is doing something. "Of course. We can't let this linger for too much longer Abdul. I will summon a gathering tomorrow."

Chapter 39

Discussion on the Onyx

aul and Tariq were both on the deck of the Black Onyx. Tariq got up to adjust the sail but noticed the expression on Paul's face. "What troubles you, my friend?"

"I'm not sure I even know where to start." Paul fidgeted a bit.

"Well, you could at least try," Tariq said as he raised the sail to catch the wind and cast the fishing net into the water.

"Does the name 'Leo' mean anything to you?"

Tariq was taken aback. *Could it be that Paul is finally getting to know his own Shadow?* He had never spoken about Leo to another person before, as everything with him had been a deeply personal and internal dialogue. *How could Paul know anything about it?*

"Leo?" Tariq adjusted the net, trying to buy himself some time. He reached for his compass in his pocket just in case.

"I'm not sure if I was dreaming or not, but I met, well, I don't even know if I can explain what exactly it was. I made contact with something. It was only a voice, but it wasn't an earthly voice. It was all very confusing, and I wasn't able to stay and communicate long because I apparently 'lowered my vibration,' " Paul rolled his eyes and grunted. He moved to help Tariq with the net, averting direct eye contact.

"Anyway, before I lost contact or whatever the hell happened, this voice told me to ask you about Leo. It said that would help me make sense of what was going on." Paul sighed and looked back up.

"I'm sure you must think I'm crazy now," he grumbled, looking down at the net, where a couple of fish were frantically trying to gain their freedom.

Tariq didn't know if he was thrilled or annoyed. While it would be nice to have someone to share this with, he couldn't help feeling a bit disillusioned that he wasn't the only one who had a Shadow, his ego liked the idea of him being incredibly special. *Who am I to feel this way? I should be grateful I am not alone, that Paul also has this relationship.* Tariq felt uneasy with his emotions that were surfacing. To distract himself he quickly pulled up the net to land the first couple of fish for their dinner.

"*Tariq, we have been through this before. Everyone has a Shadow and their own process to waking up and embracing it is a unique journey. Only a few are able to connect, integrate and balance with them because it requires a willingness to acknowledge their existence,*" he heard in his mind's eye.

"*Leo, will you help me to guide Paul however I need to?*" Tariq appreciated Leo for helping him to make his unconscious, conscious, and remembered how confusing it was when he first encountered him. His heart filled with empathy and compassion for his friend as he felt guilty over his initial reaction. He tossed the recently caught fish over, still struggling and slippery, to his first mate and best friend.

"I've never expected anyone to ask me about Leo. The fact you have is amazing, so I want to start with that. To get to a point where you were willing to acknowledge and meet your own 'Shadow', something incredible must have opened you up to it."

"Okay, Tariq," Paul grumbled, as he started to gut and clean the fish. "You're making me uncomfortable and sound exactly like whoever it was I talked to. The only 'incredible'," he said, waving his hands around in the air to emphasize the ludicrousness of it all, "thing that happened was I decided to try out the Clarity potion and ended up having the most confusing conversation of my entire life."

"The Clarity potions! What a brilliant idea!" Tariq responded. "I had almost forgotten about them!"

"Well, I'm glad one of us is amused," Paul said. "I wonder why I thought talking to you about any of this would be a good idea?"

"Paul, calm down," Tariq sensed his friend was taking his excitement from him in the wrong way, as ridicule.

"I know this must be confusing. When I met Leo for the first time, it was at one of the hardest points of my life. It took me a few years before I processed it all and was able to come to terms with who he was, and what our relationship should be."

Paul fell silent.

"I know events seem unreal right now" Tariq sat next to his friend. "Leo surfaced, or should I say, I first allowed myself to acknowledge him when Cora passed. I connected with him in an effort to deal with everything that was going on. I didn't know it at the time, but working with him allowed me to be aware of things within myself that I needed to shift and accept in order to become whole."

Paul remained silent for a moment. "I remember hearing of Cora," he engaged slowly.

Tariq was relieved. *I will take that as interest.* "Leo is my Shadow. I believe you have just met your own. In your case, you haven't had to go through a dark period to completely surrender and come back into the light. Taking the Clarity potion was a brilliant idea!"

"I didn't know what I was doing," Paul shrugged. "I'm struggling to find words, Tariq, let alone believe what happened," Paul shifted uncomfortably again.

"I asked for clarity about how you always seem to be guided into knowing what is next. The next thing I know, I'm having a conversation with my Shadow?" Paul was exasperated.

"Paul, I know this is tough, and confusing, but I promise it will make more sense in time. I have been through this."

Paul paused and took a few deep breaths, Tariq realized he wanted to say more, so he silently encouraged his friend to continue speaking whatever lay on his heart.

"The name of the Ring we found is the 'Ring of Infinite Wisdom,' at least that's what my so-called 'Shadow' told me. He also said that it could only be used by the 'Two of the Royal Heart' of which apparently you are one," Paul spoke hesitantly.

"This was what you were trying to tell me at the market?" Tariq asked Leo, silently.

"Yes," he heard in response, *"I will explain in due course."*

Paul then recounted their mission.

"Bridging the divide that exists between the Worlds of Light and Dark?" Tariq couldn't help but speak aloud.

"Apparently. Whatever that means," Paul replied, echoing Tariq's exact thoughts.

Tariq smiled again. "Paul, I know this is a confusing time for you, that half of my words and the words of your Shadow don't make sense yet. But I promise you they will. You aren't alone on this journey. I am here in any way that I can as you work through this," he said earnestly.

"Thank you, Tariq, I appreciate that." .

With that, they both quieted down and became lost in their own thoughts. Tariq returned to what had been occupying his mind all day; Akasha.

Chapter 40

Sophia's Frustration

I don't know why I expected this to be easy," Sophia said quietly to herself as she walked inside their cottage. "Like I could press some magic button and automatically have access to the Spirit Realm."

"Soph? Are you okay? I have been so worried. I didn't want to follow you, but I was prepared to if you didn't come back soon." Akasha was immediately by her side and put her arms around her. Sophia could sense Akasha's concern and was comforted by it, causing her to open her heart and express her pain.

"Oh, Akasha. I feel so lost! My conversation with Thomas confused me and I felt nothing during our toning session. I went up to the Well and all I felt there was cold. I feel so cut off, separate, confused and alone, like I'm not worthy of everything that you are receiving." Sophia felt a huge sense of relief in being able to say these things. *There is such a release in being able to express how I am truly authentically feeling.*

Akasha tightened her hug around her sister and kissed her cheek.

"Oh, Sophia. I know this must be hard for you. It is the same for me, but you aren't lost and you are never alone. You are deeply loved, and have the same access that I do."

"I wish I could see things the way you can, and I don't even know what it is you saw! I didn't realize how affected I was until the conversation with Thomas the other day. He said that I do have access, but what's holding me back is my own disbelief. Why can't I just believe, Akasha? What is wrong with me?" Sophia embraced her sister and continued to allow the true expression of her emotions.

"Sophia, this is something that is brand new to you. It takes time to learn, to get adjusted, and to accept it as a real and natural part of your life. It doesn't come easy. I still struggle understanding it all, especially with everything that has happened recently."

Sophia quieted a bit, listening.

"Earlier this week, I had a vision at the *Temple of the Holy One*," Akasha said. "I had no idea what was going on, but I trusted and followed my own intuition. When I came out of my meditation, it was one of the most confusing moments of my life."

"Akasha, I have been wondering about what happened to you at the Temple. You had a vision? Are you finally willing to share?" Sophia was amazed, this was much greater than she had expected.

"I think it might be time to tell you about someone I've met recently named Esmeralda," Akasha said. "It might help." She gently guided them to sit down by the fire.

Sophia calmed down. *Oh, thank goodness, she is finally opening back up.* It was immediately soothing to know she wasn't alone in this, and she had been desperate to hear more about her sister's week, to finally feel like she had her back.

�֎ ✷ ✷

Akasha reached for her sister's hand. "Oh Soph, I know how it feels. I have felt isolated and disconnected myself, many times. I felt it quite strongly when I didn't join you at the market." Akasha knew that the fears and darkness she had been caught up in wasn't the truth of who she was, they were only an aspect. "When I am in a meditative state, it's easier to feel connected because I am entering a state of alignment. I can let my worries go and be released from my ego, especially when I am cleansing my energy centers and tuning in with my heart. Then it's hard to imagine feeling any other way but incredible," Akasha said softly.

"But then life happens, Soph, and we get caught up in our own thoughts and we start believing that our thoughts are who we are. Our minds tell us that we aren't connected, that we aren't enough, and we start to believe it. But the thing is, we are." Akasha rubbed her forehead. *I wonder where all of these thoughts are coming from? I seem to be telling Sophia things I need to hear myself. But they don't seem to be helping, her mood doesn't seem to be lifting.* Akasha saw Sophia's diminished body language and continued to speak.

"I have been forgetting that Sophia. I have been judging myself. I have felt guilty about not being there for you, and I realize now, not being there for myself. I have been incredibly frustrated due to my lack of understanding and clarity," Akasha was beginning to see she needed to have more compassion for herself, to appreciate there were a lot of things happening. "You know Sophia, some-times it's okay to not be okay, to not feel aligned, to not feel connected. Instead of getting angry and frustrated with ourselves, instead of thinking of how horrible we are. I need, we both need to get to a space where we are showing ourselves some sympathy and compassion to just be with ourselves, without judging. There isn't anything wrong us or anything that needs to be fixed." she said in an effort to comfort her sister, but also herself.

"How did you realize that Akasha?" Sophia looked up and made eye contact with her for the first time during this conversation.

"My Shadow." The words came out of Akasha's mouth before she even consciously realized it.

"Tell me about her, Akasha."

Akasha took a deep breath. "Well, in all honesty, I don't know what I believe. I know I will sound like I have lost my sanity when I tell you about her."

"Akasha, I promise you that you won't," Sophia encouraged.

"I met Esmeralda that morning at the Temple on the way back from Cleopatra's Obelisk, although I didn't know it at the time. I heard a voice in my head telling me I needed to shift my thinking. She told me that I needed to stop focusing on what I think I lack and start thinking about how I am going to become whole. I don't know what allowed me to meet her, which I know doesn't help you, but I promise you, you have one."

Sophia took a deep breath.

"I was angry and scared of Esmeralda, Sophia, in fact, I still kind of am. My relationship with her has not been easy. I feel like she isn't actually helping me." Akasha was slowly starting to realize that Esmeralda was shining a light on areas within herself she didn't want to see. "I haven't wanted to truly allow my pain to surface, or most recently the judgement I had been placing on myself. It angered me, and I'm starting to realize now that I was suppressing that anger. Sophia, I don't know how to explain this, but I am terrified, angry, and grateful for her all the same time." Akasha saw that it was only through talking about this with her sister that she was slowly starting to make sense of the nature of her relationship with Esmeralda. "She still feels so unknown to me, so mysterious, and frankly, sinister. The more I am aware of her, however, the more familiar she becomes." Akasha paused for a second, lost in thought.

"It takes a lot to work with her, and usually ends up with me having to take a look at transforming some area of my life, whether I am ready or not." Akasha wasn't sure where all of this conscious processing was coming from, but she hoped it made some sense to her sister.

"So, your Shadow helped you process Raoul's death?" Sophia asked, intrigued.

"Yes, I would say so, my Shadow and another being I met named Leo. Although I didn't realize it at the time." Akasha wished silently that Sophia wouldn't ask about Leo as she had no explanation for who he was herself. "I don't know I fully understand yet, but I suppose through just having this conversation with you, I'm making these mental connections. I am slowly starting to accept that she is a part of me." Akasha finally saw that Esmeralda made her aware of her inner world. "She keeps telling me that she is there to help me become whole," She closed as she stroked her sister's hair and Sophia put her head against her shoulder.

"Akasha, thank you for telling me this. Thank you for being here and listening to me. Thank you for everything. I am sorry I've been so upset. I just so deeply want to be able to connect to the Spirit Realm like you do."

"Oh Soph, please don't ever apologize. I will always be here for you. And I know you want to connect. Start with the meditations and cleansing. Do them regularly and that will help, I promise! I love you unconditionally, no matter what, and I'm here to help in any way I can. Perhaps, tomorrow morning we might visit the *Temple of the Holy One* together before we open up the shop?"

"That would be lovely," Sophia responded while smirking. "Although, I am a bit nervous about seeing Thomas again. The last time I saw him, I nearly threw a book at his head!"

Chapter 41

The Unfortunate Encounter

lejandro sat at his desk as Rashid shuffled nervously into the room.

Alejandro looked at him incredibly annoyed and marked his place with a heavy pyramid shaped metal paperweight also given to him by his father. He couldn't hide his frustration as he wanted to continue his work. He felt he was getting close, but he wouldn't know until he dove a bit deeper and was anxious to complete this before he encountered Abdul again.

"I saw Abdul leaving and I wanted to check in on you," Rashid said warily.

"I'm fine," Alejandro said abruptly. He stared at Rashid, expecting him to excuse himself. His pathetic excuse of seeing Abdul earlier did not justify interrupting his work, and he didn't care enough to know his real reason for disturbing him.

Rashid just stood there. "Alejandro, you haven't seemed quite like yourself lately," he said uneasily.

Alejandro said nothing. *Why isn't he leaving? Isn't my lack of engagement and response enough? I want nothing to do with this young recruit, he is proving to be like the others, quite useless.*

"It's just that we are responsible for the death of a human being," Rashid said quietly, looking down at the ground.

Apparently, I'm going to have to deal with him anyway as he continues to speak out of place. Alejandro heaved a heavy sigh and turned to face him just as Khalid entered the room.

"You've what?" Khalid startled both Alejandro and Rashid.

Alejandro's face went white, but he recovered quickly. *Damn this fool Rashid!* He proceeded to glare as he slammed his papers down. "That is absolutely none of your concern, Khalid," his voice calm but firm as he rose to stand from his desk, his fists tightly clenched behind his back.

"Alejandro, you should watch your tone of voice with me. You forget that I am second in command in the Order." Khalid stepped forward.

"I've forgotten nothing of the sort!" Alejandro's voice rose with his frustration levels. He had had enough, he was tired of the so-called authority of the order. "This Order stands for nothing anymore! It's a pitiful example of what it used to be." He took a step forward to match Khalid's stance. *I will not be threatened or intimidated by this man.*

"Alejandro!" Khalid raised his voice. "This is not how we have taught you to behave. This is not why we asked you to join us in the first place and become one of our brothers. Is this how you treat those who've welcomed you? Those who have cared for you? Those who have taught you everything you know?"

"And what exactly do I know?" Alejandro seethed. "That the leader of the Order now believes in magical potions? That we have lost sight of every single thing my father told me we stood for in the first place?" His anger took over. "This order is a disgrace!"

"And what do we stand for then, Alejandro? Human death?" Khalid asked.

"I do not have to take this! I will not be disre-spected!" Alejandro bellowed, slamming his fists down on his desk. Was Khalid threatening him?

"This is exactly what I was worried about," Khalid said, keeping his tone even. "You are so closed off to anyone but yourself, so blinded by your own anger, it is causing harm to you and others. Alejandro, if you would just listen to me. I am not being disrespectful to you, however the same can't be said of you. I came here tonight out of concern."

Alejandro's rage reached his boiling point. "Concern? You call threatening me acting from a place of concern?" he spoke with such vehemence he almost didn't recognize his own voice. As Khalid continued to move closer to him, he reacted, registering what he thought to be danger, he picked up the paperweight and took swift action. *I will not be told what to do by this man, I will not be threatened, I come from a long line of strong men and I will protect myself and my lineage!*

Khalid took one more step forward to say something.

With Khalid's step, Alejandro's animal instincts kicked in. Without another thought, he raised his hand and slammed the paperweight into Khalid's skull. Khalid lifted his hands in reflex to block but was too late. His voice started to form a scream but before the sound could exit he collapsed on the floor.

Alejandro stood over him, blood pouring out of Khalid's head feeling absolutely no remorse. In fact, he wasn't sure he felt anything. He had not heard Khalid's words at all, he had only heard his own projections, fear and anger. Instead of listening, he read all of Khalid's efforts as a threat because he himself felt threatened. Time paused. The world paused, but Alejandro seethed as he stood, oblivious to the fact that he had just taken Khalid's life.

Chapter 42

Leo and the Secret Entrance

ariq eventually emerged from his thoughts, and realized how late in the night it was. He said goodnight to his friend and made his way down to his bed. He lay down, closed his eyes and was almost immediately greeted by Leo.

"Well, hello!" Tariq smiled at the memory of some of their first interactions, when the last thing he could have possibly imagined was being grateful to see him.

"Tariq, something unexpected has happened."

Tariq was immediately on edge, as he sensed Leo's thoughts and emotions.

"The second in command of the Order, a man named Khalid, has just been murdered by a younger member."

"I don't know why that should upset me." As far as Tariq was concerned, the Pragmatists were threatening and dangerous. *If they managed to rid themselves of one of the top men in the Order, how could that be a bad thing?*

"Tariq! I expected more of you! Khalid was working on bringing the Order back to what it used to be, a balance with the Light," Leo said abruptly. *"You, of all people, should know better than to rush to judgement, especially where the loss of human life is concerned."*

Tariq sighed. While he appreciated Leo, almost every single conversation with him revealed something he needed to integrate. In this case, it was his automatic judgment of the Pragmatists. He forgot that that was the nature of his relationship with his Shadow, and with all Shadows. They work with you to bring light to the darkness, to lead the way to integration, balance and love.

"You are right as always, Leo, but I sense that's not all you've come here to tell me."

"You are correct. There is a secret way into the Pragmatists' Cave of Wonders, which is why I wish you had listened to me earlier, but now is not the time for that. With the death of Raoul, Akasha's first love, and now Khalid, we must keep an eye on them."

Tariq thought he was going to be reawakened completely from the shock of what Leo had just said. It explained Akasha's violent response to him in the market.

"*Akasha,*" he paused, gathering his thoughts, "*had a first love named Raoul.*"

Leo waited, not interrupting him.

"*Who died recently, and it was because of the Pragmatists,*" Tariq finally finished.

"*Correct,*" Leo said.

His heart felt torn. Part of it was filled with compassion because of what he had been through with Cora. Part of it was relief at having some understanding of Akasha's vehement reaction to him. But, part of him was, well, if he was being completely honest with himself, part of him was jealous.

"*So that explains why, she reacted so strongly when she thought I was a member of the Order,*" Tariq went on.

"*Yes. It also means that we need to keep an eye out as there have now been two deaths. The Pragmatists need our help. One of their members, Alejandro, has lost sight of his relationship with humanity and we need to make sure it doesn't get worse. He continues to seek things that are beyond rational comprehension through violence. As he has no knowledge of his Shadow, we fear this will only get worse and we have no way of monitoring his behavior.*"

Khalid has entered the Spirit Realm and informed us, but we need to make sure no other lives are lost. Alejandro is capable of anything without his connection to his own Shadow."

Tariq paused. He still wasn't quite sure why he needed to do anything to help the Pragmatists. Spying on them today was one thing but helping them was another. They had not only just killed one of their leaders, but they had also apparently murdered Akasha's first love. His stomach churned at the idea. *"Why does it have to be me, Leo, can't someone else do it?"*

"Tariq, do I need to go into this with you again? You can't judge one thing as 'good' and another as 'bad' and not worth your help. The Pragmatists aren't 'bad.' Bad things have recently happened within the Order, but that is exactly why they need our help. And it needs to be you because you are one of the very few people who has access to their Shadow and the Spirit Realm.

"We need you and Paul to go through a secret entrance and make sure he isn't planning any additional attacks. We have no way to communicate with him because of his disconnection from his own Shadow, so you must be our eyes and ears. You can always get a hold of me through your compass and your pure intention. With the

loss of Khalid, who was one of the few Pragmatists aware of his Shadow, it's become more important than ever."

Tariq sighed, he knew there was no getting out of this request. *"Your wish is my command. Just tell me where to go and Paul and I will head over before sunrise."*

Chapter 43

Esmeralda's Dragon Stone

kasha lay down in her room later that night and focused on her heart center. Breathing in and out, she soon realized that Esmeralda had joined her. *That has to mean something, doesn't it? I now sense Esmeralda's presence, and I'm not immediately afraid? That is progress, right?* Akasha thought to herself even if she didn't particularly want to hear anything Esmeralda had to say.

"Yes. Akasha. It is progress."

Akasha was still cautious and weary of Esmeralda, but a lot had shifted for her tonight with her earlier conversation with Sophia. She found her heart more open to the idea of her than in the past.

"You need to come to a state of acceptance, that allows our relationship to deepen." Esmeralda knew that Akasha wouldn't be as triggered by her reflection of her innermost thoughts once she saw the nature of their relationship. *"I only want to help you understand and embrace all of who you are, what you deem as 'good' and what you deem as 'bad'. I work with you to become aware, to learn to love, integrate and balance the whole of your being."*

Akasha was alarmed. She had known this before, but the idea that someone else had access to all of her innermost thoughts was daunting. *"You can see everything?"*

"Akasha, breathe. I am aware of every single aspect of your life because..."

"You are a part of me," Akasha finished as she slowly started to comprehend.

"Correct, and the sooner you truly accept that, the easier this will become."

"I exist amongst the things that you aren't consciously aware of," Esmeralda continued. *"Your every thought and action is influenced by what is going on in the background; your unconscious mind. Most people are not aware of this. What they don't realize is their thought*

patterns control their lives both for and against their own good." She moved closer to her.

"By accepting me as part of yourself, you will allow me to work with you, Akasha. It won't always be easy, some of it will be quite daunting, challenging, and scary. In the end, however, you will be amazed at the person you are inside. This person I already know and see, even if you haven't been able to fully realize it within yourself yet."

"Through working with me, we break through some of your limiting beliefs that block you from fully living from your heart, the authentic nature of your being." Esmeralda stood by her side.

"So, what do I have to do?" Akasha asked hesitatingly, daring herself to be brave and continue to be open and receptive to this conversation..

"It starts with believing in the fact that I do exist, and our connection is real."

"And then?" Akasha asked, not sure if she really wanted the answer. *I might have had enough bravery for one day.*

"Akasha, you are meant to do great things, but first you must step into the whole of who you are. That means that you have to embrace all of me."

"All of you?" Akasha said slowly, remembering Esmeralda's terrifying flames. *You have to be kidding me.*

"Know that I would never do anything to hurt you; only heal you."

Akasha quickly changed the subject, unsure if she was ready to hear more about Esmeralda's flames and she still had a number of questions. *"What is all of this talk of vibrations that everyone seems to be so fond of?"*

Esmeralda smiled. *"Vibrations are tied to your energy levels and emotions. When you are at what is called a 'higher vibrational' state, you are more easily able to connect to all there was, is, and ever will be, including the Spirit Realm. You are then closely connected to me. It also feels good physically in that state because you are more authentically aligned to who you are. When you lower your vibration, either by resistance, fear, anger or doubt, it makes connection more difficult."*

"And who am I exactly?" asked Akasha.

"I cannot answer that question for you, Akasha. You will understand in time."

"There's that wonderful phrase again," Akasha replied with a huff.

Esmeralda started to fade, and Akasha caught herself. She tried to concentrate on being grateful for their interaction. That was an easy way for her to recenter, finding gratitude in the moment.

"You know when you don't feel good and you know when you do." Esmeralda continued tapping into her thoughts, *"Do what you can to get to the place that feels good, even if that means staying with the uncomfortable emotions and seeing what they have to show you. Loving them because they are a part of you, a part of you that just longs to be seen."*

"Take the advice you gave your sister tonight. Make sure you are always approaching yourself with a sense of love and compassion, remember that you are unbroken, there is nothing you need to fix, especially when you are feeling low. Gratitude helps as you just intuitively showed yourself. That is the other thing, Akasha. You already have all of these answers within. You have just forgotten them. You are your own best teacher as long as you start to listen."

"But then what does that make you?"

"I am also your own best teacher..." Esmeralda paused.

"Because you are a part of me," Akasha finished.

"Correct." Esmeralda smiled.

"And this man at the market? What do you know about him?" Akasha felt drawn to ask about the person who had been occupying her heart from the moment she

laid eyes on him. She was grateful that for the first time in their interactions she was seeking Esmeralda's guidance.

"I know him Esmeralda, but how do I know him? It is like I have fallen for him, but he has only just entered my life. I feel like I am betraying Raoul. And he is from the Order!" Akasha was confused about having strong feelings for someone who in everything but name she saw as the enemy. She felt all of her questions rush out in a whirlwind of emotion.

"Oh, Akasha, wait until our relationship grows deeper and we are truly connected. For now, I want you to have this," Esmeralda handed her a piece of dragon stone, a small half oval shaped stone that was dark grey along the sides and a shimmery metallic blue-green on the top with flecks of gold that sparkled with movement.

"When you are feeling scared, or if you just want my help, hold it, think of me and I will be there. The acknowledgement you have given me tonight has allowed me to give you this piece of me."

Akasha had no words but knew she didn't need them. She took the dragon stone and placed it in her pocket as Esmeralda faded away. *But I wasn't ready for that conversation to end, I still have so many questions!* She thought as sleep rapidly took her over.

Chapter 44

Tariq's and Paul's Eavesdropping

 ariq woke in the middle of the night with a nagging feeling in the pit of his stomach. He had made a commitment to Leo, but there was a difference between making a commitment and following through with it. He begrudgingly got out of bed knowing he couldn't ignore his Shadow as he made his way to Paul's chambers. *If I'm already feeling this uncomfortable, I may as well wake him up and get this over with.*

"I had a visit from Leo, and he left us with a tall order to complete," he said before his friend was fully awake.

"Leo?" Paul said, slowly emerging from sleep, taking a second to get his bearings.

"We need to go to the *Order of the Pragmatists*, Leo has shown me a secret passageway. It seems a younger member in the Order murdered their second in command. We have been asked to monitor their activity," he said abruptly, not giving Paul much choice in the matter. He wasn't particularly excited about this mission either, but he knew they needed to go, and the quicker he could rouse Paul, the better.

Paul snapped out of the dream state, and sighed.

"Right. Of course. Us against God knows how many Pragmatists. Sounds entirely safe, and exactly what I would like to do in the middle of the night," Paul grumbled. "I know we have been commanded by your Shadow but why do we have to be put in danger?"

"Paul, you realize your grumblings will get you nowhere right?" Tariq asked sharply, and was answered with silence.

"We need to move before the sun rises, to avoid being seen. Leo has shown me a passageway once we are inside, but we need to move now," Tariq nudged Paul as they put on their black robes and made their way ashore, finding the same place that Tariq had previously tied up the boat.

"Paul just follow my lead," Tariq whispered.

"Easier said than done in the pitch black," Paul whispered back.

Tariq placed his foot in the crevice he had used before and instinctively followed Leo's guidance as he scaled to the ledge where the cave was located.

He crawled over the ledge and onto the path then crept forward, hoping his steps wouldn't echo. There didn't seem to be anyone else around. *That's peculiar, I know it's late, but shouldn't there be someone on guard? Maybe he is on a patrol?* He slowed his pace, hoping his eyes would adjust to the darkness around him.

He crept along slowly when, suddenly, he was bundled over. His reflexes kicked in ready to fight, then he noticed who had run into him. "Paul!" he hissed silently as his companion inadvertently stumbled into him. Rocks and pebbles scattered down the cliff making sounds that to them were deafening, as they scrambled to remain on the ledge.

Holding their breath, Tariq silently cursed his friend. *Did they hear us? How could they not have?* At the sound of footsteps, Tariq grabbed Paul's arm and pulled him inside the entrance of the cave. They remained there for a few seconds catching their breath. The footsteps grew louder and Tariq's heart leaped as he led them around the corner and into the passageway that Leo had revealed, grateful for the cover of darkness. They hunched together and waited.

"Did you hear anything?" A male voice said only a few feet anyway from them.

This could be it, Tariq thought. *And for what? Leo, for what?* He heard nothing back.

"Hmph," another male voice said in response. "Rashid, and it is late. You must have been imagining things."

"Strange things have been happening though."

"If by strange you mean are keeping me from my bed because of some imaginary crash you thought you heard then I would agree."

"I suppose you are right. You can retire if you want to, but I will keep guard. "

"Suit yourself," the older voice said as his footsteps faded into the distance.

Tariq and Paul waited, before moving stealthily in the darkness to the hidden chamber.

They heard the person called Rashid on the other side of the entrance. It seemed like hours passed, although it was only a matter of minutes before they heard his footsteps moving away too.

Chapter 45

Rashid's Inner Conscious

ashid stood silently. His own world was now altered forever with his witness of this murder. For the first time since he had entered *The Order of the Pragmatists* he felt afraid.

Why didn't I just tell the guard what happened? What was I fearful of? Of course, he isn't going to want to stay on guard when I say 'strange things' are going on. This Order is going mad. I'm going mad. Rashid no longer felt safe.

He wasn't sure if he trusted anyone and was frustrated at being on his own. *I'm guarding this cave for what?*

*Why am I protecting it in the first place? What's there to
stand for anymore? Should I tell Abdul? Did Alejandro
see me? Alejandro seems to have completely lost his mind.
I'm not even sure if he is aware of what he has just done!*

Rashid struggled to decide at which point he would
be finished. What was the final straw to make him leave
the Order? He had so many questions and there didn't
seem to be a way to answer them. He kept pacing, until
he suddenly heard footsteps and a loud thumping coming
from inside the cave.

He was instantly on edge. *Is he already disposing
of the body? Will we not even be able to grieve and honor
Khalid?* With so many thoughts swirling, Rashid sensed
the severity of the situation, and the danger of being seen
by the murderer. He dashed over to where he knew he
would be safely out of sight from the cave's entrance, but
still able to hear. He sighed deeply as Alejandro appeared
down the hallway, dragging a life-less body with him.

Chapter 46

Alejandro and the Body

lejandro gathered himself and walked down the hall, dragging Khalid's body. He had wrapped it up like a mummy to contain the odor and the blood. He was still in a state of shock, not fully present, nor giving a thought to what might happen if anyone saw him.

"He made me do it!" Alejandro said to himself, trying to make himself feel better. "And if anyone questions me about this, they will be made to understand." He grunted at the weight of the body, determined to get it outside and dropped into the sea.

"He threatened me! I did it for my own protection!" He continued, hoping that if he said the words out loud, he might start to believe them. He struggled with his thoughts, trying to make sense of the situation and decide what to do next.

He stopped and let Khalid's body fall to the ground. He needed a break. *If only I could remember the ancient chant my father told me that could change the weight of something.* He took a few deep breaths before continuing. *Where is everyone? Normally there is at least one guard on the night watch. How very strange.* He didn't give it further thought, however, as he was approaching the entrance and it would only be a few short minutes before he could safely drop Khalid's body off the edge.

"Who could help me decipher these patterns?" Alejandro thought out loud as he continued to haul the body. "Who knew Raoul better than anyone else?"

"Akasha!" He continued speaking aloud as he reached the caves entrance. "Of course! I don't need the others in the group to help me! If I can make her help me with these patterns, I can figure this all out!" he said, working himself into a state of excitement.

"I will set off at sunrise," he grunted, as he shoved Khalid's body over the ledge leaving a loud splash behind him.

Chapter 47

Tariq's Death Wish

ariq, s-stop!" Paul grabbed Tariq and hissed into his ear. "If you go after him, you will get us both killed. We are outnumbered here. The Pragmatists haven't seen us and they don't know who we are. I can't believe I am going to say this but why don't you call on Leo or something for guidance?"

Tariq paused and breathed deeply, his heart was racing. *I am so angry. I could kill Alejandro. In fact, I could kill Paul for stopping me from killing him! I need to protect Akasha.* He had never felt this passionate about anything.

"Tariq, you must calm down. If you want us to survive, you need to think rationally. Going after him right now, will not help. It will only put us in danger. We need to form a plan." Paul spoke slowly.

Tariq did not want to listen. "*Leo, Akasha is in danger. I can't just stand by and let this man hurt her. I can't! You can't ask me to!*"

"*No one is asking you to stand by and do nothing Tariq,*" he heard Leo's voice saying. "*Paul is just asking you to not be so rash as I did when you insisted on exploring the cave alone. There are others that can help you,*"

"*I don't want to sit around making plans! I want to stop this man!*" Tariq could not let go of his anger or his rage, fueled by his fear of not being able to keep Akasha safe. He knew he should listen to Leo, but his reasoning was too clouded. In an instant he was up. He had decided to go after Alejandro, determined to stop him and not caring about the repercussions.

"*Leo, I need your help. Please tell me what to do next.*" He wanted his Shadow to provide him with guidance. He didn't know where Alejandro was nor how he could stop him. He tried to slow his breathing, in and out, in and out, in and out. He needed to calm down and get centered before he would be able to connect and hear anything from Leo, so he waited.

Leo's voice was firm, loud, and clear, and finally knocked some sense into him. *"Go to the Temple of the Holy One and seek out Thomas. He will help. Do not pursue Alejandro"*

Tariq anticipated hearing more but there was only silence. Reluctantly, he returned to collect Paul. *I don't suppose I'll do much good protecting Akasha if I am dead.*

"We need to pay a visit to the Temple, Paul."

"I am happy to go anywhere that will keep us alive."

Tariq could hear the relief in Paul's voice but just grunted as they slowly made their way out of the cave and back down to the boat.

Chapter 48

Abdul and the Clarity Potion

bdul sat in his chambers with his bottle of Clarity. He hadn't found an opportunity to be alone until now, and although he was afraid of what he might have to face, he knew he couldn't stall any longer.

Everything about the bottle reminded him of Isis. Although they hadn't been together for many years before her passing, he still missed her terribly. She had been the love and light of his life. When she passed on, he had felt a piece of him did as well. He hadn't taken the time to think about this in quite a while.

His heart was heavy, but he felt drawn to the potion. He didn't expect everything to be resolved with one sip, but he hoped for a little guiding light. *Now, more than ever, I need this before the Order dissolves into more chaos.*

He read the label on the bottle:

"This potion is designed to help you with clarity. After consumption, spend some time focusing on the item about which you are seeking additional knowledge and information. If you can, go to a quiet space where you will not be disturbed to allow the answers to unfold."

He smiled and his lips held the smile until he felt it in his heart. The words sounded just like Isis. It was almost as if she was in the room with him.

"Okay, Isis," he said aloud, "I would like some help with my Order, and bridging the divide. Is that too much to ask?"

He breathed into his heart and slowly drew the potion to his mouth. He took a swallow then lay down on his bed, hoping the answers would come.

As Abdul closed his eyes, the veil lifted and he felt the falcon's presence. Juliet was with him again.

Abdul smiled, but his heart felt heavy. The last time he had been in contact with Juliet, Isis and her own Shadow, Manu, had been with him.

"Hello, my old friend," he greeted the falcon.

"Abdul!" Juliet exclaimed coming to land on his hand with sheer gratitude to be united. *"I have missed you."*

"And I, you," Abdul responded quietly, the connection between them was strong.

She paused as she sensed Isis' connection and presence with her. She beamed with gratitude as they connected so Juliet could update Abdul on all he needed to know. Isis smiled silently from the Spirit Realm.

"I know Isis' passing was hard on you and you didn't mean to shut us all out, but Abdul, I miss you. I miss being with you, and we all need you," Juliet said, relaying Isis' message.

"Your daughters are both starting to awaken," Juliet paused for a moment, giving him the time to absorb what she was saying.

"Akasha has had a vision of the Crown, although she does not yet realize what it means to be One of the Royal Heart. She is also getting to know her Shadow, Esmeralda, but she is very angry with you and the Order.

Sophia is struggling to believe in herself and could really use you."

"Akasha has met Esmeralda and seen the Crown?" Abdul was astonished.

"Yes, it really is quite extraordinary! It has only been a week and already Akasha is coming to terms with the fact that Esmeralda is a part of her. It's only a matter of time before she is ready to receive her flames. We have been careful with the knowledge of the Crown, and not overwhelming her with the duties involved in being One of the Royal Heart. But it is Sophia we are worried about. She is the one who needs you. Akasha's heart is too angry at the moment."

"Does she know about the flames? Does she know that she needs to be baptized in the essence of the fire to wash away the old, purify, and step into the new? Does she understand the link to the Crown?"

"She has seen Esmeralda's flames," Juliet confirmed. *"But Abdul, you are not listening to me. Akasha is not open, or ready to accept you. It is Sophia who needs you. She doesn't understand what is going on in her world. She believes she is unworthy. Things have been tense between her and Akasha, and she needs her father."*

Abdul had always known that Akasha's work was tied to the Crown in some way. He knew that if the Ring of Infinite Wisdom also resurfaced, the possibilities were endless. The Crown could link dimensional spaces, and the Ring had the ability to re-center and recalibrate its use. If the two combined with Akasha finding the other One of the Royal Heart, it could usher in a whole new world. A world of balance. A world where the light didn't oppose the dark and vice versa, they would simply hold each other in harmony and integration.

"Sophia is just starting to wake up, but she doesn't realize how valuable she is on her own, independent of Akasha. I know it won't ever seem like the right moment to get to know them, but she needs to know that you're her father, that she has support, that you have been through what she has,"

"I-I-I know," he stammered, as the words finally hit home. He longed to know his daughters, yet it didn't feel like a possibility for him, it never had. They lived in a different world from the one he did. *"Would she even be open to me if I came forward?"*

"You can't know what they think or feel unless you try," Juliet gently reminded him.

Abdul rested in silence for a moment, then quietly asked, *"What do you suggest I do, Juliet?"*

"Something has happened in the Order," Juliet continued, knowing that she needed to switch gears

now that Abdul was starting to be receptive, *"Khalid has been killed."*

Abdul gasped. "But we just spoke. He was part of the reason why I was brave enough to try the Clarity potion so I could seek guidance from you. He recognized how out of control the order is becoming." Khalid had been his closest friend; he felt like a brother to him. The sudden news of his death was a blow, and his heart started to cry out in pain. He wondered if this would break his connection with Juliet.

"I know this is hard for you, Abdul, but you must not close your heart. Your Order needs you and so does your daughter. You must take a stand. Two people have been murdered and you cannot allow any more. You have been a coward Abdul. I say this in love, but it's true. You can no longer stand by silently." Juliet might have spoken with love, but her words were hard to hear.

Abdul sighed. He had been living in denial for too long, scared to take responsibility, afraid to acknowledge how far the Order had slid from his grasp and strayed from their original path.

"I know," Juliet said, *"but that can change. You need to take action."*

"But how do I get the members of the Order to do anything? How do I get them to trust me?"

"Thomas is giving a talk on the Winter Solstice that I think you and all the members of the Order need to hear. Tell them Khalid would have asked them to go to the talk in memory of him."

"But would he?"

"Yes," he heard the word telepathically. It was Khalid's voice. *"Yes, I would. I would do anything in my power to restore the balance between the light and the dark and bridge the divide."*

Abdul collapsed into tears. Hearing Khalid's voice was too much.

"Abdul, I am always here for you," Juliet started to fade as Abdul was overwhelmed by his emotions. *"Remember our connection. Remember the glove I gave you all those years ago. Please put it back on and seek me when you need me. I am here to help. We all are."*

Her voice disappeared as Abdul heard a sharp bang on his cave walls.

Chapter 49

Rashid's Assistance

 bdul! Abdul, you must wake up. Something awful has happened," Rashid barged into Abdul's chambers without waiting for approval to enter.

Abdul sat up in bed trying to regain his composure, already aware of what Rashid was going to say. "I know Rashid, I know."

"But how? It has only just happened," Rashid stopped in his tracks and stood still gathering his breath.

"That is a story for another time. What we need to do is gather the Order immediately. I know it is the middle of the night, but time cannot be lost. Khalid was like a brother to me, and I will no longer put up with this. Will you help?" Abdul's voice was strained, but there was still power emanating from it. He knew he was asking a lot as Rashid was bound to be confused as to how he would already know of Khalid's death.

"Of course. What do you need me to do?"

Rashid's response surprised him. He was clearly tired, but willing to step forward. *This young man is what we need more of here. I must not lose sight of that,* Abdul thought as he got out of bed and threw his robe around him.

"Wake the others and ask that everyone gather at sunrise in the central meeting room." Abdul went to his desk to prepare what he was going to say.

"Rashid," he looked up as the young recruit was about to leave, "thank you for your dedication, to me and to the Order. I am sorry for the events that have unfolded. I am sorry for the recent loss of life. I am sorry for the chaos that exists, but I plan to address that head on. I appreciate your support." Abdul's voice was heavy. He didn't know if he had got his point across, but he genuinely meant his words and hoped Rashid understood his heartfelt gratitude.

Rashid nodded and backed away to sound the bells to wake the Order and bring them to attention at sunrise.

Chapter 50

The Visit to the Temple

s dawn broke, Tariq and Paul wandered up the hill to the Temple. Neither of them had ever set foot inside. Tariq found connection with the Spirit Realm through his relationship with Leo, it didn't extend beyond that.

"So, this man's name is Thomas?" Paul asked.

"That's right. According to Leo, he can help." Tariq had an edge to his voice. He was still upset that the murderer had gotten away. *Leo, I know my safety is your concern, but this man is dangerous!* His thoughts demanded a response, but he heard nothing in return.

Paul was silent as they approached the Temple, though Tariq did not know if he was afraid or in awe.

"Do we knock?" Paul asked.

"Isn't that one of the things that Temples are known for? Being open to all?" Tariq pushed through the doorway, eager to find Thomas and not in the mood for pleasantries.

They were greeted by the majesty of the Sanctum. They stood for a few moments getting adjusted to the darkness and the ambience.

"Wow!" Paul said.

It is quite a beautiful sight to take in, but we have more urgent matters at hand, Tariq thought as an elderly man appeared in the room. His white hair was dishevelled. He looked as if he hadn't slept in a few days, but his blue eyes were filled with compassion and kindness.

"May I be of service?" He was dressed in a priest's robe with a long collar draped over his torso.

He seems nervous, Tariq thought as he moved towards him, softened by his manner. *I should have known he would be here just as we had arrived.* Grateful for the synchronicity, he introduced them.

Thomas nodded and smiled, "Tariq! I have heard of you. I am happy to make your acquaintance, and more so, to do anything I can to help."

"You have heard of me? How?" Tariq enquired, a little confused. *His voice does sound genuine though.*

Just as Thomas opened his mouth to elaborate, Akasha and Sophia rushed through the door.

"Thomas?" Akasha yelled, not quite seeing him or the others as their eyes adjusted to darker lighting in the room. "Thomas, we need your help!"

"Akasha, welcome," Thomas said.

Tariq turned around. *Could this be her, again? So soon?* He went to greet her, their eyes locking again.

"Oh," Akasha said, looking deeply into his eyes.

Again, those eyes. I could get lost in them, he thought. "Akasha, it is good to see you again." He held her gaze. *We must keep her safe.*

Akasha stood still.

Why isn't she speaking? Tariq wondered.

"I, uh, I didn't expect to see you here," Akasha admitted.

"We came here out of concern for you, actually," Tariq responded gently, taking a step closer to her. "You are in danger," he found himself admitting without meaning to. *I don't want to overwhelm her, but she needs to know what has happened.*

"Danger?" Akasha raised her eyebrows, she moved towards him, brushing her hands against her dark burgundy robe. "And what kind of danger is that?"

Tariq smiled. She was so incredibly beautiful, even if she looked at him with scepticism, cynicism, and doubt.

"I don't want to alarm you again. It might be better if we talk with Thomas first."

"If you have anything to say that concerns my safety, I think I should be the first to hear it. I'm surprised you are concerned at all, considering where you come from and who you work with," Akasha responded very intently. "As far as I am concerned, the only issue with my safety at the moment is being here with you," she turned away from him and crossed her arms.

Tariq was tired of this and determined to loosen her guards, although he understood why she had raised them in place. "Akasha, you misunderstood the other day. Paul and I are not part of the *Order of the Pragmatists*. We have been asked to monitor their activities to prevent any future harm or damage to Gibraltar," Tariq explained. *This is all so uncomfortable.*

"Asked by whom exactly?" Her arms remained folded, making her look like an angry child who didn't believe a word he was saying.

"By Leo," Paul announced, looking as if he was going to continue to explain.

Tariq gave him a sharp jab. *There is no way that Akasha will understand who Leo is. This will only make the situation worse.*

"Just be present, and listen, Tariq, I have met Akasha before," he heard Leo's voice in his mind, causing a quick reaction in him. *"Akasha met you? How?"*

Akasha reacted in a completely different manner than Tariq had expected. She hesitated, holding her tongue for a moment as if she was processing something profound.

"By Leo?" She sounded alarmed.

"Leo is Tariq's Shadow," Thomas said softly.

Akasha gasped, "How on earth would I have been able to access and meet Tariq's Shadow?"

"Because of your roles Akasha, as the Two of the Royal Heart," Thomas said gently.

The meeting of Leo and Akasha suddenly made more sense to Tariq. He didn't know what being the Two of the Royal Heart meant, but it at least confirmed the reality of their connection. He allowed this to deepen within him before he began to explain why he was there in the first place. "Leo guided Paul and I to a secret part of the Pragmatist's cave to monitor their activity," Tariq said slowly, he could sense how unnerved Akasha was.

"Is Akasha safe?" Sophia asked, linking an arm with her sister to support her.

"That's why we came to seek out Thomas. Leo told me he would be able to help," Tariq said. "It appears that Alejandro, a member of the *Order of the Pragmatists*, is responsible for Raoul's death. He is desperate to get any information about Raoul that he can, and is planning to seek you out in an effort to learn more." *I hadn't planned on saying all of that at once, but the truth needs to be known.* He watched as Akasha's eyes widened even more.

Chapter 51

Akasha's Overwhelm

 aoul's name just came out of Tariq's mouth! Akasha didn't understand the depth of her emotions for Tariq. She felt guilty for even having any, and Tariq speaking his name felt like a betrayal. *Raoul has only recently passed. How can this all be happening so quickly? How is any of this happening? I am glad that Sophia is with me,* she thought as she leaned into her sister's loving presence.

"Akasha, maybe we might sit down?" suggested Sophia.

"Akasha and Sophia, I think it might be best if you stay here for the next few days," Thomas said, ushering them to one of the aisles so they could all be seated, Akasha looked overwhelmed. "You will be safe here as the Temple is protected by the ancient divine right. Tariq, Paul, and I can work on a plan to deal with Alejandro."

Alejandro? Who is this Alejandro? And why is he now after me? I don't understand. Akasha felt numb, but she followed Sophia's guidance and sat down almost without realising what she was doing. *I'm in danger? Tariq isn't from the Order?* Confusion overtook her as she realised that she didn't hate him. He had been seeking to protect her all along. *Leo is his Shadow, but somehow, I interacted with him before my own?* Her mind was spinning; none of it made sense.

"Akasha, are you okay?" Sophia pressed gently, as they sat down. This was a lot for any of them to take in.

Akasha did her best to get control of her senses; she needed to concentrate on what was being said. She looked around and met Tariq's eyes again. *Those eyes. They know me. It feels like they can see inside me.* She looked down and took a few deep breaths to try and center herself.

"Not at the moment, Soph. But, I will be." She slowly looked back up at the group, acknowledging the danger of this situation.

"It's just a lot for me to process. If I'm in danger, then so is Sophia," Akasha said, slowly recalibrating herself and gathering her strength. "Thomas, I don't want to put you out, but I think you are right. It might be for the best if we stay here." She was exhausted and hoping that she would be able to sleep within the Temple walls. Remembering what had happened to her earlier this week she couldn't help but voice her concerns. "I just hope I don't get another vision of the Crown within the next few days, as I don't know how I'd handle it."

Chapter 52

Tariq's Understanding

t was Tariq's time to process. *The Crown? Did she just say the Crown? As in the Crown that is to be paired with the Ring of Infinite Wisdom? How was she linked to the Crown?*

Thomas saw confusion on his face. "The nature of the Crown Jewels, and how you are the Two of the Royal Heart, I think, will be a story for another day," he said, looking specifically at him.

Tariq nodded, sensing he needed to keep the Ring and his connection to it a secret for now. *Thomas seems to know a lot more than he is saying aloud.*

Tariq did not ask the questions on his mind as he did not want to further overwhelm Akasha. He also didn't want her out of his sight. *It is incredibly unnerving how important she already is to me. I don't know if I like these emotions Leo. I am not used to wanting to protect anyone other than myself.* Leo remained silent.

"Akasha, please, let me take you and your sister up to the sleeping quarters where we can make a place for you. The Temple walls are protected by a spell cast in the Ancient of Days, only those who wish no harm can enter. Tariq and Paul, thank you for coming to warn us. I will need to make sure these ladies are settled, as you can understand."

"Thank you, Thomas. We appreciate that," Tariq acknowledged, although every membrane in his being was longing to not be separated from her. *I'm also really uncomfortable with this need to be around her!* "Would it be okay if we came back later to speak with you? I have a number of questions."

"Of course," Thomas responded. "Both of you will be welcome."

With that, Thomas guided Akasha and Sophia through the back of the room to their new home for the next few days. Tariq watched them leave, completely unsettled.

Chapter 53

Akasha's Resistance

I know a lot is happening, but I need to be alone for a few minutes," Akasha said, stepping away from Thomas and her sister. "I am feeling a little overwhelmed and need some fresh air. I will be in the Garden. I'm sure I will be safe there." Without waiting for their response or approval, Akasha walked swiftly into the garden. She was proud of herself for voicing how she was feeling and taking action to center herself, she hadn't been doing enough of that recently.

Akasha pulled out her dragon stone unintentionally and stroked the smooth blue-green grey surface as she sat in a wooden chair in the Temple garden. She wasn't feeling like herself when she suddenly heard Athena's voice, *"Akasha, are you alright?"*

I'm not sure if I'm ready to talk. In fact, I'm not sure about anything at this point, she thought as she stayed silent trying to gather some sense of equilibrium before communicating with her. *"I know Athena, you are my 'Protector,' but I'm exhausted. I miss feeling safe and in control."*

"But you were never really in control, Akasha. You were only ever under the illusion that you were," Athena said as Akasha suddenly sensed her presence in the garden even though she could not see her.

Akasha waited, growing more tired by the minute. *"Athena, you have yet to bring me any comfort. Why do you always seem to show up when nothing makes sense?"* This visit from Athena continued to agitate her.

"That is part of the reason why I appear, Akasha; to make sure that you are okay. You might have been wondering what I am protecting you from."

"Might I? I don't think it matters. You will tell me anyway," Akasha sulked.

"Akasha, you are acting like a child!" Athena's tone hardened as she came into Akasha's sight. *"In addition to*

protecting you from others, I am also protecting you from yourself. The mind is a very powerful thing, and you are going through a major transition. You have a role to play, Akasha, and I am here to make sure you are ready and willing to play it."

"A role to play?" Akasha stood up and started pacing the garden not caring if it looked like she had lost her mind. "Additional responsibility, when I can barely hold myself together?"

"Have you ever wondered what your vision of the Crown means? I know we have told you it is larger than you." Athena's voice hardened again.

"Of course. All the time. It's not like I enjoy feeling the way that I do! I hate not understanding."

"And what don't you understand?" Athena asked.

Akasha stopped, lost in thought for a moment, then raised her hands in frustration and said, "Everything!"

"I think you understand a lot more than you think, if you look a little deeper. You already know of your connection to the Crown and to the Ring of Infinite Wisdom.

"Akasha, you have all the answers within when you are ready to receive them. I came here to remind you that I'm here. I am always here to help and guide you. You are meant to do great things, but most important is that you feel whole and complete. You need to know who you are *and to believe in yourself. My request is that you please take care, be easy on yourself, and know that you are loved and supported."*

Akasha was silent for a moment. *"Athena, I just want to be alone."* Akasha didn't care if anyone else heard as Athena disappeared and Esmeralda came into view.

"Esmeralda, I am falling apart currently. I know you gave me this dragon stone to help, but right now it's all too much. I don't want to be reminded of how terrible of a person I am or have anything reflected back to me," Akasha struggled to keep her thoughts straight and hoped she was communicating clearly enough.

"Do I reflect things back to you? Tell me, how exactly does that work Akasha?" Esmeralda mirrored her tone.

"By just being here." Akasha started to pace the garden again. She was upset and surprised that her emotions were not breaking their connection.

"And doing what exactly?" Esmeralda was not backing down. She moved and stood firmly beside Akasha.

"I just told you! I want to be left alone!" Akasha was nearing her boiling point.

"And what exactly is being alone going to do for you? When you try and escape truly feeling your difficult emotions and don't allow for the healthy expression of them, you create your own suffering. You have responsibilities,

Akasha. As Athena has just reminded you, this is so much larger than just you." Esmeralda paced beside Akasha, matching her steps, her words, her thoughts and actions.

"You know what, Esmeralda, I asked for NONE OF THIS. NONE. I don't want any responsibilities. I don't want the stupid Crown. I don't want to be One of the Royal Heart. I certainly don't want to have to deal with Tariq and whatever is going on between us. I want to sit here and miss Raoul and be alone. That's it! That's all. Aren't my vibrations, or whatever the hell you said before, supposed to impact us? Shouldn't my anger and my complete and total disgust send you on your way? Isn't my vibration low enough that I can actually be left IN PEACE?" Akasha reached down to find a rock or anything to throw at Esmeralda and make her point but looked up to see that she was alone yet again.

Chapter 54

The Walk to the Black Onyx

 ariq and Paul left the *Temple of the Holy One* and began making their way back to the Black Onyx.

"Do you think Akasha will be safe at the Temple?" Paul asked.

"Yes," Tariq said after a moment. "Although, it will take her time to adjust and start to feel protected." The question he wanted answered though was, how safe was he? *How can I love this woman I barely know?* He knew he had a connection with her, he had known it from the very moment he laid eyes on her, but he was struggling with the depth of it, with the realization that they were both tied to the Crown and she apparently had the ability to connect with his Shadow.

They walked in silence for a while until Paul spoke, hesitantly, "Tariq?"

"Yes?" Tariq sensed that Paul had something on his mind, but the encounter with Akasha had completely thrown him off. He shifted his focus and paid attention to his friend as they walked along the beach.

"Will you tell me more about your relationship with Leo?" Paul asked.

Tariq could tell he wasn't grasping the concept of his own Shadow and wanted to help. So, he put all of his emotions about Akasha on hold to devote his time, effort and energy in the present moment to his friend.

"Yes, Paul. Sorry. I meant to tell you about it earlier. It's just that we got caught up in other things." Tariq put his hands on his compass in an effort to gather his thoughts as he took a deep breath.

"My life was falling apart when I opened up to Leo for the first time," he admitted as they walked down the beach. "I felt no hope for the future. He emerged one night and was terrifying. I didn't know what to do. I didn't know him, but I could sense his power. He was more than anything I had ever witnessed in this physical realm and it scared me."

Paul gave Tariq his full attention. Tariq hoped he could communicate what he was finding hard to put into words. "I shut him out Paul. I was aware he existed, but I wanted nothing to do with him. If I could turn back time, I wish I had been more open to building a relationship with him at the start, but I didn't understand. All I knew was my own fear, resistance, and hopelessness."

"So, what changed?"

"I changed," Tariq said. "One day I woke up and realized I couldn't keep living the way I was. I knew I would always miss and love Cora, but I was shutting off my life by living that way. I woke up, and I knew I needed help, although I didn't know how to get it. So, I asked. I sat down one night and begged, prayed for help."

"You've never struck me as the type of person to seek out help, Tariq."

"I'm normally not, Paul, but I was at my breaking point. I didn't know what to do. That very night Leo appeared again, but by that time, I was finally open to what he had to say. My relationship with Leo has never been easy. He is constantly showing me things about myself that I have not previously been aware of, helping me to see what doesn't serve me. It was through my embrace of him that I have this compass, and how we found the Ring of Infinite Wisdom."

Paul paused, "Leo, your Shadow, led us to the Ring of Infinite Wisdom?"

Tariq smiled and nodded.

"I guess there must be more advantages to this Shadow thing than I thought!" Paul said, smiling as they arrived at the harbour and jumped aboard the ship.

Chapter 55

Alejandro's Discovery

lejandro was out for a walk and immediately recognized Tariq. He had been determined to find out more about him, so he followed the two men overhearing their entire conversation. He couldn't be bothered with understanding what the Shadow things were but was delighted to uncover who would be kept safe.

Akasha is in the Temple of the Holy One, he thought after he watched them climb aboard their ship. *How very convenient! I just need to wait for her to leave. I'm sure it won't be long.* He quickly changed course and made his way back to the cave to gather a few things for his wait outside the Temple.

❈ ❈ ❈

Alejandro camped out in front of the gates for the day, hidden behind an olive tree with food, a warm wool blanket and a mat to sleep on if he needed it. He hadn't seen anyone coming in or out of the Temple. That was unusual. *How long should I wait for Akasha to leave? No one else had been as close to Raoul and she could hold the key to figuring the codes out.* He was considering tampering with her third eye if she was not forthcoming. *I might even uncover something interesting about her ridiculous potions.*

Alejandro was so blinded by his quest for knowledge that the connection to his Shadow was moved even farther away, causing him to be even further controlled by this unconscious desire. Worse, he was not even aware of any of this.

"Will the other members of the Order have noticed that I am missing?" Alejandro said aloud, lost in his own thoughts. He was tempted to enter the Temple himself, although something about the place unnerved him. So, he sat back against the tree, the sun was hot and he was grateful for the shade. He made the decision that if there was no movement by nightfall, he would go inside and find her.

Chapter 56

The Connection to Sophia

 ophia curled up in bed, and decided to meditate. A lot had happened today, and she wanted to see if she could find any sense of peace. She breathed deeply and worked on letting go of her thoughts. It was sometimes tricky for her to get to that state where she wasn't thinking, but remained aware. She was so worried about her sister that her mind was scattered, but she slowed down and breathed deeply. She focused on her chakras again, her energy centers, as her sister had only recently taught her.

She thought of the color red and imagined it encompassing and surrounding her root chakra, the energy center located at the base of her spine. Once she felt herself to be grounded, her thoughts moved up to her sacral chakra and she imagined a healing orange energy cleansing and purifying it. Next, she moved on to her solar plexus and imagined a sunshine yellow energy and light swirling around her belly button. She spent a few minutes there and then finally moved up to her heart center and imagined emerald green. It felt so peaceful, so calm and so loving. *This is so nice, I can't believe I'm finally feeling this, instead of the absence of it,* she thought as she continued to breathe deeply.

"*Sophia.*"

She heard her name spoken very softly. Her heart jumped, as she continued to breathe deeply.

"*Sophia, my dear Sophia. Can you hear me?*"

Again, the words were feathery soft, resembling the voice of her mother, Isis.

Sophia's eyes began to tear up. She didn't think she would ever hear that voice again, she was deeply touched.

"*Mother?*" She didn't say the words aloud, only sent them telepathically through her third eye. When she was connected and in tune with it and her heart, she was able to open up and be aware of the Spirit Realm.

"Yes, my dear! I am so glad you can hear me," her mother said. *"I have come so you know we are all here, watching, and waiting to help as you need us."*

"Who do you mean by 'we'?"

"That will make more sense in time, Sophia."

Sophia had so many questions for her mother, so much guidance she wanted to seek from her, she almost didn't know where to begin. *"Mother, do I have a Shadow?"*

"Yes, and she very much longs to meet you."

"Then how do I connect with her? Why haven't I been previously able to when I have been trying so hard?" Sophia felt sad but also thrilled to be with her mother, even though she didn't understand what she was doing now that she hadn't done before.

"Well, Sophia, you start with having love and compassion for yourself, not judging yourself. Then you open yourself up to the possibility that your Shadow does exist and is a part of who you are." Her mother's voice felt like a gentle wind of comfort.

"What stopped you before my dear, sweet child, was the idea you kept telling yourself that you were doing something wrong, that you didn't have access. You do, my love, you always have. You connected with your heart center today and let go of your fears and doubts, which is what enabled me to be able to speak to you."

"I'm grateful to have connected with you mother," Sophia said gently as their connection started to fade. For the last few days, she had been telling herself that she wasn't enough, that the Spirit Realm wasn't meant for her, so it felt wonderful to be able to connect with the things she had been dreaming of.

"You are worthy of love, worthy of connection, and of everything your heart longs and desires. It just starts with you believing." Isis' voice slowly disappeared as Sophia continued to breathe and remain in that state of gratitude.

Chapter 57

Paul and the Heart Stone

 aul went below deck. He wanted to use the Clarity potion again, eager to connect if he could. He took a sip and said aloud, "it is my intention to meet with my Shadow." He breathed deeply as he lay down and felt his body getting heavy. His awareness started to expand and he seemed to sink a little deeper into the moment.

"*Paul.*" He heard, felt and recognized the same voice and presence from their previous meeting. It was clearer than before, but it remained a little distant.

"Who are you? Paul asked warily. "I know more about the idea of you now, but I am struggling to understand what it all means."

"My name is Rocky, let's begin with that."

Rocky stepped into Paul's sight and he saw an immense wolf ahead of him. The creature instilled in him a sense of wonder and of power, but he also felt like something outside of himself, something unknown.

"So, according to Tariq, I need to embrace you? This all seems so stupid to me," Paul said. He was glad to be able to see Rocky and to meet him, but he would be lying to himself if he didn't acknowledge how weird he felt. "I'm not scared of you, but I'm not sure if I believe in you. I don't know if I believe in any of this."

"It's your doubts, Paul, and your lack of belief that are making this feel unreal to you. Everyone's experience with their Shadows is unique to them. When we first appear, we force you to look at an area of yourself you have previously repressed or kept hidden. We ask you to embrace it, as it is through embracing that aspect of yourself that you will come to know me," Rocky said.

Paul paused to think.

"I know this is confusing for you, Paul, but please know that this is real; that I am always with you and I long to help you."

Paul still didn't understand and felt incredibly sceptical. *Rocky is here with me however, so I should at least try to get to know more.*

"And how do I get to know you, Rocky?" He tried to be open to the idea that he was communicating with a giant talking wolf.

"*You just believe that I am here, as I am. I am always with you Paul.*"

Paul grunted. He wasn't sure how he could just make himself magically believe.

"*Well, it begins with questioning that thought. Why don't you believe? What is holding you back from accepting me? Why do you think you need the Clarity potion to connect to me?*"

"*I don't know, Rocky! If I knew that we wouldn't be having this conversation in the first place!*" Paul said, annoyed and frustrated. This conversation wasn't helping.

"*Just breathe, Paul. Calm down. Don't lower your vibration. When you start to doubt this in the future, ask yourself why. See if you can shift your thinking.*"

"*You make it sound so easy.*" Paul was starting to feel annoyed. It wasn't as if he knew of some miraculous way to immediately lift his vibration and his mood, he felt the connection between them begin to dissipate.

"Well, if you believe you have help and assistance from us, it becomes much easier," Rocky said, as his presence started to fade.

He placed a green stone in the shape of a heart into Paul's hand. *"This will help. When you feel you are starting to question and doubt your connection with me and the Spirit Realm, place your hand on this stone to help ground and center your energy."*

Paul didn't have a chance to thank Rocky, but the stone remained in his hand as Rocky disappeared.

Chapter 58

Abdul and Rashid Unite

bdul's mind went to the glove that Juliet had given him so many years before. He had buried it in a drawer when he lost Isis and hadn't thought about it until she had reminded him moments ago.

He got out of bed and opened the drawer and shuffled through his belongings, wondering if it was even still there. He dug amongst the contents until he felt the comfort of the soft black leather glove. He sighed deeply as he pulled it out.

Smiling as he inspected it, he took a large breath and felt Juliet's loving energy. He really had missed it. *There are so many things to do, I haven't prepared my speech for the Order. Do I have time now? Khalid's murder must be accounted for. We can't spiral into further darkness.* His thoughts circled around him as he struggled to focus.

He heard footsteps at his door and looked up to see Rashid standing there.

"Abdul, I have summoned the Order. They are waiting in the main meeting room," Rashid said with urgency.

Abdul was glad he had found Juliet's glove, knowing that he would need to lean on her for help. He had thought he would have had more time to prepare but knew he must face the Order. He needed to listen to his deceased friend and take action.

"There is more you should know, Abdul, that I did not tell you last night." Rashid spoke truthfully and swiftly as he told Abdul about the secret council, and of Alejandro's previous murder.

Abdul stood up. "I had suspected Alejandro when I saw what looked to be the alchemical knife in his chamber. Khalid came to me last night, asking me to call a meeting, to stand firm, but I was too late." His voice was filled with anger and sadness. "Do the others continue to follow him?"

"I believe the others have lost heart with the death of Raoul. Unfortunately, that did not seem to deter Alejandro."

"Do you know where he is?" Abdul repeated.

"I do not, but the others are gathered. We need you Abdul; we need a leader. We need someone strong, before all hope is lost," Rashid pleaded.

"Khalid, I am so, so sorry," he said to his friend. He looked down at the glove in an effort to center himself. Rashid just watched in silence as they walked to the main meeting room.

Chapter 59

The Chat with Leo

 ariq felt unsettled, even though his heart was full after seeing Akasha earlier that day. *I don't like this feeling of needing her, needing to know she is safe. I am used to taking care of myself and not worrying about anyone else, especially after the loss of Cora.* Of course, he wished the circumstances were different, but he was glad to know she was protected. Akasha seemed to be on guard, but his connection with her still overwhelmed him. *How is it that I have such strong feelings for her?* He lay in bed, unable to get up and focus on the day until he cleared his head. He

placed his hands on his compass. It made no sense. He had only just met her, yet it felt like he had known her all of his life. It felt like she was a part of him.

"It's pretty powerful, isn't it?" he heard Leo say.

Tariq was startled, although he was used to having access to him. His confusion over the depth of his emotions for Akasha had placed him in a different world. He was grateful for his presence though as he needed help sorting through this.

"Powerful is a bit of an understatement, but I don't understand it, Leo. It's unnerving, I am starting to feel out of control." Tariq focused on his heart so that he could tune into his connection with Leo more clearly.

"There are many things you won't be able to explain or control Tariq. What exists between you two is a deep love that goes beyond time and space."

"Is she aware of it? And how were you able to connect with her? Nothing about this woman or our connection makes any sense to me!"

"She is aware of a deep connection with you, but like you, she doesn't understand it. Be that as it may, her soul knows you and she recognizes you when she looks into your eyes. But, she hasn't allowed herself to process it yet. I was able to meet with her because of your connection.

I went to her to make sure she was okay in the absence of her own Shadow."

"She mentioned this in the Temple, but how is that possible? I didn't think others could see you. I thought I'd be the only one aware of your presence."

"Usually, yes, but as you are the Two of the Royal Heart, we are able to access one another, just as you will be able to access Esmeralda once Akasha has fully embraced her."

Tariq still couldn't believe that his own Shadow had been able to spend time with Akasha, let alone whatever this 'Two of the Royal Heart' might be.

"Don't be unnerved, Tariq. I went to make sure she was alright. She wasn't coping well with Raoul's death and needed support to accept her emotions and work to release them. She was not yet aware of Esmeralda, and as you had already fully accepted me, I was able to step in, in Esmeralda's place."

Tariq was quiet, taking in what he could. This was not a light load!

"The Crown Jewels are part of yours and Akasha's destinies. Akasha will need to work with Esmeralda to manifest the Crown which will be paired with your Ring. Once you are both standing in your authenticity, they can be used in partnership. What this means is that you and Akasha will need to align your intentions to travel to LionsGate where your mission will begin." LionsGate existed in the Ancient of Days and if successful, their mission could reconnect the worlds of the past, present, and future, but Leo was careful to only reveal one piece at a time. *"As I said before, your mission is to bridge the divide that exists between the Worlds of Light and Dark."*

Tariq was curious about this mysterious place called LionsGate but for now his thoughts drifted back to Akasha.

"She will be safe within the walls of the Temple. We will look out for her, but it's important that she gets to know and trust you."

"This feels very much like my initial relationship with you," Tariq said, raising an eyebrow as Leo smiled and faded away.

Akasha's Moments of Clarity

kasha woke up the next morning not feeling much better. She had spent the rest of yesterday carrying through the motions with her sister and Thomas. She ate the food prepared for her, talked when she was spoken to, but she still felt alone, in danger, and overwhelmed. Sophia slept soundly in the bed next to her, her sister's soft breathing unmistakable. Akasha didn't want to disturb her slumber, so she quietly

headed to the Sanctum. There she sat among the pews and took a few minutes to calm herself and go within.

She slowly breathed in and out as she began to meditate. She felt her world expand as she sunk deeper into her connection with herself. When she felt what she could only describe as a shimmering white light surrounding her, she knew she had cleansed and purified all of her energy centers to get to that state and was comforted.

She stayed in the shimmering light for a few minutes, feeling surrounded in love and a warm embrace from the universe.

"That was beautiful, my dear, you have always done that so well," said Isis. Akasha was dumbstruck as she felt her mother's loving energy enter into her space for the first time since her passing.

"Mother! You're here? How?" She didn't know if she wanted to laugh or cry. She hadn't anticipated ever being able to be in her presence again, and was grateful to commune with her.

"Keep your breathing steady to stay in this place my dear" Isis responded as Akasha felt her unconditional love.

Isis was able to be with both of her daughters as they were entering the powerful time of the Winter Solstice Portal. Both women were starting to wake up to who they truly are, and their connection with the divine was increasing. Every time they leaned into their heart space and lived from the authentic nature of their being, the veils between the worlds were lowered and the Spirit Realm was revealed in a more conscious way. *"You are doing so well, Akasha, we are all so proud of you. I know how tough this last week has been."*

Akasha listened, unable to express in words her joy at hearing her mother again.

"I have come about your own relationship with Esmeralda. You need to seek her as this will be vital in the days to come. Esmeralda is here to help and assist you to connect to your wholeness. I know you are frustrated, and you feel she is invading your space, but ultimately she is there to allow you to love and embrace all of who you are."

"I'm not sure I understand," Akasha said. She was only too aware that their last interaction had not gone well.

"I know. That understanding will come. I would encourage you to spend some time with your dragon stone and with her. It's important my dear, that you come to think of her as someone who is working with you and not against you."

Akasha listened, realising just how much she missed her mother.

"I miss you too, my dear, but I am always here watching over you with Athena, Esmeralda, and the others.

Know that," she said. Their time was coming to a close as their heart connection started to fade.

Akasha was left in a state of wonder, which left her more open to the idea of her Shadow. She wondered if she should try taking her mother's advice.

Akasha took the dragon stone, turned it over in her hand, and thought of Esmeralda. Almost in an instant she appeared, like magic, before her.

"Is it always going to be this easy to connect to you?" Akasha asked, surprised she was there so suddenly.

"When you are open to it, in alignment, and grounded, yes." Esmeralda placed herself next to her.

"And how do I deepen my relationship with you?" Akasha posed the question that had made her uneasy for days. *I suppose I really should try and learn more about this, trying to close her out has not done me any good,* she thought, realizing her mother would not have appeared for the first time since her passing for no reason.

Well, for one, you should see that I am here to help and not hinder you. Let's start with your relationship with Tariq. What do you feel about him?"

Akasha was determined to stay open to this conversation despite her discomfort, *"I don't know,"* she answered honestly, *"There is a deep connection, but it's terrifying because I don't understand it, and I am scared of being hurt."* This was the first time she had realized that. Was that what this was? She was scared?

"And that is exactly why I am here with you," Esmeralda said. *"To help you make sense of those things that confuse and upset you, so you see that these feelings are natural, and should not be repressed or avoided. They may be uncomfortable to begin with, but when you sit and work with them, with help from me, we can transform your reality. Your relationship with Tariq is a perfect example. You need to spend some time discerning your emotions and the depth of that connection, rather than pushing it away."*

"I'm not pushing it away!" Akasha was defensive as she slowly started to shut herself back down.

"Akasha, you can't hide things from me." Esmeralda said. *"You are pushing your emotions away. You're not willing to recognize them because you are scared of how they might make you feel, of having to be vulnerable, of admitting that you have feelings; crazy, passionate feelings for someone else."*

Akasha said nothing, but allowed Esmeralda's words to sink in.

"Our relationship depends on you allowing me to help you work through these challenges, including your relationship with Tariq and with the Crown."

"*And what is my relationship with the Crown?*"

"*It is part of your destiny. You are One of the Royal Heart which I know you don't understand yet. When you are able to connect with the Crown, it will help you to travel to LionsGate to bridge the divide that exists between the dimensions and the Worlds of Light and Dark. Your work will bring balance, order and ultimately love between all.*"

"*Was anything you said just now supposed to make any sense? And what is LionsGate?*" Akasha asked.

Esmeralda laughed. "*I think we can leave it at that. It will make more sense as we work together. But for now, I suggest you spend some time thinking about your connection with Tariq. Also, spend some time thinking about your vision of the Crown. You already have all of these answers within you, Akasha.*"

Akasha had one last thought on her mind: Esmeralda's flames. Esmeralda decided to address it before departing.

"*There will come a time, Akasha, when you will need them, when you will need to identify with them. You need to know and accept that nothing about me is designed to hurt or hinder you, only to allow you to expand into who you are meant to be. My flames are a part of that. For now, let's take this one step and one breath at a time. Thank you for calling me and being open.*"

With the closing words of her Shadow, Akasha took a few more deep breaths and came out of her meditative state. She came back to the present moment grateful for their expanding relationship, but frustrated Esmeralda had not told her more about LionsGate. Everyone kept mentioning she would travel there, but she had no idea what 'there' actually was. Thomas had assisted her before and so she decided to lean on him for guidance yet again. She wandered the Temple until she found him in the library.

Chapter 61

Lesson on LionsGate

"Thomas, what do you know about LionsGate?" Akasha spoke quickly.

Thomas jumped in surprise. He had anticipated helping, but knew the situation was quite delicate. Silently, he sent a request to Peter for guidance. He put down the book he was looking at and turned to address Akasha.

"LionsGate is a powerful place that exists in Egypt. It is heavily linked to the energy of our powerful spiritual sun, Sirius." Thomas knew this was the first time that Akasha had heard of Sirius, our sun's spiritual sun and of

LionsGate. There was so much magic and mystery associated with both, Thomas and the others had decided to reveal it one piece at a time to not cause her overwhelm. "Sirius is the spiritual sun to our sun, acting as a governing and guiding body. Sirius and the Earth's moon have always been connected to LionsGate. Humans realized this connection in the Ancient of Days, but it had been lost in translation since then." Thomas paused to look for a book that would provide Akasha with a understanding of what would start when the Crown Jewels were both physically manifested on Earth.

"It is an extremely potent place in terms of aligning your energy and causing shifts within the dimensions," Thomas continued, as he searched through the library.

"A lot of this won't be easy to grasp just yet. On the Winter Solstice there will be a powerful portal that you and Tariq will have the ability to access. As the Two of the Royal Heart, you will be able to travel there." He hoped these words wouldn't startle her but he intuitively knew they needed to be said.

❊   ❊   ❊

Akasha was confused, but glad to at least know a little more about her mission. The thought of traveling anywhere with Tariq both excited and terrified her at the same time. She realized that she really did need to do exactly what Esmeralda had told her; spend some time being with her emotions.

Thomas nodded at her. "I know this a lot to take in Akasha. I wish there was more I could do to ease this transition for you, but you are doing amazing and undergoing a powerful awakening period. It is up to you to process it all."

Akasha took in the words and bowed, knowing that she needed to be alone with her thoughts. *Will any of this ever make sense to me?* She thought as she returned to the garden.

Chapter 62

The Garden and the Beach

 kasha found herself back in the garden and shifted her focus to her heart center; breathing in and out of it to reach a state of deep alignment between her brain and her heart, what she liked to call heart coherence. It allowed her to step into the authentic nature of her being. She spent a few minutes there and in turn felt her awareness expand. Her thoughts shifted from where she had anticipated gaining more clarity and focus on, which was Tariq, to Raoul. She followed them, *I do miss Raoul. I miss him and I feel guilty about Tariq.*

She felt her energy shift again and found herself on a beach. Knowing she was traveling through her mind's eye, she allowed herself to relax into the situation. The warmth and the sand beneath her feet felt lovely. The sound of the waves soothed her soul and for the first time in a week, she was at ease. She felt the wind blow through her hair as she gazed out at the water, watching the beautiful reflection of the sun as she walked along the shore.

She suddenly came across someone and halted. She knew that body, and face, even from a distance. She took a deep breath and smiled, her stomach churning in anticipation, as he looked deeply at her.

"Akasha," Raoul greeted her, and that was all she needed.

"Oh, Raoul!" Akasha said and ran to him, throwing herself into his arms. She was so comforted by his presence, by being able to place her head on his heart. Comforted and unnerved at the same time.

"How are you here?" Akasha felt everything at once. *"How have I managed to connect with my mother, Esmeralda, and now you?"*

"You tapped into your heart space and the authentic nature of your being which allowed us to meet here," he explained. *"The power of the Winter Solstice is also aiding with these connections."*

Akasha started to feel her heart sink as she was reminded of the reality of their situation. Raoul wouldn't be there when she came out of her meditative state.

"Akasha, please stop. If you lower your vibration now, we will disconnect, and I don't have long. I wanted to see you one last time before I transition to join the others."

"Why wouldn't I be able to see you again? She asked as she rested her head against Raoul's shoulder, his arms around her. She felt such a broad spectrum of emotions. Comfort and love to be in Raoul's arms, sadness in knowing this moment would not last, and unease in her newly discovered feelings for Tariq, she felt proud of allowing herself to feel them.

"There is a lot you aren't ready to understand yet. What I want you to know, and this is going to sound strange coming from me, is that your feelings for Tariq are real. They are okay. You shouldn't be scared of them. You shouldn't repress them."

Akasha's head snapped up. This was not what she was expecting. Raoul, the love of her life, was telling her that it was permissible for her to have feelings for another man. She couldn't control the profound confusion and anger from rising and taking expression.

"What? You left me Raoul! You left me alone! And before we have even had your burial, you are talking to

*me about my feelings for another man? I don't even know
what to say any more. I really don't!"*

Akasha pushed herself from his embrace and
walked away, towards the water. She wasn't sure why she
was so upset, but his words had hurt her.

*"Akasha, I didn't mean to upset you. I would love to
spend hours with you in my arms. The problem is I don't
have a lot of time. I need to join the others. There is a lot
going on in the Spirit Realm and we need to prepare for
the events before the Solstice."*

*"I know how confused and scared you must feel.
I know you probably haven't even allowed yourself to
consider what's going on with Tariq. I needed to make sure
that you knew that what is most important to me is your
happiness,"* Raoul spoke softly, speaking gently into her
ear as he put his arms around her once more.

"How do you even know of Tariq?"

*"It's a completely different realm here, Akasha. I
have a level of awareness of all kinds of things that I didn't
in the physical plane."*

*"But how could you possibly be fine with me even
considering someone else?"* Akasha asked. She suddenly
realized why she was so upset. She felt wounded and
hurt by Raoul suggesting she be open to someone else. It

made her feel like their relationship and his feelings for her meant nothing.

"No, Akasha. It's not like that at all. I love you. I will always love you," Raoul said gently. "But my time has come, and I am needed in the Spirit Realm. We were brought into each other's lives for a reason and I will always be grateful for everything we had. But your happiness is what is most important to me. Many things will unfold in the next few days and will start to make sense. Tariq will be one of those things. I want you to understand that you shouldn't hold back, feel guilty, ashamed, or embarrassed because of what we had."

Akasha really wasn't sure what to think or feel. She just wanted to be in Raoul's arms. She leaned in as the beach slowly faded away and she found herself back in the garden.

Chapter 63

Abdul and the Order

bdul looked down at Juliet's glove as he took one last breath for strength and stepped into the main gathering room. *I am grateful Rashid stepped in to help organize this, I could not have done it on my own,* he thought as he tuned into Juliet's unconditional love for additional support and inspiration.

As he reached the center of the room, he noticed Alejandro's absence and debated on addressing it directly. He took a deep breath and began, "I consider you all family and it is with deep sadness that I call you together. As you know, we have just lost someone I considered to be my brother, someone who helped me run this Order, someone I leaned on for support. Khalid was an amazing man who will be deeply missed." Abdul paused to gain his composure and touched Juliet's glove, rolling his thumb over the leather. He felt a surge of love and protection.

"Khalid was an extraordinary man. He had an inner knowing and ability that drew him into the *Order of the Pragmatists* in the first place. He understood that there was more to all of this than it seems, but he craved the knowledge to scientifically prove it." He made eye contact with each member of the Order, hoping that his words were resonating.

"When Khalid joined, those of the Light were his friends. We worked with them, and what they took in faith, we used as an incentive to study. The divide, animosity or hatred that currently exists was not present then. So I am asking all of you tonight to suspend your judgement of those of the Light. Suspend those thoughts of us being 'right' and them being 'wrong'. Try not to see them as the other, as separate or different from who we are."

He stood still for a moment to get a sense of how his words were being taken in. Surprisingly, every member of the Order was listening. Maybe this was something they could relate to. He remained hopeful. "I want to tell you a story about Khalid. Years ago, his closest friend was a man named Thomas. They grew up together, spending their days playing in nature and enjoying life. One night, they experienced something neither of them could explain. This event caused them both to make decisions that determined the course of their lives. Thomas processed the events of the evening by joining the service of the Temple, while Khalid joined us.

"I won't go into the details of what happened that evening because it is not my story to tell. The point I am trying to make is that they both experienced the same life-changing moment, and took actions they believed to be sensible in light of that experience. Neither of them was right or wrong.

"Thomas knew him before we did and he is going to honor Khalid's life on the evening of the Winter Solstice by telling that particular story.

"I have asked you all to suspend your judgement of those of the Light and the Temple. For one night, I ask you to join me in honoring Khalid by going to a place where his childhood friend can honor him. It is a place where we can meet and hear the story that brought him to us, where we can work to no longer be divided, but to unite in our love and honor of this amazing man. I know many of you have been looking to Alejandro for wisdom recently, but you will notice that he is absent tonight after taking Khalid's life. I ask for your compassion and openness."

Abdul paused as he knew his official announcement of the murderer would shock them. He took a deep breath and continued. "Will you all join me?"

The group was silent. Abdul was asking a lot of them. There had existed a distrust and disdain within the Order to those of Light, and many had gravitated to the secret leadership of Alejandro. But, he also knew that deep down they'd all loved Khalid.

"I will join you," Rashid said, standing up to show his support. "Khalid cared about us all and deserves to be honored."

With his words the energy in the room seemed to shift.

"And I."

"And I."

"And I."

Slowly, one by one, everyone in the Order stood to show their support. Abdul smiled. He felt thankful for Rashid, for Juliet, and beyond grateful for the love he felt for every single member of the *Order* that night. With the exception of one.

Chapter 64

Sophia and Mystique

ophia woke up to an empty room. She felt her spirits lift as she remembered the connection with her mother the night before. *I did it!* She thought ecstatically. *I connected with the Spirit Realm.* She was overjoyed to know she was a part of it all. She breathed in a deep sigh of relief. *I have a Shadow. A Shadow who longs to meet with me. I wonder if I can connect with her? I wonder if the meditations might work now that I more firmly believe?* She knew she should find her sister and make sure she was alright, but she desperately wanted to connect with her Shadow for the first time.

She lay back down and closed her eyes, connected to her heart center, and followed the meditation her sister had given her a few days before. She let go of her expectations of what it might look like and before she knew it, she felt her level of consciousness expanding. While she knew she was still on her bed in the sleeping chambers of the Temple, she felt as if some part of her awareness was above that existence, beyond time and space. She breathed deeper, allowing herself to experience and connect to the depth and love she felt surrounding and engulfing her. She slowed her breathing, staying in this space as her mother had taught her to do.

"*Sophia. Can you hear me?*"

The voice was soft and unfamiliar, but she wasn't afraid of it.

"*That's amazing!*"

"*What's your name?*" Sophia asked timidly. She was still uncertain, but she wanted to understand how to access the Spirit Realm and meet her Shadow. Sophia deeply longed to see her for the first time.

"*My name is Mystique,*" her Shadow said, appearing before her in the form of a beautiful black panther. She was immense and powerful.

Sophia expected to feel terrified, but she was more intrigued. She felt a childlike sense of wonder and tingles all over her body as Mystique approached her. Sophia was awestruck as Mystique radiated power, beauty, and love.

"*You are beautiful,*" Sophia said as she gently stepped forward to touch her.

Mystique smiled.

"*I am a part of you. I am amazed at your reaction to our first encounter, Sophia. You are more receptive than most as you are open to this experience. You are already close to a state of acceptance in the nature of our relationship. You don't seem to feel fear in my presence and know me already. I am so delighted.*" Mystique stepped forward to allow Sophia to come into contact.

"*But why was it so hard for me to meet you, Mystique, when Akasha found it so easy to meet Esmeralda?*" Sophia asked as she looked around. An evening sky of stars and planets swirled around them. *We seem to be a long way from Gibraltar,* Sophia thought.

"*Akasha was able to connect with both Leo and Esmeralda because she was so caught up in her grief over the loss of Raoul. She set her ego aside and surrendered to the universe in asking for help. That allowed them to come through, help her process the loss, and be able to connect to us and all there was, is, and ever will be.*" Mystique moved closer to Sophia and looked up at the sky with her.

"I have always been with you. You just needed a little divine assistance to fully believe it. That appeared with you connecting to your heart center and reconnecting with your mother for love and guidance."

"I always thought I was doing something wrong, that I was missing something, and I wasn't good enough to have a connection to the Spirit Realm; only Akasha was," Sophia said slowly and sadly as she looked in Mystique's eyes. *"I believed I wasn't worthy."*

"I know," Mystique said. *"You and Akasha have different roles in the events to come, but you have always been worthy, and are deeply loved and guided by the Spirit Realm."*

"So my lack of belief, prevented me from accessing it and you?"

"Yes," Mystique said quietly. *"But the important thing is that you believe now."*

"I want you to know, Sophia, most people take years to reach a state of acceptance in their relationship with their Shadow. You have taken just a few moments. Because of it, I can give you this moonstone to call on me whenever you need me." Sophia reached for the moonstone and placed it next to her heart, smiling with gratitude in the realization that she wasn't unworthy; she was deeply loved.

"*Thank you, Mystique, I am so grateful to have met you,*" Sophia said as she stepped forward. With that acknowledgment and embrace a white light shimmered, surrounded, and engulfed them, connecting the two on an even deeper level.

Sophia smiled as she felt her vibration raise and she returned to connect with her body lying on the bed. She opened her eyes and looked down at the moonstone. Although Mystique was not physically in the room with her, Sophia knew she was there, and that felt wonderful.

Chapter 65

Akasha's
Conscious Processing

kasha came out of her meditative state and sat in the garden for a minute to collect her thoughts. So much had happened in the last few weeks. It had been nice to reconnect with Raoul, but also confusing. *How can he tell me that my feelings for Tariq are okay?* Next, she thought of Leo, who she now saw had helped her release her pain on the night of Raoul's death.

Then came Esmeralda. *It was her voice I heard when I had my vision of the Crown.* She thought back to what Esmeralda had first told her, *"That is the wrong question to ask. The questions to ask are how do you integrate from here? What do you do next? How can you use this pain you currently feel?"*

She had also seen the Crown and a brilliant ruby red Ring that evening. *I still wish I knew more about them. People keep telling me that I am One of the Royal Heart, but what does that mean?* She sensed this was connected to her future but couldn't clearly see any more. Next came Athena, her 'protector' throughout this transition. *Apparently, she is protecting me from myself.* She couldn't make sense of it at all.

She thought of her mother and was grateful to have a few words with her, even if they were to galvanize her to be open to Esmeralda.

She had asked Esmeralda about the Crown and the Ring. What had she said? She thought hard and touched her dragon stone and the words were repeated in her mind.

She still didn't understand half of it. *What's this 'divide' I will have to bridge? What are the dimensions?* She assumed the Worlds of Light and Dark had to do with those of the Light and the Pragmatists. She was beginning to understand that the 'Ring of Infinite Wisdom' was the same as the ruby red Ring she had in her vision. *I still don't understand the whole concept of Sirius and this place called LionsGate though!*

Her mind was reeling as she slowly returned to what she knew she should be processing; her relationship with Tariq. Even thinking of him made her heart jump. The feelings she had for him were hard to put into words. When he looked into her eyes, she felt like he saw deep into her soul. It was like she knew him deeply even though she didn't know him at all. She remembered when she had first seen him at the market. *I was so angry! But I had thought he was from the Order.*

She calmed herself down, noticing she was starting to get upset again. When she did that, she tended to cut off her emotions and lower her vibrations as everyone had been so fond of telling her recently. *Although I still don't really understand what that means.* She realized though that when she didn't allow herself to feel the emotion, to be with it, she tended to get swallowed up in it. *I feel a sense of disconnection, which is exactly what Esmerada had said. I guess she has been right.*

"Damn it!" Akasha said out loud, smirking as she saw that she was going to have to get used to Esmeralda proving her wrong. She grasped what Esmeralda had snarled at her before, that when she didn't deal with her emotions, she caused herself additional suffering.

Her mind circled back to her meeting with Tariq yesterday evening. *He seemed so concerned about me. He came to make sure I was safe.* Her heart fluttered again. What was going on? It was almost like she loved him. *But how is that possible? Raoul has only recently passed away and I barely know him!*

She sat for a few minutes deep in thought until she suddenly felt her sister's presence.

"Akasha! I have news!" Sophia said, appearing beside her, with a huge smile on her face.

Akasha snapped herself out of her reverie and focused. Sophia was so happy, her smile so genuine, that she couldn't help but feel her mood and confusion lift as she smiled back.

"Yes? Tell me." She motioned for her sister to sit down next to her.

"I've met my Shadow! Her name is Mystique and she is a gorgeous black panther. She gave me this!" Sophia said, pulling out her moonstone to show Akasha.

"Oh Sophia! That's fantastic! I knew it would only be a matter of time!" Akasha admired the moonstone, it fit delicately into her palm, the shape of an oval. It's coloring soft and creamy with swirls of warm amber running through it.

"It's amazing you have already received something from her. It took a couple of meetings with Esmeralda before I was ready to accept my dragon stone. You are one incredible human being, you know that?" She gave her a hug. It felt good to reconnect with her sister.

Sophia beamed. "The most astonishing thing happened, Akasha! When I fully embraced and accepted her as part of myself, we were surrounded by a breathtaking, healing, beautiful, shimmery white light. And now? Now I know that she is with me always."

"Sophia, you have just met your Shadow, and have already surpassed my relationship with my own. That is phenomenal. Can I ask you something?"

"Of course, Akasha. You know I'll help you however I can."

"Was it scary?" Akasha asked. "Part of me is still a little fearful of Esmeralda. She has told me that she would never cause me any harm, and that she is here to help me, but it is hard to fully accept."

Sophia took a few seconds before responding.

"No, Akasha, it wasn't scary at all. I think the difference for me was I realized tonight that I hadn't thought I was enough before. I thought the Spirit Realm was being denied to me because I wasn't worthy, that there was something wrong with me. So, when I was finally able to connect with Mystique, I was just grateful. She is definitely powerful and otherworldly, but I was more in awe than afraid. Accepting and embracing her came naturally."

Akasha knew she should open up and seek help more often It felt wonderful to be comforted and inspired by her sister.

"And the moment I fully accepted and embraced her, the feeling was so incredible. I couldn't put it into words even if I tried."

"I am so happy for you, Sophia. I can only hope to experience something similar soon."

"Don't just hope for it, Akasha, make it happen! If I have learned anything these last few days, it's that anything is possible as long as you believe."

Akasha wrapped her arms around her sister. "I love you Sophia, you know that, right?"

"I do," Sophia grinned.

Chapter 66

Akasha and the Crown

idday came and Akasha felt the need to go to the Temple's gardens again, it had become her sanctuary. "Sophia, I'm feeling a little uneasy about not being at the market today. I think I might go and spend a few moments in the garden to try and ease my mind."

"I know. It is strange to not be there when it is open. We haven't missed a day since we lost mother, but our safety has to come first, Akasha."

"I know, I know, my dear sister." Akasha smiled. "I just want to try and quiet down my mind a little. I will be in the garden if you need me," she said as she walked out.

If she was being perfectly honest with herself, Akasha was nervous about more than just their absence from the market. She had never been in danger before. *I know Thomas will keep us safe here, but I am still afraid.* She didn't want to burden Sophia with this as well, so she made her way to the garden.

Akasha sat down, touching her dragon stone for comfort. She thought of both Athena and Esmeralda. If Athena was also protecting her, then she could use her assistance right now. She breathed deeply and closed her eyes, connecting to her heart center. She sat there for a few minutes until she felt her consciousness expand. She sensed the loving, healing presence of all there was, is, and ever will be. She spent a few minutes in that space, calming her mind and breathing deeply.

Instead of seeing Athena or Esmeralda though, she saw the Crown and her mind began to race. She took a few deep breaths to maintain her meditative state.

"We wanted to take this time to explain a little more about your relationship to the Crown, the Ring of Infinite Wisdom, and what it means to be One of the Royal Heart," she heard Athena's voice say.

"Is the Ring of Infinite Wisdom the same ring I saw in my vision just after Raoul's death?" Akasha asked, although she already knew the answer.

"Yes, the very same one and it is currently in Tariq's hands," Athena confirmed.

"Tariq has it?" Her heart started to beat rapidly.

"Yes. Leo helped him find it," Athena said.

"And I aspire to help you, Akasha, to manifest the Crown," Esmeralda said, showing herself to be there with Athena.

Akasha remained quiet, wanting to understand, waiting to hear more.

"Together the Ring of Infinite Wisdom and the Crown make up the Crown Jewels. They disappeared from the physical realm after the death of the King in the holy wars. They will ultimately be used to bridge the divide that exists between the Worlds of Light and Dark. As Thomas told you when he introduced you to the Book of Records.

"What we want for you today is to understand what being One of the Royal Heart is, and what your mission and destiny will be. The Crown has similar properties to the Ring of Infinite Wisdom. The Ring provides the ability to recalibrate and re-center your energy and your being. The Crown allows you to cross the boundaries of time and space. It was why we waited to tell you about LionsGate,

as you will need to cross both to begin. The Crown Jewels are needed together – the Crown to cause the forward movement and the Ring to balance the energy the forward movement brings," Athena explained.

"What is this divide that I need to bridge?" Akasha asked, not fully grasping how she and Tariq were meant to travel through time and space.

"The divide exists on many levels. On the physical level it manifests itself in the animosity and hatred that exists between the Light Workers and the Pragmatists, with the idea that one group is 'right' and the other 'wrong', and the idea that they are separate from one another. Ultimately, it has a deeper level, where one can see that all of the thoughts and beliefs we consider outside of us, appear in us as well, but translated in different ways." Esmeralda didn't want to overwhelm Akasha, so she concluded with, *"There shouldn't be a divide, a separation or a feeling of difference."*

Akasha could feel herself becoming agitated. If there wasn't any separation that would mean she was being asked to accept everything on the planet. *No divide at all. Is she implying that I should suddenly love all thing? That would include things I currently hate, like, for example, the Order?*

"*Esmeralda, do you expect me to come to see myself in those who murdered the man I loved? You expect me to see myself in people who are determined to cause destruction?*"

"*Akasha, breathe. Remember if you lower your vibration, you will lower your connection with us,*" Athena said.

"*Akasha, listen to me,*" Esmeralda said. "*You have a deeper connection to the Order of the Pragmatists than you are aware of. I don't expect you to see yourself in the murder of Raoul. Anything can be taken to the extremes. But I want you to think about the founding values of the Order of the Pragmatists.*"

Akasha slowed her breathing and thought deeply, unsure of what she knew. She stayed in that space for a few moments, asking for help and clarity, and sensed another presence joining her. She felt the love of her mother and welcomed her.

"*Oh, Mother! I always seem to forget I have the ability to connect with you now too.*"

"*Akasha, my dear, like the others, I am always with you. But, when you are connected to your heart space, the true authentic nature of your being, I am able to come through the veil and be with you during the Solstices,*" Isis said.

Akasha paused, focusing on her gratitude for the present moment, despite all her current confusion.

"Akasha, there is something you need to understand about the Order of the Pragmatists. Your own and Sophia's connection runs deep within it. The Order was not founded on the disharmony that exists today. It was established to work hand in hand with those of Light, to study and provide the scientific backing for the things we take in faith. In the past we worked together successfully."

"What is this connection that we have, Mother?" Akasha suspecting that her confusion was only going to grow without answers.

"It is probably time to tell you. You come from a long line of royalty, both from my side as well as your father's," Isis said, slowly.

"My father's? You mean the man who abandoned us and left us after Sophia's birth?" Akasha had few memories of her father. The last time she'd seen him she had only been two years old. She had a memory of a loving man with dark hair and a gentle smile, but the pain she felt in his absence was still a very strong wound in her heart.

"He separated from us, yes, Akasha, but for reasons that will be difficult for you to understand. His love for you, for me, and Sophia has never changed. It became necessary for him to step in and lead the Order."

Akasha was shocked as her mother's words sank in. *"My father,"* she began.

"Is Abdul," Isis quietly finished the sentence.

"My father is the leader of the Order of the Pragmatists?" She felt her vibration and energy start to shift as she absorbed the news, her very being trembling as it set her reeling.

Despite this, Akasha didn't come directly out of her meditative state. Instead she saw the Crown again. This time, she could see it outside the Temple. It felt like it was waiting for her to collect it from the Well of Remembrance. It was calling out to her. *Will the Crown help?*

She immediately returned to her physical reality and conscious state of mind. She knew she shouldn't leave the Temple without telling Thomas and her sister, but she felt she had no other option. They wouldn't let her go, and with the discovery of the identity of her father, she had far more questions than answers. If the Crown could cause forward movement and shift, then she needed it now, more than ever.

She looked around to make sure no one was watching as she made her way around the garden and outside the Temple walls. She was determined to get to the Well of Remembrance.

Chapter 67

The Pursuit
and Transformation

hey gathered in the Spirit Realm as they watched Akasha leave the Temple.

"What happened?" Athena asked. *"How did the Crown just appear like that?"*

Khalid and Amadeus, Isis and Manu, Athena, Esmeralda and Leo were also confused.

"Perhaps it appeared because Akasha needed to adjust her views after learning about Abdul? It might

be calling her to Egypt and LionsGate to educate her?" said Leo.

"But it's not safe for her out there! Alejandro is still outside the gate!" said Athena, becoming alarmed.

"We are all concerned," said Isis slowly.

"She does have her dragon stone with her," Esmeralda said. "We all know that Akasha ultimately needs to accept me as part of herself before she can physically touch and manifest the Crown. I could step closer to assist her if she should call on me?"

"That is a good idea," Leo said as they watched Esmeralda depart to the physical realm.

Alejandro became alert as he saw Akasha leaving the Temple. *She is alone! I can't believe my luck!* He quickly packed up his things and leapt up to follow her. She was moving quickly, heading for the hill where the Well of Remembrance stood. He followed in rapid pursuit, not letting her out of his sight.

Akasha would settle for nothing less but getting to the Crown. She remembered the dragon stone in her pocket but was moving as fast as she could to get to the hill.

Suddenly she heard a rustling behind her and stopped. Sensing someone was following her, she turned around to face whoever it might be.

"Akasha," the man said. "I was hoping to find you. My name is Alejandro and I would like to speak with you."

Akasha jumped with the recognition that this was the very man she was hiding from. He looked much younger than she had imagined. It was strange that instead of being afraid, she just felt anger and frustration at having to pause in her quest for the Crown. *This is the man responsible for Raoul's death? I hate him,* she thought as a rage coursed through her veins.

"I couldn't say the same," she said coldly, narrowing her eyes at him. "If you will excuse me." She turned her back on him and continued to walk quickly up the hill. She put her hands on the dragon stone as a precaution.

"Akasha, I don't know what I could have done to upset you," Alejandro followed behind her.

Akasha could sense his ill intention, but she was determined not to be afraid, and to continue on her quest.

"Akasha, please stop. I just want to ask you a few questions about Raoul," Alejandro pleaded.

Raoul's name spoken aloud from his mouth was her breaking point. She immediately flung herself around to face him, looking him directly in the eyes.

"Don't you ever mention his name in my presence again! You should be absolutely ashamed of yourself! You killed him. You murdered my first love! I want nothing to do with you! I will answer no questions! Now please leave me be!" Akasha yelled angrily, unable to control herself, her fire rising within her.

Instead of having the reaction she had hoped, her anger seemed to fuel Alejandro's pursuit of her.

"You should learn to watch your words with me, Akasha. I will not be disrespected," Alejandro exploded.

Akasha felt concerned as she saw something dark and irrational surfacing in his eyes. She quickly turned again and kept walking, silently asking Esmeralda for help.

Alejandro grabbed her arm, forcing her towards him.

"Run!" she heard Esmeralda silently say to her. *"Run towards the Well of Remembrance. I will be there waiting. Know Akasha, that nothing within me is meant to hurt you, just to transform you into who you are meant to be."*

Akasha ripped her arm free of Alejandro's grasp. She looked into his eyes, saw hatred there and knew that was her cue. She ran with all her heart and soul towards the Well, and the Crown. Alejandro followed close behind her, but Akasha felt an inner strength that carried her despite her fear. Alejandro was catching up, but as she dashed up the hill, she saw her.

Esmeralda was standing beside the Well, powerful and otherworldly, her wings stretched and her flames rising to surround her. The Crown rested just beyond her on the Well. Akasha didn't stop for a moment. She believed within every membrane of her being that Esmeralda would help her, that the danger she felt from Alejandro would disappear by her reunion with her dragon. She propelled herself forward and, without hesitation, dove into the deep indigo blue flames of Esmeralda, sensing that they would lead to her safety, her baptism by fire enabling her to physically manifest the Crown.

The minute she stepped into them she felt transformed. It was like the sensation Sophia had described to her, although the light was a deep shimmery indigo blue rather than a brilliant white. She felt a warm embrace, a deep transformation, a purifying fire that burned away all fears and worries, and allowed her to fully accept Esmeralda.

The world stopped and her relationship with Esmeralda deepened. Akasha emerged shimmering and shining, in a brilliant indigo blue dress, and without thinking she grabbed the Crown. The second she touched it, she felt time and space shift as she and Esmeralda were surrounded in its majesty and transported from the physical realm.

❊   ❊   ❊

Alejandro was left standing in the dust in confusion. One minute he had been chasing Akasha, and the next there was an explosion of shimmering blue dust. When it cleared she was gone. His frustration increased. He had no clue what had happened. He let out a loud, angry scream as he stood alone at the top of the hill and kicked the Well.

Chapter 68

Preparation for the Solstice

homas sat in his office. The Winter Solstice was only two days away and he had written no more than a few words. There had been so much going on within the Temple walls, he hadn't found much time to focus on his talk. Peter had told him to start small, with curiosity and a childlike state of wonder. He thought back to the night of the full moon where he had first met him, and of Khalid who'd met his own Shadow, Amadeus.

Thomas and Khalid had been sitting in the Temple garden, staring at the full moon.

"It really is something to behold, isn't it?" Thomas said. "I have heard that there is an element of magic on the nights when the moon is full." Thomas had recently felt there was more to him than just his body and his thoughts. He hadn't accessed the Spirit Realm yet, but he sensed it.

"Really? I don't know if I believe in magic," Khalid had replied. They had spent practically every day together out exploring and studying the natural world.

"I wonder if we might try an experiment," Thomas had suggested, knowing his friend loved anything to do with science. "We could try meditating on the moon. I know this sounds a bit strange, but I wonder what would happen if we spent a few minutes imagining that the moon does have energy that can surround us in a magic we can connect to?"

Khalid shrugged. His mind was much more focused on logic than the subtle energy of the moon, but he decided to humor his friend.

What happened was a shock to both of them. Thomas' energy centers had been active for a few months, but he wasn't sure how it all worked. It was through his belief, and his unwavering love for his friend, that they found themselves transported back in time to LionsGate, standing in front of a beautiful pyramid with a geometric pattern located at its based, the wind engulfing them with dust and sand that scratched at their faces.

"Thomas? What just happened?" Khalid said, clearly growing alarmed.

"I am not sure, Khalid, but let's not be scared. We are together and for some reason we were meant to travel here tonight." Thomas remained calm, surprised he didn't feel any fear, but he had a sense in the last few weeks that something like this would happen, something inexplicable.

Khalid stopped short as they suddenly both sensed other presences, powerful presences. Their Shadows came forward, Amadeus, the immensely regal white stag, and Peter, the unflinchingly loyal mountain dog. Both Khalid and Thomas were silent and stood there, gaping.

"Breathe, Khalid and Thomas. We didn't come to harm you. We have come to introduce ourselves," Amadeus said.

Neither could find any words to speak even if they wanted to, but Amadeus and Peter knew their jumbled thoughts.

Amadeus continued, *"You are at LionsGate. You have been transported back to the Ancient of Days from Thomas' desire to connect to the Spirit Realm and his belief in the healing powers of the full moon. Khalid, you were able to join him, not because of your own belief, which I hope we can cultivate through the deepening of our relationship, but through Thomas' unconditional love for you."*

"We know we seem foreign to you now, but we both exist deep within you. Thomas, you and I are deeply connected and the same goes for Amadeus and Khalid," Peter explained.

"I don't understand," Thomas said, finding his words.

Peter continued. *"We don't expect you to understand yet. We just want you to know we are here. There will be a time, Thomas, in the years to come, where you will help the Two of the Royal Heart to travel here to LionsGate. They will need to be here to embark on their mission to bridge the divide that exists between the Worlds of Light and Dark. The female will embrace her own Shadow and connect to the love and light of Sirius the great spiritual sun. The male with the moon. You will guide the way for their return. I know you do not understand now, but we wanted to introduce ourselves to you in the place where the magic will unfold."*

Thomas and Khalid were beyond confused, and slowly, that confusion turned into fear, their vibrations were lowered and they found themselves transported back to the gardens of the Temple.

Thomas came out of his thoughts. Somehow, he had forgotten Peter's final words to him that day, about the role that he needed to play to help Akasha and Tariq return to LionsGate, about the power of the moon and Sirius. He had remembered earlier that week while talking with Isis about the portal being accessible during the Winter Solstice, but he had failed to remember the uniting factor of the energy of Sirius the spiritual sun as well as the moon.

His talk needed to be powerful, but coming out of his reverie he wondered how he had not made the connection before. He got out his pen and paper and frantically began to write.

Chapter 69

Akasha's Journey

kasha took a deep breath as she emerged in the desert. She wasn't sure where she was, but she saw a huge pyramid in front of her. She didn't know how it was possible, but she felt completely transformed. She was wearing an electrifying, shimmery, and elegant indigo blue dress, and her long, dark, wavy hair blew in the wind around her.

Esmeralda stood by her side. *"Akasha, thank you."*

"Esmeralda, I should be thanking you. I feel incredible. I feel otherworldly. I feel so in touch with who I am, who you are." Akasha laughed and whirled around to

see her shimmering dress sparkle in the wind. She had temporarily forgotten about the danger that stood back in Gibraltar.

"It happened because you welcomed me with open arms. You weren't scared of my flames or of me and allowed yourself to be baptised by them. You trusted and released all of that fear and tension.

Akasha was more aware of Esmeralda.

"By embracing me, you have stepped into your wholeness. You have acknowledged and embraced all of who you are that allows us to work together in levels not previously accessed before."

"However, I'm feeling and whatever knowing I awakened, I don't ever want it to stop!" Akasha said, smiling widely. She couldn't remember the last time she had felt this exhilarated and free. She took a deep breath and looked around.

As she slowly returned to reality, she remembered the escape from Alejandro, the embrace of Esmeralda and then reaching for the Crown. She looked down. The Crown was still in her hands. It was incredibly beautiful, made of gold with gorgeous emerald green and lavender stones embedded in it. She had almost forgotten that she had it and she wasn't sure what to do with it now that it was physically with her.

"*Embracing my flames not only transformed you, Akasha, but allowed you to step into who you really are, to step into your destiny, which is why we are here at LionsGate and why you are holding the Crown in your hands,*" Esmeralda said slowly.

"*It's beautiful, Esmeralda, absolutely beautiful. But what does it mean? And why am I here?*" She fully took in the scene around her.

"*This is the transformative place we will need to come back to with Tariq at the Winter Solstice to start your mission. We have traveled to the Ancient of Days to connect you to the magic and mystery of this place. It is important for you to have a connection ahead of your next journey here.*"

"*What happens on the Winter Solstice? And what am I supposed to do with this Crown?*"

"*Well, it didn't physically manifest to be worn on your hand!*" Esmeralda chuckled as Akasha carefully put it on.

When the Crown touched the top of her head, the wind picked up. Akasha gasped and scooted closer to Esmeralda for reassurance and comfort. Esmeralda smiled and wrapped her dragon wings around her, as any trace of Akasha's fear vanished.

A magnificent bright blue star appeared on the horizon. It rose in the sky like the sun, but Akasha knew that it was not the same sun she was used to seeing in Gibraltar with its majestic blue beams.

"That is Sirius." Esmeralda answered Akasha's unspoken question. *"Thomas told you about it before."*

Akasha stood speechless as she felt Sirius' beautiful rays surround her and Esmeralda. She felt a warmth and love she didn't think would be possible after she had embraced Esmeralda, but this moment was more. She was connected to all there is, was, and ever will be. She felt infinitely blessed and grateful, like she was ready to conquer anything, whatever her destiny might be.

"Well, that's wonderful Akasha, because there is much ahead of us. It's work you will not be doing alone, you will have me, Tariq, Leo, Sophia, Mystique, Paul and, of course, Thomas, but you will also need to come to know and accept Abdul."

Akasha scowled at the sound of her father's name, but the Sirius sun beams causing a shimmering golden yellow and blue light distracted her. She slowly breathed the energy in and out, not focused on anything but its loving light. She wasn't sure what she was doing but followed her intuition, the same intuition and inner knowing that had led her to the Temple the morning after Raoul's death.

"You are accepting love and blessings from Sirius. You are connecting with Sirius' energy and boosting your own inner light and vibration," Esmeralda explained.

Akasha knew she would remember this moment forever.

"Welcome, my child."

She heard a deep female voice and looked at Esmeralda to make sense of it and understood she was now able to communicate with Sirius.

Akasha listened to the inner language of her heart and wondered if she could find words to physically express the depth of what she was feeling. "I don't know what to say to you other than I am honored to be received and acknowledged by you," Akasha said aloud, speaking the words that authentically rang true for her. There was a lot she couldn't explain about the current moment, but she was beyond grateful for the love and embrace she felt standing in the light of Sirius' sun beams.

"You hold a great destiny, Akasha. The Crown upon your head signifies that. With our work together we can accomplish wonders. You will return on the night of the Winter Solstice, with Tariq. You will call upon my energy again so that I can aid with your work to bridge the divide that exists between the Worlds of Light and Dark. But for now, is there anything you need, or I can assist with?"

Akasha sensed that the ability for Sirius to provide was limitless, but she had no idea what to ask for, so she leaned on Esmeralda for support.

"Esmeralda, is there anything I can do for you or the other Shadows?" the voice asked.

"I wonder if it might be useful for all of us, including Isis, to take a physical form for the next few weeks to assist Akasha and the others as best we can?" Esmeralda asked, also enfolded in Sirius' divine love and light.

"Consider it done. If anything else is needed, please call on me during the Solstice and I will return," the voice spoke as the light gradually faded behind the pyramid.

Both Esmeralda and Akasha stood for a few moments in a state of complete and total gratitude.

"Esmeralda, what happens on the Winter Solstice?" Akasha asked again.

"I will explain the Winter Solstice to you in time. The bigger question for you right now is whether you are willing to work with Tariq. Have you accepted your feelings for him and that the two of you make up the Royal Heart? Your work together will play a key role in the upcoming events."

Akasha felt her heart quicken as she thought about Tariq. The connection with him was powerful, even though she had only met him a few times. Embracing Esmeralda had allowed her to overcome some of the fears she had about him. People kept telling her that she was One of the Royal Heart, and he made up the other half of it. She didn't understand what that meant, nor how it was tied to them traveling back on the Winter Solstice.

"That is part of your shared destiny with Tariq. You are both deeply connected in mind, body, spirit, heart, and soul as the Two of the Royal Heart. When you are in alignment with your true self and Tariq is in alignment with his, you can accomplish wonders.

"The start of this part of your destiny was manifesting the corresponding pieces of the Crown Jewels. For Tariq, it was with finding the Ring of Infinite Wisdom through his trust in Leo, and for you, it came with being baptized in my flames to manifest the Crown."

Akasha thought about her relationship with Esmeralda and saw how she had made her aware of her fear of her love of Tariq. She had been scared to allow them to surface because she was projecting herself getting hurt.

"Yes Akasha, you resisted and suppressed them. You channeled your feelings into anger and fear rather than love. You must realize there is such beauty in acknowledging and accepting that now. It's okay to be afraid. Loving someone else in an authentic heartfelt connection

*can be incredibly vulnerable and unnerving, but you have
me and you have the others to help you work through it.
Ultimately, you need to find that love within yourself first.
Tariq will help you, too, as he loves you just as deeply as
you love him."*

Akasha felt her heart begin to soar. *"He does?"*

Her mind shifted, and she thought of Raoul. She
knew she had only recently lost him, so how was it possible
for her to feel so deeply for Tariq?

*"Raoul is fine, Akasha. It was his time. He is with
us now in the Spirit Realm continuing to love and support
you; he cares for your happiness most of all. He also under-
stands the nature of your relationship with Tariq, even if
you haven't come to terms with it yet."*

"And what exactly is my shared destiny with Tariq?"
Akasha wanted to understand what it meant to be One of
the Royal Heart.

*"I wouldn't ask something you are not ready to
hear the answers to yet,"* Esmeralda said gently. *"And now
we really should be getting back. I am glad you have been
able to connect with the energy of this place, and that we
had the opportunity to connect with Sirius. I have a few
parting words I know you aren't fully ready to hear, but I
am going to say them anyway. At some point soon, you
are going to need to be willing to listen to your father."*

Akasha felt her spirits immediately begin to diminish, she didn't want to talk about him. She didn't want to deal with him. *"All I feel towards this man who is supposedly my father Esmeralda, is anger, hurt, resentment and pain."*

"Be patient with yourself Akasha, in terms of your emotions for Abdul. Know that it's O.K. to feel the way you are feeling. You have only just found out who he is and you currently consider the Order of the Pragmatists to be something completely different from who you are. You identify them as a group of individuals that caused Raoul's death.

Akasha sighed, not really wanting to listen to anyone of this, but Esmeralda continued on.

"Consider for a moment that they aren't different, that they were actually founded on principles which you could relate to, even if members of the Order have diverted from their original intentions. Consider that there were outside factors that ultimately caused your father to separate from you, but that he still loves you with all of his heart, even if he hasn't been able to physically be there." She swooped Akasha up with her wings and placed her gently on her back preparing for flight.

"Be compassionate and allow yourself to think and feel the way you authentically do. Do not repress or shut anything out because it's uncomfortable. Work through it

and know that I and the others are here. In terms of your emotions with Tariq, it's alright to feel fear, but remember the love that exists between the two of you. That is the most powerful and healing energy in the world. Not to mention the love you two share exists beyond time and space. And, in terms of your father, all I ask is you try to keep an open mind." Akasha wrapped her arms around her Shadow in loving support of her guidance as Esmeralda slowly took off soaring into the sky and transporting them back to the Well of Remembrance.

Chapter 70

Tariq and Paul Return to the Temple of the Holy One

ariq and Paul arrived early. Thomas was expecting them and led the way to his office. "I will leave you both for a few moments, but there are a few passages from the *Book of Records* that I think will be very clarifying for you." He pulled the book out of his desk, leaving them alone once he had shown them where to look.

"It appears that you and Akasha have some work to do," Paul said as they were both reading. "I wonder if Sophia and I will play a role?"

Tariq was utterly lost in thought and did not hear his friend as he sought his Shadow's help. "*I know I love Akasha, I knew that from the moment I laid eyes on her. Leo, I am scared to want and need her though.*"

"*She is your destiny Tariq, and you have a mission to complete, together...*"

Thomas returned to the room after a while, offering them tea.

"Where is Akasha? How is she?" Tariq asked, making his inner thoughts known.

Thomas smiled. "The last time I saw her she was out in the garden having a quiet moment. We can check on her shortly, but first I wanted to address any questions you might have for me."

"What is the work Akasha and Tariq need to do?" Paul said. "And I'm having problems understanding what it means to operating from the authentic nature of our being?"

"Yes, authenticity is a confusing concept, especially when you are first introduced to it. It means that your behavior and intentions align with the essence of who you are, your most authentic sense of self. This is manifested in different ways for different people," Thomas answered.

"Does it mean people have connected with their Shadows?" Paul asked.

"In a way, yes," said Thomas. "That is at least the first step, the acknowledgement, acceptance and embrace of all of who you are. It means stepping into your own personal sense of truth and power, but it also means operating from your heart with intentions that ring true to the core of you. It's not just knowing your Shadow." Thomas paused.

"As humans, it is easy to forget who we are and get caught up in things that don't serve us. It is easy to lower our vibrations. Operating from the authentic nature of our being means accepting this, but also accepting that we will never be perfect. We will always be exactly as we are, and that in and of itself is perfect. It's the power of connecting and living from our hearts, realizing there is nothing within us that needs to be fixed, and operating as best we can from a state of wholeness."

Paul still looked confused.

"Will anyone ever explain to me what it means to be of the Royal Heart?" Tariq asked, changing the subject, anxious to get some of his own questions answered.

"I cannot tell you what you and Akasha will need to do to start your mission other than to believe and go to LionsGate on the evening of the Winter Solstice. I will aid that transition during my talk here at the Temple. More will be revealed to you both in time. Trust that you are being led, guided, and protected by more than just your Shadows. Let us check on Akasha, shall we?"

Chapter 71

Concern over the Return

kasha! Where are you?" Sophia yelled as she ran through the Sanctum and out into the garden. Her sister was nowhere to be found and she started to worry. She entered at the same time as Tariq, Thomas, and Paul came out of the Temple.

"Is everything alright, Sophia?" Thomas's tone matched the concerned expression on her face.

"I can't find my sister," she confessed, unable to contain her fear.

They all immediately reached out to connect with their Shadows in the hope they would be able to assist.

With that, Mystique physically appeared, alongside a large beautiful lion with a powerful golden mane and deep golden black eyes, a beautiful black and white mountain dog with shaggy hair and eyes that seemed to reach directly into her soul, and a gorgeous brown wolf. Golden loving energy permeated through each one of them.

"Wow!" Sophia said, taken aback, completely in awe.

"Sophia, meet Leo, Peter and Rocky" Thomas said with a grin.

"I didn't realize this is possible, that I could see other people's Shadows." She said hesitantly as she went up to stroke Rocky. *Is this OK? Am I allowed to touch someone else's Shadow?* Rocky moved towards her in a way that appeared to be encouraging the greeting.

"It is not normally possible," said Mystique. "However, Akasha manifested the Crown today and received a special blessing from Sirius which allowed us to be physically here," she answered.

❊   ❊   ❊

Tariq stammered. "The Crown has resurfaced? And what exactly is Sirius? If the Crown has appeared doesn't that mean something has happened with Akasha? Is she alright?"

"Yes," said Mystique as she recounted the events of the day.

"But, what of Alejandro?" entreated Tariq, only half registering the idea and concept of Sirius. "It is not safe outside of the Temple walls for either Akasha or Sophia. Where is she?" He was growing more alarmed every time he inhaled, and his heart was racing.

"Alejandro is a concern, that is true. When Akasha and Esmeralda disappeared, he was left incredibly angry," Leo said slowly.

"Then what the hell are we doing here, just standing around talking about it? We need to keep her safe!" Tariq said.

Isis spoke calmly, appearing in their midst. "She is not back in the physical realm yet. She and Esmeralda are traveling back from LionsGate. They will emerge from the Well of Remembrance shortly."

"Mother!" Sophia exclaimed.

"Hello, my dear, it is wonderful to see you," Isis said as she wrapped her arms around her daughter. "But Tariq is right to be concerned. Akasha could be in danger when she returns."

Tariq didn't wait for any additional pleasantries, "I think that is more than enough for me. You can all stand around if you would like, but I need to make sure Akasha is safe." With that, he turned and ran as swiftly as he could out of Temple gardens and up the hill.

Chapter 72

Isis' Ask

ariq! Wait!" Sophia implored, knowing it was useless. Tariq was already outside of the Temple's walls.

"He will not listen, his heart is set on her protection." Isis continued, "Before any of you do anything else rash, the one thing I request is that you seek Abdul's help."

"Why on Earth would Abdul want to help us?" Sophia asked, although for some reason she wasn't as surprised as she thought she would be hearing this request, considering he had just recently purchased a Clarity potion.

"Sophia," said Isis, "I revealed this to your sister earlier today, and we think that may have been what ultimately caused the Crown to reappear. You both come from a royal line on my side and from your father's. This will not be easy for you to hear, but it is important you know. Abdul is your father."

Sophia was dumbstruck. "Abdul? You mean the leader-of-the-Pragmatists Abdul?" She asked, absolutely and completely shocked. She looked around the garden for somewhere to sit, worried her knees were going to give out on her. This was a lot to take in.

"Yes, Sophia, but your current projections of who you think he is, and who he actually is, are two completely different things," Mystique offered.

"He deeply loves you and longs to know you, but situations have not permitted it," Isis said. "I won't ask you to try and understand yet, but what I will ask is you seek him out now. He would want to protect Akasha and you from Alejandro, and he may be able to reason with him in a way no one else can."

"I will go with Tariq to keep him safe," Leo said. "Isis brings up a very good point. Thomas, Paul, and Sophia, I think it would be a good idea if you do head over to the *Order of the Pragmatists'* cave."

"But what about Tariq?" Paul asked. "He isn't listening to anyone right now, and when that happens, he tends to put himself in danger." He wanted to stay with Sophia but he also knew he needed to protect his friend.

"I will go with Thomas," Sophia said bravely, never imagining she would set foot in any place that had anything to do with the Pragmatists. "And Paul, you should follow Tariq and try to prevent anything untoward from happening. I don't think Akasha could handle losing him. Even if she hadn't come to terms with the fact that she's in love with him, the rest of us have."

"Consider it done," Paul said as he ran through the garden and after his friend.

"We will be with you Sophia, if you need us," her mother said quietly as she slowly faded away leaving just the Shadows behind.

Sophia and Thomas looked at one another realizing they had no idea where the Cave of the Pragmatists was.

"Let me lead the way," said Juliet appearing before them. "I am your father's Shadow. It is a pleasure to meet you, and I would be honored to facilitate your reunion with him. But let's hurry."

Sophia was even more surprised. Her father had embraced his Shadow? Maybe there was more to this Abdul character than he seemed. Maybe Mystique was right after all.

Chapter 73

Akasha's Return through the Well of Remembrance

ow could she have disappeared?" Alejandro growled, stamping around the grass in front of him, he looked around for something to throw, but there wasn't much vegetation on the top of the hill. "I was so close! And what had she been running towards?"

He had seen her run, reach down and touch the Well, and the next thing he knew, she had vanished into a whirlwind of dust. It was infuriating! Even though a few hours had passed, he was still pacing around, trying to make sense of it. He suddenly heard movement and quickly turned around.

Akasha slowly emerged to the present in her shimmery indigo blue dress. Alejandro was startled. He caught his breath but couldn't speak. He had difficulty dealing with her disappearance, and had no way to comprehend her reappearance. She seemed to have a glow unlike anything he'd seen before.

Suddenly, he noticed the Crown placed on her head. His eyes widened. Could this possibly be the Crown that his ancestors had created the alchemical knife for? The one that his family line had always wanted to replicate?

❈ ❈ ❈

Akasha rose from the Well, stepping out with her dragon by her side and immediately noticed him. She felt a pang of fear but did not let it show. She was grateful for Esmeralda and still felt the powerful beams from Sirius protecting her.

She stood still, wondering how she was going to avoid any conflict with him, how could she get back inside the Temple's walls?

Esmeralda spoke with urgency through Akasha's mind's eye. *"Tariq is on his way. Thomas and Sophia have gone to get Abdul. If you need to, just stall him but do your best not to anger him. Do not speak until he speaks to you. He has no insight about our travels or the light of Sirius which still surrounds us in the form of love and protection."*

"Where did you go? Alejandro said, coming to his senses. "How did you just appear out of thin air?"

Akasha remained silent. She did not want to say something that might trigger him to move in on her again. She followed her Shadow's advice.

"Are you not going to answer me?" his voice grew more hostile.

"Anything I might say will not make sense to you," she said looking directly at him, taking care that there was no edge to her tone. She remembered the hatred she had seen in his eyes before she embraced Esmeralda.

"And why would you say that?" Alejandro stepped closer.

Akasha's heart raced as her fear increased. She made a conscious effort to not show it as she took another step back and found herself pressed against the Well.

"We can't just disappear and go back to LionsGate, can we?" she silently asked Esmeralda.

"Unfortunately, not. The Portal opened today to permit you to travel back during the Winter Solstice. We cannot come and go as we please. LionsGate is only

available at certain times when the stars, sun, the great spiritual sun, and the moon, are aligned," Esmeralda replied.

"What is that on your head?" Alejandro said mischievously as he took another step towards her.

Akasha's worry was increasing as she looked down the hill and saw movement. Her heart leapt as she saw Tariq running towards them, a look of pure anger on his face. Akasha did not want to answer Alejandro, but she knew she needed to allow Tariq to reach them.

"What can you tell me about Abdul?" she asked, bringing up the first thing that came to her mind.

Alejandro huffed. His manner seemed to shift from maliciousness to disgust. He appeared to be distracted from Akasha while forming his thoughts.

"Abdul has lost sight of what the Order should be."

"And what should the Order be?" Akasha asked politely, deliberately, keeping any disdain from her voice.

She saw Tariq with his fists clenched ready to attack, but the last thing in the world she wanted was for him to be injured. Again, she was careful to hide her reaction.

"Everything that it is not right now!" Alejandro bellowed, answering her question as his anger increased. "We should be experimenting, analysing, and assessing, not sitting around and buying your potions!"

He approached her once more, but then heard something behind him. He quickly turned and met Tariq's eyes right at the moment that Tariq threw himself upon him. Alejandro's arms reached out in reflex to block.

Tariq hit Alejandro as hard as he could, his fist flying at his head as he threw the hardest blow he was able to right at Alejandro's Temple. A massive rush of adrenaline coursed through his body. Tariq was not normally one to act in violence, but protecting Akasha was no ordinary thing. He stood silently as Alejandro collapsed, his head hitting the Well with a sickening thump. He looked down at Alejandro to make sure that he was no longer moving, before making eye contact with Akasha.

Her reaction wasn't what he expected. Instead of relief, he sensed anger, although he knew there had to be a reason for it. It was strange, this new ability to pick up on her emotions.

"That is because your connection has deepened," Leo said as he bounded towards him.

Akasha was beyond mad. She was beyond anything she had ever felt before if she was being honest with herself. She wasn't though and was currently only in tune with her anger. She wanted to explode, unable to believe the depth of her feelings for Tariq. She couldn't believe how easily she could have been parted from him. Alejandro had lost his rationality, and anything could have happened. Tariq had only recently come into her life and she didn't want to lose him before she really knew him.

"I cannot believe that you thought that was a good idea!" she faced and scowled at him. Tariq stood there silently, waiting. "And now you aren't going to say anything?"

✠   ✠   ✠

He just looked deeply into her eyes, tuning into her emotions. He was able to feel what she seemed to be unwilling to say, her love for him.

"Tariq, what you just did was incredibly dangerous!" she said as her voice rising until she was almost yelling.

"Akasha, breathe," Tariq finally replied, stepping a little closer to her. He knew her anger was because of her concern for him, her fear of losing him.

"Do you just think a few deep breaths will make what you did acceptable? Do you know how hard it is for me to lose people I love? I will not have you just throwing your life away!"

He moved even closer.

"I knew what I was doing. I knew I was going to be safe, and most importantly, I had to keep you safe." He could sense the depth of her despair and concern for him. Similar feelings had stirred in him when he had first met her, but he hadn't really allowed them to surface until now.

Tariq put his hands on her face and brushed her dark hair away from her eyes.

❋ ❋ ❋

"Tariq, I don't know," she spoke hesitantly. She had calmed down, but a whole new set of emotions had taken over. She wanted Tariq. She loved him, but she was scared. She looked into his eyes and knew there was no way to go back. She breathed a contented sigh.

"Akasha, I have wanted to do this from the moment I first laid eyes on you." His hands brushed her cheeks.

She closed her eyes. The next thing she knew his mouth was upon hers and her world stopped. Time stopped. Everything stopped but their heartbeats. She felt his lips on hers, and not only was there a fiery passion ignited within her, there was also a sense of inner peace. A deep inner knowing that this was right. This was true. This was, well, *love*.

Chapter 74

Paul's Acceptance of Rocky

 aul was lost in thought, struggling to make sense of the concept of Shadows and even more confused because of the new ability to see and interact with the others.

"You are being too hard on yourself, Paul. You know and understand a lot more than you think you do. You have stepped in and accepted our relationship on a much deeper level. The fact that I am standing here beside you to have this conversation is proof of that." Rocky spoke gently through his mind's eye.

"I wish it felt more natural to me," said Paul silently as he continued to follow after Tariq, whom he could no longer see. *"I wish I didn't have doubt. I'm half expecting to wake up and find these interactions to be a dream."* He sincerely wanted to be able to let that go, to truly believe that everything happening around him was real. *"Maybe I'm struggling because I don't know how to tell myself to stop. I don't know how to get myself to fully acknowledge you."*

"And you are judging yourself harshly along the way," Rocky said. *"What if you adjusted your thoughts for this moment and accepted that there is nothing wrong with the way you are currently thinking? Perhaps questioning and doubting things, is what you need to accept and embrace our relationship."*

Rocky's comments made sense. If he didn't think there was anything wrong with the way he was building his understanding of Rocky, then the relationship felt better. Everything felt better. If he accepted the fact that his doubts were there for a reason, and part of his life's journey, that also felt better. He spent some time reflecting on this and how grateful he felt.

Suddenly a shimmering light surrounded both of them. The light felt incredible, like nothing he had ever experienced before. Rocky smiled. *"And, that my friend, is how you learn to truly embrace me. Not by forcing it, or thinking you are doing something wrong, but by accepting your process just as it is and being open and aware of my help and availability. Welcome to stepping into your wholeness."*

Paul felt a huge surge of energy as he ran as quickly as he could, back up the hill. He slowed as he saw Tariq and Akasha in one another's arms and a lifeless Alejandro laying a few feet away from them.

Chapter 75

The Cave

ello. We come in peace. I am an old friend of Khalid's and am hoping we can have a few words with Abdul," Thomas said as he saw a young man heading in their direction, with Abdul following behind him. The young man's eyes grew wide as he took in their Shadows.

"He can see us," Peter said to him silently. *"Akasha enabled that earlier today. He can't touch us, but he can see us and hear us if we choose to speak out loud."*

"Remarkable!" Thomas thought. *"This will make my speech on the Winter Equinox so much more powerful."*

❈ ❈ ❈

"Juliet?" Abdul said, stepping out from behind Rashid.

"We don't want to overwhelm Rashid," Juliet said to him silently as she flew to him. *"Akasha unlocked an ancient portal through Sirius' blessing, which enabled all of us to start the process ahead of the Winter Solstice. That means, however, that everyone can see us, including Rashid, and since he isn't exposed or aware of his own Shadow yet, we need to be careful what we say aloud."*

"Understood," Abdul said silently, still mystified that Juliet was physically with him since he hadn't summoned her.

It was also not lost on him that Akasha had made the journey to LionsGate, which meant she must have embraced her own Shadow, been baptized by Esmeralda's flames, and gained access to the Crown.

"We've come because Akasha is in danger and we don't have much time." Sophia's words snapped him out of his thoughts.

"Alejandro is after her to get as much information about Raoul as he can. We must go to the Well of Remembrance immediately," she finished, shuffling her feet nervously as she now knew who this man was.

"She will be returning soon with the Crown. Tariq has already gone to her, but we came to get you in the hope you might be able to reason with Alejandro,"

Abdul noticed that Rashid was looking very confused beside him, and couldn't stop staring at their Shadows.

"Rashid, I must go now and make sure that Akasha is safe. I know these beings don't make any sense to you. It will become clearer when we go to the *Temple of the Holy One* for the Winter Solstice to honor Khalid. I have been told that the speech will be very powerful, and will help answer some of the questions you must now have."

"That's wonderful news!" Thomas affirmed. "I did not know you were all attending."

"Father," Sophia said, "We must go. Akasha needs us." She wasn't even fully aware of the fact that she'd spoken those words aloud until they were out of her mouth. That was the second time being in his presence had done that to her.

Abdul looked at his youngest daughter, his eyes widening.

"She knows?" he silently asked Juliet. He realized that he loved having Juliet beside him, not only for the proximity, but because he could communicate with her more easily.

"They both do. Isis has told them. But Abdul, she wasn't kidding when she said Akasha is in danger. We must go," Juliet said back to him.

"You don't know how I have longed to hear you call me that," Abdul said, not wanting to take his eyes off Sophia. "Both of you. This is a historic moment, but you are right. We need to make sure your sister is safe. So, let us go."

With that, they all took off running as fast as they could back to the Well of Remembrance, leaving a very stunned Rashid behind.

Chapter 76

The Reunion

ariq looked up. He kissed Akasha on the forehead as Paul approached. He kept his arms wrapped around her as he greeted his friend. "She is safe."

"I am very glad to hear it," Paul said.

Akasha felt surreal standing in Tariq's arms, but she smiled at Paul, noticing a giant mountain dog beside him. "Who is this?" she asked, introducing herself to Rocky, properly greeting Leo and then allowing herself to come back to the gravity of the situation as she looked down at Alejandro's body.

"The Winter Solstice is just a few days away and all we know is we are supposed to go to LionsGate," Akasha said "Will anyone be telling us exactly what we need to do?" She was starting to get worried that they had no idea what their mission really was.

"We will work through all of that together," Esmeralda said, "Thomas' speech tomorrow will set the stage and we will go immediately from there. Tariq will need to work with the moon, and you will need to call on Sirius."

"Where are the others?" Tariq asked.

"Isis asked them to find Abdul for help in reasoning with Alejandro, but it appears that such an intervention won't be necessary," Paul said as he gestured at Alejandro's inert body.

Akasha stiffened. *Sophia is seeking out our father? She is placing herself in danger by entering into the cave of the Pragmatists!*

"Akasha, keep in mind your own judgements and biases here. What you currently think of Abdul and the Order is not the truth of who Abdul is or what the Order stands for," Esmeralda said to her gently. *"He is your father. There is a reason why your mother loved him. I know it seems like he abandoned you and your sister, but there*

were greater factors at play. Ultimately, he just wanted to keep you safe."

Akasha wasn't sure how to deal with this information. She had been so angry with the idea of her father for so long. To know he was not only alive, but also the leader of the Pragmatists, was a lot to take in. *Has everyone forgotten that the Order of the Pragmatists were responsible for Raoul's death?*

She stepped out of Tariq's arms as she was starting to get upset. He placed his hand on the small of her back.

"Akasha, there is a difference between an individual being responsible for his death and placing blame on the entire organization. Anything can be taken to extremes," Esmeralda said softly. *"Alejandro lost all sight of his humanity. He is unaware of any connection to all there was, is, and ever will be, and does not know his Shadow. He became so caught up in his quest for knowledge and understanding that which cannot be readily explained, that this unconscious desire took control of his life. He blocked any responsibility for his actions and also any possibility of his own understanding. You need to remember that Alejandro's thoughts and actions do not represent those of the entire Order."*

Akasha started to speak but stopped as she saw her sister approaching with a beautiful black panther by her side.

"Sophia! I am so glad you are safe! I was so worried," she said, running towards her and wrapping her in her arms.

"Oh Akasha, I felt exactly the same. I am so relieved to see you. And look at you, you've completely transformed, what is this beautiful Crown and your dress?"

Before Akasha had a moment to respond she looked up and saw Abdul slowing from a run to a walk. He appeared to be nervous. *Well, good! He should be uncomfortable!* she thought as she locked eyes with him.

"Akasha, this is Abdul," Sophia said gently, "our ..."

"Father," Akasha finished. "Yes, I am aware. Mother informed me." Her tone was firm and harsh, as she hadn't fully decided how she felt about this mysterious, powerful man that stood in front of them.

Chapter 77

The Family Introduction

bdul paused, trying to gather his words and his thoughts with both of his daughters standing in front of him. They knew who he was and Akasha had already stepped into her destiny by manifesting the Crown. He knew the role he had to play in helping her understand her mission and his heart felt heavy at not being able to be there for her sooner. He silently called on Juliet for help, taking a few moments to form his words.

"I don't know that I can explain how I am feeling," he finally spoke hesitantly, hoping they would listen. "For so long, I have longed to know you, but your mother and I agreed long ago that with the first sign of descent and judgement of the Light shortly after Sophia was born, and until the *Order of the Pragmatists* were contained again, they were a potential danger and threat to you. To keep you safe we decided to keep my identity hidden and I maintained my distance." He spoke slowly, trying to gauge their reaction. Sophia seemed open and responsive. Akasha on the other hand, seemed closed.

"I know you may not understand, nor do I expect you to immediately feel comfortable forming a relationship with me, but I hope to gain your trust and love in time," Abdul said, his eyes beginning to water. He was getting emotional, but at the same time, he had not anticipated this interaction with his daughters.

Abdul saw Alejandro's body and knelt beside him. "Alejandro, I hope wherever you are now, you are well, and able to find the peace that you were seeking in this lifetime." His tears flowed freely. Alejandro had been like a son to him and he had hoped to bring him back on track, but he knew now that it was too late.

Akasha reacted violently to her father showing compassion for Alejandro. "That's all well and good, but your Order murdered my first love, and this man you hope finds peace came very close to hurting me. You may say that you kept your distance to protect us, so far it seems your protection has not done us any good!"

"Akasha, breathe and be careful of your words. Consider for a moment that Abdul might be in as much pain as you are. Please try and sense the depth of Abdul's despair, I am repeating my request for you to open your mind to see things from his perspective." Esmeralda said.

Akasha was unwilling to listen, unwilling to forgive, or even remotely begin to let Abdul in. She was comforted, however, by Tariq's loving presence beside her.

"Father, I know this must be hard for you," Sophia said soothingly as she saw Abdul's tears.

"We won't begin to understand everything yet," she continued, "but the one thing I ask is that you give us some time. For so long we believed that our father abandoned us. It is quite a shock to hear the reality is so different, let alone that you are our father and the leader of the *Order of the Pragmatists*."

"I understand," Abdul said softly.

"It has been a long and eventful day for all of us," Thomas said. "Why don't we all go back to the Temple and have a meal together?"

"Abdul, I would love you to join us," he finished, gesturing that they should all return and leave the complication of this moment behind them.

Akasha stiffened again, but this time she responded to the love that Sophia, Tariq, and Esmeralda and the support they offered her, which helped to calm her.

"Akasha, I know this is painful," Sophia said softly. "It is for me too, but I think we should hear him out. We owe him the opportunity to talk to us,"

Akasha looked into Sophia's eyes and saw such love and compassion. She sighed and knew she was right. She looked at her father and slowly nodded her head.

"I would love to join you, if that is alright?" Abdul asked hesitantly.

Akasha and Sophia both nodded, and together they all walked away from the Well, leaving Alejandro's still body on the ground.

Chapter 78

The Last Supper

hey entered the Temple and made their way to the kitchen. Thomas gathered the ingredients to start preparing a stew while the others collected around the old oak dining table.

Akasha was exhausted by everything that had unfolded that day. Although she still didn't fully understand the complexities, she was grateful that Tariq was there with her. Tariq pulled in close. *It's almost as if he can sense my thoughts*, she thought as he whispered gently into her ear, "You can lean against me if you want." Akasha sighed, still facing forward as she rested her back against his chest.

There was such comfort in his presence and their physical touch.

She had not forgotten about Raoul. She still felt slightly uneasy about it all but remembered that he was the one who'd told her this moment would come. In fact, she realised her connection with Tariq ran much deeper than it ever had with Raoul. *Raoul had told me the emotions I feel for Tariq are natural,* she thought as she stopped resisting and leaned in against Tariq, allowing herself to take in his love, comfort and support. Tariq felt like home to her.

"Tell us what happened after you touched the Crown," Sophia asked as she sat beside her sister. She reached over to peel some carrots to help Thomas.

"We traveled to LionsGate," Akasha said, "I don't know how to explain. It's an unimaginable, magical place. The energy is amazing, I felt it even before I connected with Sirius, the great spiritual sun. The Central Pyramid will take your breath away, it is an incredible work of art, beauty and architecture." She said as she recounted the rest of their adventures."

"Sophia and Paul, you will need to hold space for them when they return," Rocky said as she finished.

"What does holding space mean?" Paul asked. He pulled a seat next to Sophia and began to chop some potatoes, grateful to hear they would be doing something together. She turned and smiled at him and he responded back bashfully.

"Tariq and Akasha will not be able to return immediately. There are a number of things they need to accomplish," Leo said carefully.

"While they are there, they will need you and Sophia to remember them, to hold the vision, so to speak. So that when they have finished, they can return through the Well of Remembrance. Holding space means remembering who they are, envisioning their highest good, and holding them in unconditional love to allow for safe return."

"But what is our mission?" Akasha prompted. "I have been told we need to bridge the divide and bring balance between the Worlds of Light and Dark, but I don't understand."

"Perhaps Abdul can assist?" Thomas suggested as he gathered the carrots and potatoes and added them into the stew.

Both daughters looked at their father expectantly, *I suppose I can give him a chance, although, I'm still not convinced that I can trust him, no matter how helpful he is trying to be,* Akasha thought as she continued to lean against Tariq.

✖ ✖ ✖

Abdul took a deep breath, looking at Juliet to help him guide his words so that they would be received in the way he intended. "I'm not sure where to begin. Perhaps I'll start with the reason we named both of you as we did. Your mother and I knew of your destinies long before your births. As the high priestess, Isis had always been able to connect to the Spirit Realm in ways that I have not. I come from a long line of people who have been ruling, serving, and guiding this planet from the *Order of the Pragmatists'* perspective.

"Akasha, you and Tariq comprise the Two of the Royal Heart. Your mother and I knew before your birth that you were one half of the pairing but we did not know if you would find your counterpart."

Abdul looked at Tariq, "There is a place called the Akashic Library. It holds the Akashic Records. You will need to seek this place out during the Winter Solstice to find your answers. Namely, what being the Two of the Royal Heart means and what that journey looks like individually for each of you. You will be able to access the Akashic Library through your work in LionsGate. You should know, however, that the Library is not in this realm." He paused, allowing for this information to be absorbed as the smell of the delicious stew slowly filled the room.

"Sophia, your role has its own destiny, which is why I am delighted to have made your Shadow's acquaintance as it begins with your belief in it," Abdul looked at his other daughter. "You are named after Divine Wisdom. It is ultimately your wisdom, emotional intelligence, and understanding that was told at your birth and will continue to play a prominent role in this journey."

"I cannot tell you what it is that will enable you to locate, enter, and access the Akashic Library," Abdul continued, "but I do know, Akasha, it is your destiny to do so. The Crown you wear will enable your return to LionsGate. There you will begin the mission. The Ring of Infinite Wisdom will assist Tariq and help with what should be done next."

"Like what is written in the *Book of Records*? If I remember correctly, it says we will be guided and asks us to keep an open mind, heart, and will," Akasha said. She was starting to realize that a lot of their mission work, they would have to take in faith.

"Correct," Abdul said. "Sophia, we always knew that you would aid Akasha by holding the space to enable her return. We did not realize that Paul would also be here to assist."

He paused to look at his daughters and continued.

"I must also tell you my own story and connection to the *Order of the Pragmatists*." Abdul felt the energy in the room go tense, but forced himself to continue. "I have a lifelong love and passion for science, rationality, and order. My family has led the *Order of the Pragmatists* for years, but when I was younger, I resisted. Many years ago, I met Khalid and he told me of his Shadow but I did not understand. My world was based on facts, things I could physically see and explain. Khalid's Shadow was not one of those things. It was through that encounter, and the deep friendship that emerged, that I found myself called to the Order. Khalid was determined to prove the existence of his Shadow, and I wanted to support him in that endeavor.

"Unfortunately, that time and now are very different. My point is that the *Order of the Pragmatists* were not founded on the extreme practices and experimentation that Alejandro conducted. Previously, those of the Order and those of the Light worked together in harmony to balance one another. Your mother and I are examples of that.

"As a disconnect in the Order grew, and because of your destinies, your mother and I agreed that it was best to keep you as safe as possible. That meant distancing myself until you, Akasha, were ready to fulfill your destiny. My role is to help in any way I can upon your return and also equip you, as I am doing now, with all I know that may be of use before your journey."

Akasha was glad she had Tariq by her side because this was a lot to take in. Her mother and father had known of her destiny at her birth? She needed to stay in LionsGate until they found the Akashic Library, whatever that was? *And mother worked in alignment with the Order of the Pragmatists?* She looked at her sister who seemed to be just as taken aback.

"Akasha, breathe," Esmeralda told her silently. *"It will be okay. We will be with you, physically, and able to support you in any way we can. When we return, we will be ushering a whole new era of peace and prosperity,"* Esmeralda communicated to her silently. Akasha looked up at her skeptically.

"What if I don't want to go?" Akasha asked aloud. She didn't want to disappoint anyone, but if she had learned anything recently, it was that she needed to be honest with herself. And, right now she was feeling exhausted and overwhelmed.

"We will not force anyone to do anything they aren't willing to do," Thomas said, making some final adjustments to the stew as he covered it up and let it sit until it would be ready to serve later. "I ask only that you don't make any decisions tonight. You will need to rest and have a clear head."

Abdul nodded in agreement. "Thomas speaks wisely. I must thank you both for listening. I know that this is a lot to absorb and I am grateful you heard me out. The last thing I want you to be aware of is the Pyramid in LionsGate itself. It is an ancient energy center named Tajarat. You will need to learn to harness your power and energy there if you choose to go. I think it's important you know it is an additional resource for you on your journey."

With the explanations done for the moment, Thomas and Abdul made eye contact and smiled, both grateful that the group was together ahead of the Solstice so Abdul had the chance to begin to impart his knowledge.

Chapter 79

Akasha and Sirius

few hours had passed and Akasha and
Sophia were both back safely in their cottage.
Tariq and Paul were back on the Black Onyx.
Akasha and Tariq had kissed goodnight and agreed to
meet the following day to discuss what to do next.

Akasha felt immense relief to be in the sanctuary of
her own home. She curled up in bed ready to go to sleep,
but decided to quickly check on her sister.

"Sophia, are you okay? You were quiet at
dinner tonight."

"I think so. I am still not sure how I feel about Abdul being our father. It's a shock to hear that he and mother knew our destinies before our births and named us accordingly," Sophia pondered. "It's overwhelming for me, so I can't imagine how it is for you. I've been wanting to ask you the same thing, but I didn't want to disturb you. How are you, Akasha? It appears that you and Tariq have, um, worked through a few things." She had a sly smile on her face as she had noticed they had been at each other's side the whole evening. Sophia had also been present for Akasha and Tariq's kiss goodnight. Similar feelings stirred inside her for Paul, but she didn't know if she would ever act on them.

Akasha blushed, thinking of Tariq, and laughed as she saw her sister's smile.

"Somehow, I knew I could count on you to lift our moods," she teased. "I am as okay as I can be. I don't know if I will ever trust Abdul, but I didn't know that I would ever trust Tariq. Honestly Sophia, my feelings for Tariq concern me because they are unlike anything I have ever felt before. Now it's becoming harder for me to picture my life without him." The depth of their connection unnerved her but she was learning to just trust it. With the Solstice rapidly approaching she wished she more clearly understood what was being asked of them. "I don't like the thought of leaving you. I am grateful that Esmeralda, Tariq, and Leo will be with me, but the thought of leaving you behind, even for a short while, truly upsets me."

"I know, Akasha. I don't like the thought of you not being with me either, but it appears this is part of our destiny." Sophia understood that part of her role in holding space for Akasha meant encouraging her to go. She wondered if they might have some form of communication along the way. "We already have the ability to sense each other's feelings, so maybe that will exist in different dimensions. Don't you think you would regret it if you didn't go; if you didn't step into who you are meant to be and your destiny?"

Akasha paused, thinking how amazing it was that Sophia always knew the right things to say and had the ability to calm her down, and soothe her.

"You have given me some things to think on, Sophia. I promised everyone that I won't make any decisions tonight. Tariq and I will have a discussion tomorrow, but I appreciate your thoughts and, more importantly, your unconditional love, more than you can ever know.

Akasha soon fell asleep and found herself by the Well of Remembrance with Athena and her mother. They must have seen the events of the day and she was unsure of how they were going to react. She stood there silently, worried they might be angry with her for not automatically agreeing to go.

"Of course, we aren't be angry," Isis said gently. *"We love you unconditionally. We called you here to make sure you realized that, but also to tell you about the Well of Remembrance."* Akasha was relieved as she felt her mother's embrace.

"The Well has been with us since the Ancient of Days," Athena said. *"It provides a link between then and now. What we will ask you to do tonight is to drop the bucket in and focus on any question you have. When you pull the bucket back up, there will be something inside to answer that question. If you decide to go on your mission, this will also serve as a means of communication between you, and those you leave behind. Your sister was very wise earlier tonight. Although you will not physically be together until you return, you will still be able to sense each other's emotions, and to communicate via this Well."*

"We will leave you some time alone to think of your question, but we want you to know that we are very

proud of you. You showed immense bravery today," Isis said lovingly.

"Mother, can I ask you something?" Akasha needed to get this off her chest. She recognized her progress in not bottling up her emotions.

"Of course."

"I don't know if I can ever trust Abdul. I don't know if I can ever get over feeling abandoned by him. I'm still shocked knowing that he is my father. I guess I am wondering if you have any advice for me? I know I can't force it, but as Athena said when we first met, if I hold on to anger and resentment, it will only hurt me. I have discovered this more deeply by getting to know Esmeralda, so I'm hoping for your thoughts too."

"Oh, Akasha," Isis said, "I know this must be very difficult and confusing for you. I wish there had been a better time to tell you, but with Winter Solstice rapidly approaching, it was important you made the connection. Abdul is a kind, compassionate, and wonderful man. I know you don't see or believe that yet, but he loves you and his heart has been broken by the separation. He longs for nothing more than to build your trust.

"You are absolutely right that you can't force it. You should allow yourself to feel how you are feeling. Be angry. Be mad. Be sad. But work with Esmeralda to see *how it might serve you and how you might best process it. Don't suppress it, be with it and see how you can trans-mute and integrate it with yourself. Remember Abdul is eager to help you however he can, if you choose to go. He has more information that he needs to share with you if you are willing to listen. Remember also that I am here, we are all here with you always,"* Isis said as she and Athena slowly started to fade away.

Akasha stood for a few moments taking in the words before moving towards the Well. She picked up the bucket and dropped it in the water and said aloud, "Please tell me anything that might help me make my decision for the Winter Solstice. Please give me any additional guid-ance I might need."

She focused on each of her energy centers starting at the root, moving to the sacral, then on to the solar plexus, heart, throat, third eye, and crown as she slowly retrieved the bucket.

She placed her hands in the bucket and retrieved a golden key with the image of the sun on the end of it. She looked at it with wonder. The bucket also contained a note that appeared to have the same blue glow as the beams of Sirius.

"This will allow you to access the Akashic Library when the time is right. It is sent with love from Sirius and also to remind you that you are the Key."

She was the Key? What did that mean? She remembered Sirius' loving rays and energy. She remembered the magic and mystery of the place. She remembered how powerful she felt standing in Esmeralda's flames and truly stepping into her wholeness and personal sense of power. She looked down at the key in her hand as she felt the Crown on her head and knew beyond any doubt that she would go. She was destined to.

Chapter 80

ᏠᎾriq and the Ϻoon

ariq and Paul had instantly fallen asleep without discussion. Tariq abruptly found himself with Leo, gazing at the moon, with all its magnificence, beauty and light.

"Should you decide to go tomorrow, you will need to call on her, it is important that you begin to understand the power of the moon," said Leo. "The moon plays a vital role with Shadows, enabling us to come in contact when the intentions align. She is at her most powerful on evenings of the full and new moons. The moon's power is also amplified as the lunar cycle coincides with the Solstice."

Tariq had previously sensed the energy of the moon. Through his connection with Leo, he was able to sense the energy of all living things. He had yet to intentionally call on the moon or work directly with her, it felt a bit strange to him, a bit foreign.

"Focus on her energy. Open yourself up to a new experience," Leo led.

Tariq felt silly trying to sense and feel the moon, but Leo had not misguided him before.

"You feel uncomfortable because you are in a state of resistance," Leo said. *" What if you accept the fact that you are resisting and then make the attempt?"*

Tariq sighed again, knowing that Leo was right. He took a few deep breaths and closed his eyes, focusing on the rhythm of each breath.

"Try and align with your energy centers as I have taught you," Leo continued.

Tariq slowly breathed into each, starting with the root and working his way up to the crown. He felt such a state of peace and then suddenly he felt so much more.

Leo smiled as he watched the moon's energy shimmering down around Tariq like a silver light. It felt wonderful. It felt hopeful. It felt encouraging.

"Should you go to LionsGate tomorrow," a powerful female voice said, *"you can call on me. I will assist with your*

relationships with Shadows. You will come to work more directly with me if you should so choose."

"That is the voice of the moon," Leo said. *"Because you are open to her energy, you are able to receive input directly from her. Sophia holds a moonstone from Mystique, so she has the same ability to tap into the moon's energy. You will need to talk with Paul about this tomorrow, as there will come a time when you will work together with the moon's energy in both dimensions. Paul and Sophia will do this together in Gibraltar."*

Tariq felt a powerful moonbeam surround his body and heard the female voice again.

"I will leave you with this token of our connection. It will be needed when you get to LionsGate and will also connect you both to those in Gibraltar."

Tariq opened his hands and his eyes and saw an exquisite silver crescent moon in his palm, a medallion made of mother of pearl and moonstone.

"Thank you," Tariq murmured, not fully understanding but grateful to receive it. In the glow of the moon, he knew with every atom of his being that he must go to LionsGate.

Leo roared with pleasure as Tariq fell into a deeper sleep.

Chapter 81

Before the Winter Solstice

ariq and Paul rose early the next morning with the sun. They ate a quick breakfast and made their way into the village to meet Akasha and Sophia at the Temple. With their Shadow's by their side, they took a new route to avoid the stares of the townspeople.

"I had an interesting dream last night," Tariq said as they wandered in the opposite direction of the marketplace.

Paul walked on, knowing he would hear about Tariq's dream whether he wanted to or not.

Rocky smirked beside him. Paul was becoming accustomed to having Rocky by his side and hoped that it wouldn't soon change.

"We need to be careful with others seeing us," Rocky said silently. *"In general, humans are usually fearful of their Shadows at first, and we have not been able to take a physical form before."*

"The moon was like a being. No, that's not even the right word to describe it. The moon was like a presence I could connect with," Tariq continued, vaguely aware that Paul wasn't paying attention.

"You should listen to this, Paul. It's actually quite important. I know you will be skeptical because that is your nature, but listen to your friend. It has to do with you and Sophia," Rocky said to him through his mind's eye. With the mention of her name, Paul turned his attention to Tariq.

"She was a real presence with a loving energy that I could connect to. At first, I resisted, but when I let go, it felt magical, a bit like the moment when Leo and I first bonded. She told me I would need to call on her and that Sophia has a moonstone which links to her energy. If Akasha and I decide to go tomorrow evening, which I have a feeling we might, then we will need to channel the moon's energy."

Tariq smiled and saw the amused expression on Paul's face. "I know this sounds strange, Paul, but I am telling you because you will need to work with Sophia on connecting with the moon as it will connect you with us."

"Very good," Leo said to Tariq silently as they walked on.

Paul's expression went from amused to confounded, causing Tariq's smile to deepen as he knew how Paul processed information. He knew eventually Paul would reach a state of acceptance.

They rounded the corner and arrived at the Temple door only to see that they were not alone. Abdul was there with Juliet pacing back and forth, lost in thought.

"Good morning, Abdul," Tariq said quietly.

Abdul jumped, surprised by Tariq's greeting.

"Good morning," They had caught him in a quandary. There was more he wanted to reveal to his daughters, but he knew they would need time to process it, and time was running out. His pacing stopped as the door opened and Akasha and Sophia stepped outside. The sisters had arrived earlier that morning to spend a few moments in quiet meditation at the altar, they both looked weary at seeing their father so soon.

"It seems you have something you need to tell us," Akasha said stiffly to Abdul. She had agreed to listen to her mother's advice from her dream the night before, but she was only willing to take it one step at a time, starting with listening to what he had to say. She led the way inside and the others followed.

Abdul gathered his breath and his thoughts and began to speak, "Tonight is a very powerful night. LionsGate is a place that exists at all times as part of the Ancient of Days, but the magical portal within it is only active during the Summer and Winter Solstices. This will allow you to use the Crown Jewels not only to travel there but also to start your mission. We have talked about this, but it's important that you understand before traveling that it exists on many levels and many dimensions. What you see and are exposed to in LionsGate may be completely different to what you understand here." He took a few more deep breaths to gather his thoughts, knowing the importance of communicating this accurately.

"I cannot speak to it myself, as I have never been, but it's important you remain open to everyone you encounter and every conversation you have, as you will be guided along the way.

"There is more I need to say about Tajarat, the Central Pyramid. It will play a key role in helping you to connect with the energy and resonance of the area. Hopefully, that role will become clearer upon your arrival." He paused, taking a deep breath, pleased they were paying attention.

"Akasha, it is important you realize your connection to both the 'Light' and the 'Dark'. It is through this connection that you were baptized by Esmeralda's fire. You had to fully embrace your darkness on a much deeper level than most. You were asked to step into something that frightened you, then come to know you could trust it, that it was a part of you. This powerful realization on your behalf enabled you to not only embrace Esmeralda but also physically manifest the Crown.

"I don't think you realize the significance of this yet, Sirius created the Crown Jewels for use of the Two of the Royal Heart, but the Crown has not been on this planet for five hundred years. It holds incredible power. You had the ability to unlock it because you yourself are a perfect balance of the Light and the Dark as you came to embrace all of who you are. Through doing so you have begun to pave the way for others to follow down the same path."

"Sophia," Abdul turned his attention to his youngest daughter, "though Akasha is meant to go, I want you to know that your role is just as important. It is your love, support, and wisdom that will allow their return."

Sophia felt tears coming into her eyes. "I don't know if these are tears of sadness, happiness, gratitude, or release."

"I think it's a combination of all of the above. But deep down it's caused by your own personal realization you are worthy and also destined to do great things," Mystique said to her silently.

"I must leave you shortly," Abdul said. "But the final thing I need to say is to remember the energy of Sirius the great spiritual sun and the moon tonight, if you should choose to go. They will be there to guide and help you along the way, as we all will."

He saw the exhaustion on his daughter's faces.

"I suggest that you rest today. You will have a big evening tomorrow," he said as he slowly began to walk away.

"Father," Sophia said after a few moments.

Abdul turned around and looked into her eyes.

"Thank you," she said genuinely, some of the harshness removed from her tone as she ran to give him a hug.

"I will see you and Akasha at the Temple, and you are welcome. I am grateful I was able to tell you what I know," Abdul also had tears as he wrapped his arms around his daughter.

✠ ✠ ✠

The rest of the day passed without anything of much consequence. Akasha told her sister of the Well of Remembrance and how they would be able to communicate through it. She wasn't sure precisely how, but since she had a special connection to her sister, she knew they would both know what needed to be done when the moment was right.

Tariq and Akasha merely needed to make eye contact with one another to know they were both going to be traveling to LionsGate. It took just one look to finalize it all, though neither spoke of their dreams from the night before, or the gifts they had received.

Chapter 82

The Winter Solstice Talk

he moment had come. Tariq, Akasha, Paul, and Sophia gathered at the doors of the Temple and slowly made their way to the Sanctum.

The entire town of Gibraltar would be attending tonight, as they had in years past, so they asked their Shadows not to be physically present, not wanting to overwhelm them.

"Is it strange to say I've missed you since I last saw you?" Tariq asked, kissing Akasha very sweetly on the forehead.

"Not strange no, but a bit soft," Akasha teased as she leaned over to give him a proper kiss. The depths of her feelings were still intense but she appreciated the comfort of being close to him.

"Okay, lovebirds, enough of that," Sophia said, smiling. As they all sat she made brief eye contact with Paul sending a soft rush to her own heart. with the fluttering of her inner world, she observed how strange it was to not have Mystique by her side, she'd grown to her presence.

They waited as the *Order of the Pragmatists* entered the room. They could sense the cynicism of most, but Abdul's face looked hopeful as he ushered them to rows that were close to where Akasha, Sophia, and the others sat. He smiled gently at his daughters. They nodded back.

✠ ✠ ✠

Thomas was in his office preparing for his talk when he felt both Athena and Isis' presence. He turned around and smiled in greeting.

"*Thomas, we have had a thought,*" said Isis. "*Tariq, Akasha, Abdul, Paul, and Sophia decided not to have their Shadows physically present with them, however, we were thinking that you could invite them to join you.*"

"You will have been speaking about what Shadows are so the audience will have some understanding by then," Athena added.

"The issue here, Thomas, is we don't have much time," continued Isis. *"Akasha and Tariq will need to leave shortly after your talk, and they will need their Shadows to help them travel to LionsGate. Neither of them realizes this yet. They are simply trusting in the process. By creating a space for their Shadows to emerge and physically be with them at the end of your talk, we are hoping to help facilitate this.*

"They can, of course, always seek their Shadows through the objects their Shadows gave them: The dragon stone, the moonstone, the heartstone, and the compass. However, when their Shadows are physically present, they are able to communicate with them at any time, as they have grown used to them over the last couple of days."

Thomas thought about this. *"I think you are both right. I had planned on leveraging the Shadows at the end of my talk, but you have just sparked an additional idea. I will make some final adjustments for my speech."* He also silently asked Peter to stay behind and not appear with him.

He was nervous, but he knew he was also supported and guided. He gathered his papers, looked at Athena and Isis before making his way to the Sanctum.

Athena and Isis smiled at one another. Thomas' idea was a good one.

❈   ❈   ❈

Thomas walked into the Sanctum and up to the altar, nodding at those he passed. He stepped up to the podium and took a deep breath.

"What if this world was more than it appeared? What if there were things going on all around you that you aren't consciously aware of, but at the same time, play a significant role in not only how you perceive your life, but also how you live it? I am here today, to help you see that both of these things are true. I am asking you for just a moment in time to suspend your judgement.

"Tonight, I want to talk about two things. I want to talk about the importance of knowing and embracing all of who you are. I also want to talk about the importance of operating from a space of authenticity and pure intention, a space where you are able to physically connect and tap into your essence. I want to talk about these things because when you are able to embrace your entire being and are authentically connected and operating from it in a state of pure intention, magic can happen." He paused, looking around the room, making eye contact with Abdul and a few of the Pragmatists.

"I would also like to take a moment to acknowledge the Pragmatists who are with us tonight. There is so much judgement, anger, and hatred in our world today, but Khalid, who was a member of the *Order of the Pragmatists*, held none of that. He had a desire to serve, to educate, to bridge the gap that exists between the world of spirit and the world of matter through scientific study and practice. Although it has been many years since I last saw him, I think of him fondly. We honor him tonight, and I personally thank you all for joining us on the Winter Solstice.

"I would like to start with two stories. The first is about the moon and the second the great spiritual sun. My story about the moon involves Khalid and dates back many years. It led to his entering the *Order of the Pragmatists* and to my own role here at the *Temple of the Holy One*. It began on the night of a full moon where two young friends lay in the garden behind the Temple, gazing up at its majesty and wondering about more. Khalid and I were childhood friends and this night we decided to hold our first full moon ceremony. I asked Khalid if he wanted to conduct an experiment as I knew of his love of science and rationality."

Thomas smiled and looked at the *Order of the Pragmatists*. He saw smiles on a few faces, felt supported, and continued, "I have always had a bit of guidance. That night we set the intention to be more, do more, serve more, and we somehow found ourselves transported to an ancient time and place in Egypt.

"Now, I know a few of you will scoff at this idea, but just for the moment, pretend it's real. Imagine that two young friends who had no idea what they were doing found themselves by the Pyramids in Egypt at a magical place called LionsGate. The winds were blowing, and the stars all shone brightly in the sky."

"We found a way to connect to parts of ourselves we hadn't previously acknowledged. In particular, we connected with what we call our Shadows. They are not meant to harm or hurt us, but allow us to become whole by accepting all of who we are.

"The Pragmatists are here tonight because they want to honor someone who was an extraordinary being. Khalid honored himself. Khalid acknowledged his Shadow. He embraced every single aspect of who he was, and we will all miss him.

"I will never forget that evening because it changed my life. I was introduced to many things I could never explain or even attempt to. That evening inspired me to join my family in serving the Temple. Khalid's method of processing was different to mine and he found he was drawn to wanting to scientifically explain what had happened, thus he joined the *Order*.

"We took different paths, but neither path was right or wrong. Both were pure and true to the essence of who we are. What I want us to remember tonight is that although we are different, we are all equal. Our paths may lead us in different ways, but ultimately there is not one right or one wrong. Things might get scary and uncomfortable, but that is part of the beauty in life, to embrace those things, all of those things. Accept yourselves as you are. Love yourselves as you are. Know that we are all connected even if that connection appears in different ways and different forms."

Thomas paused to take a breath. He looked around the room and saw they were paying attention to his words. He smiled and sent his love, light, and gratitude to the universe.

"My second story involves something that will happen tonight." Thomas slowed down to gather his thoughts as this part of his speech had not been as prepared aswith the rest. He silently called on Peter to help him with his words.

"The nights of the Winter and Summer Solstice serve as powerful portals to that same place Khalid and I traveled many years ago. LionsGate is an ancient place and holds many magical and mystical powers. It is heavily aligned to the power, infinite presence, and love of the great spiritual sun, Sirius.

"I know many of you will not have heard of the idea of a sun beyond our own. But imagine, if you will, that it exists, that it is a loving power that guides, rules and governs our sun. It has a power and majesty so great it is hard to comprehend. Sirius, in an effort to connect us and allow us to begin to understand its majesty, created and brought to life the Crown Jewels."

Thomas paused as he heard a few gasps in the audience. He knew that the mentioning of the Crown Jewels would wake them all up.

He made eye contact with Akasha to try and prepare her for the words he was about to say.

"To begin to understand Sirius, we need to step into a childlike state of wonder. I know my words might seem strange, but I ask Akasha and Tariq to join me at the podium." Thomas waited for them to rise.

Akasha hesitated, caught off guard, but Tariq sensed this was a defining moment and grabbed her hand. Together they walked forward.

Thomas continued, "You have all heard of these Crown Jewels. What I ask of you tonight is to believe in the power of the Shadows, the moon, Sirius the great spiritual sun, the Crown Jewels and the power of your own inner beliefs and thoughts.

"LionsGate opens a portal that is only available during certain times of the year, tonight being one of them. I also said that the Crown Jewels were created and brought to life by Sirius in an effort to connect us all to its light and energy. I am now asking Tariq and Akasha to physically demonstrate this.

"We have all heard that the Crown Jewels will reappear when the Two of the Royal Heart have learned to live within the authentic natures of their beings and claim and manifest them with pure intention. Well, tonight I would like to invite the Two of the Royal Heart to the platform along with their Shadows, Leo and Esmeralda."

Thomas allowed his words to slowly sink into the larger audience, not just Tariq and Akasha.

Tariq reached for his compass. *"Leo, is this okay?"*

"*It is destined,*" he heard in response. Thus, Tariq and Akasha knew what had to be done and called forth their Shadows to emerge and join them on the platform. Tariq pulled out the Ring of Infinite Wisdom and Akasha revealed the Crown.

The crowd gasped as a giant dragon and lion appeared on the platform alongside them. It was the first time that any of them had ever seen the Shadows let alone the physical manifestation of the Crown Jewels. The light in the room shimmered as Tariq put the Ring of Infinite Wisdom on his finger and Akasha placed the Crown on her head. Neither of them knew in advance what would happen. They were both stepping into the authentic nature of their beings, and trusting in their heart coherence. They knew they were being guided.

"Behold the power and beauty of not only connecting to your Shadow but also those of the Royal Heart's embrace of Sirius, amplified by the power of our own moon," his voice rose in power and passion as he connected to the energy of the present moment.

"I began by asking you all to believe in a world that is more than it appears, and tonight I have offered you visual and physical proof of this. We honor Khalid's memory by also honoring his Shadow. Amadeus, would you please join us?" As Thomas asked, the beautiful white stag that was Amadeus appeared.

The Pragmatists all gasped, unsure of the meaning of what they were seeing.

"We all have Shadows, but tonight was meant to introduce you to the idea, to show you that they are nothing to fear. They are a part of you, here to help you accept and embrace all of who you are. Tonight, we are watching destiny unfold. Tonight, we are connecting to the magic, mystery, and embrace of Sirius. Tonight, we let go of the current constructs of reality and just breathe."

Akasha and Tariq looked at one another with wonder in their eyes and reached out to hold hands with Esmeralda and Leo beside them. *"Breathe deeply. The portal is opening, and we will be leaving soon,"* Esmeralda said to them both.

Thomas resumed. "I won't ask you to understand everything I've said. We all process things in different ways. All I ask is that you be open. Tonight, we honor Khalid and the Winter Solstice by witnessing the great event transpiring in front of us. We are watching the Crown Jewels in action, calling the Two of the Royal Heart, Tariq and Akasha, to LionsGate to unlock your own Shadows and slowly start to bridge the divide that exists between us."

Thomas wasn't able to finish his words. The shimmering light became too intense as Tariq, Akasha, Esmeralda, and Leo vanished leaving the room in a stunned silence.

Chapter 83

The Portal and Connection

kasha and Tariq's world erupted into light. They continued to hold hands while surrounded in powerful light and magic. It felt like they were moving and yet not moving at all. They connected to the energy, but had no sense of time and space, only the colorful and dazzling indigo blue energy that engulfed them and their Shadows. Neither felt afraid. For a few moments, they seemed to step outside of themselves into the great unknown, directly into the power of all there was, is, and ever will be – the unifying force of the universe. Time seemed to stop, until the energy dissipated

and they found themselves at LionsGate. It was night and they were completely alone, apart from their Shadows.

"I don't know if I will ever get used to that," Akasha said. She was so caught up in the joy of the direct connection of the divine they had just experienced, that she temporarily forgot her worries and concerns.

"I don't think we are supposed to," Tariq said with a grin. He pulled Akasha into his arms and kissed her. Time seemed to pause for them both until they felt Leo and Esmeralda pulling them back to their current reality.

"While we honor and embrace your connection, we must remind you both there are things we need to do," Leo said.

"Yes, yes," Tariq said, only partially listening as he quickly kissed Akasha one last time.

"The precise alignment of the new moon will be in a few hours. Tariq, it is up to you to call upon its energy to ask for a connection," Leo instructed.

"Akasha, you will need to link with the loving and healing energy of Sirius to ask for assistance for those back on Earth," Esmeralda said to guide Akasha.

"Those back on Earth? Are we not on Earth now?" Akasha was confused.

"We are," said Esmeralda, *"but we are within a different dimension. This will make more sense the longer*

we are here, but we don't really have much time. We should begin our meditations now."

Akasha was worried and Tariq was skeptical, they often mirrored one another.

"I suppose it doesn't hurt to try," Akasha said after a few moments' thought.

With that, they stood in the sand facing the Pyramid. Akasha checked to make sure she still had the Key from Sirius in her dress pocket, and Tariq did the same with his moonstone pendant. They smiled at one another, placed their hands at their sides, closed their eyes and rested as the moon slowly started to appear above the tip of the Pyramid.

�֎ �֎ ✖

Tariq found himself surrounded by silver light. It felt marvelous, just as it had the night before when he had overcome his resistance to the process. He slowed and continued to take deep breaths, focusing on the gratitude he felt for the current moment, his connection with Akasha, and the loving presence surrounding him.

"I am glad that you have both come," the loving female voice said.

Tariq recognized it as the moon, having heard the night before.

"Tonight, is one of magic and power. This realm holds ancient magic and mystery as you will soon see, but tonight we will not focus on that. You have been called because it is your destiny to start to bridge the divide. Set your intention and consider it done," the female voice said.

Tariq took a few heart centering breaths and realized he needed more clarity, *"Is my intention to ask for all of those that attended the Temple's Shadows to physically be present?"* he asked Leo, hoping that he could still hear him and connect with him in this state of being.

"I am always with you, Tariq, and our connection has deepened in the last few days," Leo answered gently. *"But you must set your own intention and it must feel authentic. It cannot be something that I tell you to do. It has to be pure and it has to resonate with you. What do you want to accomplish while you are here?"*

Tariq thought deeply for a few moments knowing he needed to connect and believe in what he was saying. What were they meant to do during their time at LionsGate? Why were they here? *"I want others to feel the way I do. I want others to find love, feel love, connect, and know all of who they are, and all that they are capable of."*

"Think back then. How did your journey begin?" Leo asked.

"Through knowing you, and coming to love and trust you, accepting you as part of my wholeness. Before I came to know and love Akasha, I had to truly love and accept myself, which included you, Leo," Tariq answered.

"So, your intention is for others to step into their wholeness and truly love and accept themselves by coming to know and embrace their own Shadows as you have?" the voice of the moon spoke aloud.

"Yes," Tariq answered deeply, connecting to the words.

"And so, it is," the moon said as Tariq and Leo felt the power of the Moon and its mystery intensify and shimmer.

❊　❊　❊

Akasha shifted her thoughts back to the loving, powerful and healing energy of Sirius the great spiritual sun.

"Thank you for allowing me to connect with you, allowing our Shadows to be with us, protecting me on my journey back to Gibraltar, and allowing me to feel your presence," she thought as she felt her heart center expand in love and gratitude.

"*Akasha, the joy of connecting with you is beyond what we can express in words or thoughts. Know the honor is mine. Thank you for having the courage to step into your destiny. I know that much is unknown to you, but we are so proud of you,*" a female voice said which Akasha knew to belong to Sirius, the great spiritual sun.

"*We?*" She was confused. Was there more than one great spiritual sun?

She felt a loving embrace and what felt like joyous laughter. "*Your embrace and your acceptance of your destiny by receiving the Key last night has allowed you to have access to a set of beings that live here. They are called Lion's People. They originate from Sirius, but you will come across a few in LionsGate while you and Tariq are on your mission to access the Akashic Library.*"

"*Lion's People?*" Akasha wondered if she would have a moment when she didn't have a million questions. Again, she felt the loving presence of Sirius, almost as if Sirius could read her thoughts.

"*You will know them when you meet them and sense their loving energy,*" the voice of Sirius said.

"*There is still so much I don't understand.*"

"*You are deeply loved and guided, Akasha. You wear my Crown on your head and will come to understand all you need to over time. It is your destiny to be* here and bridge the divide that exists between the world of faith and the world of matter, between those of the Light and the Shadow." the voice said.

Akasha felt chills going up and down her body. "But how am I to do that? How do I start to bridge this divide?"

"You have already begun the process by being here tonight. Together, you and Tariq can accomplish miracles as you learn to live from the authentic nature of your beings. Now we need to clarify your heart and your intent. What do you want, Akasha?"

Akasha thought for a moment, and like Tariq, said, "Love. I want love. Just as I have experienced and received it myself, I want the same for others. I want others to feel the power and connection I felt when I stood in Esmeralda's flames."

"Those flames were your first introduction to me, although you did not know it at the time. You and Esmeralda have a deep connection to me."

Akasha took in those words. She had a deep connection to the great spiritual sun?

"Athena was not joking when she said you were destined to do great things. So, your heart's desire and intention is for others to know love and to step into a state of acceptance with who they truly are?" the voice of Sirius asked.

"Yes," Akasha answered.

"And so, it is," Sirius said as Akasha felt herself engulfed by the energy and power of Sirius yet again.

Chapter 84

The Departure and the Great Awakening

 lejandro woke in excruciating pain. Where was he? He rubbed the top of his head and felt a fresh jab of it.

"Ouch!" he yelled aloud, slowly sitting up as his memories returned to him.

He remembered Akasha's disappearance, and then her sudden re-emergence. He remembered the mysterious

Crown she had been wearing. He remembered being so close, and then that damn man who had been spying on the Order suddenly came up behind him.

"He will pay for this! Whoever he is! He will pay for it!" Alejandro said, standing up.

Suddenly, he saw a brilliant, bright, indigo blue light coming up from the Well of Remembrance.

"What is this?" he stepped forward, intrigued. Momentarily forgetting his anger and his pain, he moved towards the Well, drawn to the power and energy of the light. As he leaned over the edge, he felt himself pulled inside and was suddenly surrounded by it. Time stopped and the world disappeared as waves of indigo light crashed over him.

❈ ❈ ❈

Thomas looked around as he saw the indigo light activated again. He knew then that Tariq and Akasha had arrived at LionsGate and had been successful in connecting their energies and setting their pure intentions. He sent up gratitude and thanks to the universe and stepped off the podium.

Since the Portal was still open, Sophia would be able to send her first message to her sister. He quickly walked over to her, not wanting her to miss her chance at connection.

"Sophia, you must go to the Well of Remembrance with Paul. You've both connected with the energy of the moon, and the Winter Solstice Portal is now open. This energy coming through is the start of the gate being opened. There is still much to be done. Let your sister know that the process has started, that we are all safe. You may remind her that she can use the moonstone pendant which Tariq received to reach out to you. To contact Akasha, write a note and place it in a bottle in the bucket, intend for her to receive it, and drop it in the Well. While the indigo light is still shining, the note will get to LionsGate."

Thomas handed them a bottle, a scroll, a quill and some ink that he had carefully placed in his gown just before the service. He ushered them out of the room as the indigo light continued to swirl and grow brighter.

❀ ❀ ❀

Sophia and Paul dashed up the hill to the Well. They sensed there wasn't much time so Sophia quickly wrote:

My Dear Akasha,

We are all safe. Thomas asked that I write to you now so we know how to communicate with each other. On the evenings of the new moon and full moon, I will be able to write to you through the

Well of Remembrance. He mentioned the moon pendant that Tariq received. That will be your method of getting a hold of me. I know you will both be guided. The service was powerful. We have heard you have made it to LionsGate safely and stand by waiting to do whatever is needed. I am grateful to be able to connect with you and send you all our love.

Sophia

As the shimmering indigo blue light was slowly fading, she quickly dropped the bottle into the bucket into the Well and prayed that it would arrive successfully into Akasha's hands.

❊ ❊ ❊

Alejandro found himself surrounded in gusts of sand and through it he could barely make out the shape of a giant Pyramid. What was going on? He looked around, confused, as a bottle with a note suddenly emerged and dropped down next to him.

"What is this?" he said aloud as he read the letter from Sophia. His jaw dropped as he realized the letter was meant for Akasha, which meant that Akasha was here! Wherever he was, so was she!

What are these Shadows she writes about? He scratched his head in confusion and felt a sharp jab of pain again. He was exhausted and knew that he needed to rest. Akasha was wherever he was and that was all that mattered. He could find her and question her after he rested a bit.

❈　❈　❈

The Temple was inundated with energy from both the opening of the Portal as well as the pure intentions set by the Two of the Royal Heart.

"Friends, please just breathe," Thomas said. "What we are tapping into and feeling now, is the magic and power of the Ancient of Days, of a time when there was no separation, no us versus them, no self or other, nor light or dark. We were all one and everything existed in a perfect state of balance.

"Tonight, I ask everyone to suspend judgments and believe. Through the power, strength, love, and intention of Akasha and Tariq you will all be able to experience that within yourselves. You will be able to connect to a part of you that you didn't know previously existed – your own Shadow. Just as you met the Shadows of Akasha and Tariq tonight, you will be able to meet your own.

"I ask you to breathe and just be," Thomas said. "Do not fear them. They will seem powerful and mysterious at first, but ultimately, they are part of you. By embracing them, you will learn to embrace all of who you are. When that happens, we will be able to bridge the divide and magic can happen." Slowly, as the indigo blue magic began to fade away, the Shadows started to take form and appeared amongst them. The world was now permanently altered and shifted as the Shadows came to surface in the physical realm.

...TO BE CONTINUED.

CPSIA information can be obtained
at www.ICGtesting.com
Printed in the USA
LVHW031158010820
662151LV00026B/2405